DEATH of a Shipowner

DEATH of a Shipowner

THOMAS HENEGE

ACADEMY
CHICAGO

Published in 1987 by
Academy Chicago Publishers
425 North Michigan Avenue
Chicago, IL 60611

Printed and bound in the USA

Library of Congress Cataloging-in-Publication Data

Henege, Thomas.
Death of a shipowner

Reprint. Originally published: New York: Dodd, Mead, c1981.
I.Title.
PS3554.E4954D4 1987 813'.54 86-32236
ISBN 0-89733-258-X (pbk.)

For TGB
TBM
RHB

PART 1

Ballast Leg

1

Shipowner Johansen opened the frosted glass door and stepped into the freezing wind rushing down Ovre Slottsgate. The door shut behind him with a familiar click. He had come to the office early, as was his practice, and now, preparatory to meeting the Greek at the Grand Hotel, he dismissed the morning's telex traffic from his mind. He had in mind dismissing the Greek as well. However, as he had to see him, he preferred to see him at breakfast (some goat cheese, a few herrings), rather than summon him to the office, particularly at that time of day and on an empty stomach. In any event, he almost never saw the Greek in the office.

Evgenides had been managing the *Rose,* a 1970-built Freedom (dry cargo vessel of about fifteen thousand tons), for fourteen months. For the last few of these she had barely been breaking even, despite the Liberian flag and the sort of crew that only someone like Evgenides could assemble. Under normal circumstances even Paul Johansen might have been willing to give the Greek another chance, but the theft of six crates of auto parts by pirates while the *Rose* was anchored off Port Kelang had moved him to act.

Johansen turned the corner into Karl Johansgate. Although it was dark, he knew that the sky was low, and he could feel the snow in the air. Perhaps he thought he might get in some skiing at the weekend. The neon thermometer on the Grundig sign across the park showed seven degrees of frost. He did not know he was being followed by a dark Mercedes that on signal pulled away from the curb as soon as he emerged from Ovre Slottsgate. The signal was given by a man Johansen knew well but did not on this occasion see. Even if he had, he would have thought nothing of a man sheltering in a doorway out of the wind, trying to light his pipe.

Johansen also did not see the car increase speed. Nor did he see the flashes at the window on the passenger side. He did hear the ugly *snap-snap-snap* and at the same time was consumed with pain, but then a millisecond later, he felt nothing at all.

That, in any case, is how I thought it might have happened.

At the time, of course, I knew very little. I did not, for example, know that Evgenides was in Oslo. And it was Inspector Frogh who told me about the Mercedes.

I also didn't know that, having murdered Johansen, they would turn their attention to me.

At the time of Paul Johansen's death in January 1976, I was Finansdirektor of his company, P. Johansens Rederi A/S. Johansen and I were graduated together shortly after the war from the Commercial High School in Bergen. Just after graduation, I had married a Bergen girl of whom my parents disapproved, while Paul—we were good friends then—went on to study marine engineering at Durham.

I spent the next ten years or so wondering what I was doing wrong; why my wife and I didn't get along the way we had; why she didn't want my children; why she spent so much time with her mother. Then I realized I didn't like her much anymore, and that she didn't like me, so we got a divorce.

When I reached the office the morning of Johansen's death, the reception area was crowded with people I'd never seen, except for one young reporter for the *Aftenposten* who used to call on me every couple of weeks for a comment on the tanker market. Our receptionist, Liv, was in tears. I was asked for my reaction to Shipowner Johansen's death. My response was that I did not know he was dead.

"Do you live in a vacuum, Finansdirektor?" asked the young man from *Aftenposten.*

"No, I live just off Drammensveien," I snapped. "What the hell is this all about?"

I was then told Johansen had been shot. I found suddenly that I couldn't breathe. I wanted to say that it was untrue, a mistake, something that couldn't happen, but the words wouldn't come.

Inspector Frogh appeared and, taking me by the arm, led me back to my own office. As we passed down the corridor, I noticed that no one was making any attempt to work. They sat or stood in little groups whispering. Phones rang and no one answered.

I sat heavily at my desk and Frogh took a chair in front.

"Shipowner Johansen was shot to death this morning in front of the tobacco shop next to the Grand Hotel, Mr. Henriksen." He selected one of the three pipes he carried in the breast pocket of his suit coat and began to fill it. "He was shot in the back from a moving vehicle, and if I'm any judge of these things, with an automatic weapon. I can't think he suffered long." He lit his pipe with three or four matches and great spumes of smoke. "What is your immediate reaction?"

"Preposterous." I fought to keep down the nausea.

"I'm not surprised. That was my thought as well. All very orderly, planned, premeditated. Happens all the time. But not in Oslo to innocuous owners of medium-size shipping companies. It is like a gangland killing in Chicago."

"Or terrorism," I said. "The fashion of the day."

"Possibly. But to what end?" Frogh's pipe had gone out. He stared at me over the bowl of the pipe through his thick lenses. His light blue eyes looked as if they were watering.

"I cannot imagine," I said. "Hasn't it occurred to you that terrorism has become an end in itself?"

"I must say, Mr. Henriksen, that you don't seem moved by the death of the man for whom you've worked for . . . how long?"

"Thirteen years."

"For thirteen years."

"In all candor, Inspector Frogh, I'm not moved. I'm shocked, and horrified that such a thing should happen, and I'm sorry for his son. But I cannot say I'm moved."

"And why?"

"I see you didn't know Paul Johansen, even by reputation. He and I used to be friends. We were at the Norges Handelshøyskole in Bergen together. He was all right until he took over this firm from his father. Maybe that's not right either. Maybe the change happened before. In any case, he turned into a machine. Johansen was obsessed with ships, and he expected everyone who worked for him to be obsessed equally, or at least to give the appearance of it. Did you know this place is known in the shipping community as Johansens Mek?"

"You mean it's called Johansen's Engineering Works?"

"Yes. Because of the mechanical way he approached his ships and his people. Don't misunderstand, Inspector Frogh. He was a very capable shipowner, and some people thought he was the next big name in Norwegian shipping. That was before the collapse of the tanker market, when bankers used to line up outside the door begging us to take their money. He and I respected each other after a fashion. But he was a difficult man to work for."

"If he was so difficult, why did you all stay?"

"Perhaps because of the challenge. And he paid well."

Frogh cleaned the bowl of one pipe and filled another. The mosaic of Johansen's character he was constructing was clearly insufficient to explain what had happened to him. It took him five matches to get his pipe lit properly this time.

"And how about the son? Fredrik is it? How did Johansen treat him?"

"Like something scraped off the bottom of one of his hulls."

"Badly enough, do you think . . ."

"For an intelligent young man with a normal amount of self-esteem, no, because such a young man would simply have gone elsewhere. Fredrik, I regret to say, has no self-esteem that I can detect, except a sort of primitive bravado, but I don't think he has the imagination or the sangfroid to organize a murder."

At that moment my intercom crackled to life. Through Liv's snufflings, I learned that Frogh was wanted on the telephone. I asked her to put it through to my office and offered to leave, but Frogh waved at me to remain. When the phone rang, he answered. The conversation was entirely on the other end, punctuated by an occasional grunt or unintelligible mumble from the inspector.

As he replaced the instrument, he said, "The car has been found in Smestad. A black Mercedes."

"Like an Oslo taxi."

"Exactly," Frogh said. "But this Mercedes has a Kristiansand registration."

2

I think the enormity of what had just occurred struck us both at once. As outlandish as the thing had been, there had been a chance that the reasons for—and the solution to—this bizarre murder might have been confined to Oslo. But Kristiansand is two hundred fifty kilometers southwest of Oslo.

We were both staring into space, Frogh in my desk chair, I in the chair he had left to answer the phone.

"It seems to me now, Mr. Henriksen, that this is something that may go beyond Norway. Like all shipping companies, Johansens Rederi has offices and agents everywhere. Has anything unusual happened abroad recently?"

"Nothing."

Frogh shrugged and rose. "Thank you, Mr. Henriksen. We shall be speaking again. I will talk to the boy this afternoon. I understand he is quite inconsolable now." He paused at the door. "And yes, I agree with you. Terrorism has become an end in itself."

Johansen's office was next to my own. I tapped on the door, expecting that Fredrik would be inside, but I received no reply. I went out to the reception area. Frogh was just saying, "No comment," to the reporters, who then turned on me. A very bright light came on, blinding me for a moment.

"What is your reaction to Shipowner Johansen's death, Finans-direktor?" someone asked.

I squinted into the lights. "What the hell do you expect me to say?" I could feel tears in my eyes, but whether they came from frustration, from sorrow for Paul, or simply from the brightness of the light, I couldn't say.

Someone else said, "Please don't take offense, Mr. Henriksen. Violent death is news, especially in Oslo." I believe the television news that evening accurately conveyed my snort of disgust. But after all, the young man was right. Oslo, although the capital of Norway, had a population of less than half a million. One could walk from one end of the town center to the other in less than ten minutes, among tiresome northern European buildings of gray stone, concrete, or muddy pastel shades. The city, at the turn of the century, when it was called Christiania, had regarded Ibsen as a pariah. Even now this gray city was so infrequently regarded that the British journal *The Economist* had recently photographically mistaken the parliament building for the bourse. Of course violent death was news in Oslo.

I opened the door to Johansen's office. The inconsolable Fredrik was sitting at his father's desk humming tonelessly and tapping the blotter with a letter opener. He was younger than his twenty-two years and overweight, and he looked soft.

"So, Henriksen. Life must go on, eh? Bring me the morning telexes, and let's discuss them."

Poor Fredrik. He hadn't the foggiest idea how to run a Volvo agency, much less a shipping company. Or perhaps, *au fond,* his father had treated him so badly that he simply didn't care.

"Stop talking nonsense, Fredrik," I said. "This firm is in trouble. Your father's death is, forgive me, only an additional blow."

Fredrik deflated visibly, like a sack leaking air. He began to cry quietly, large tears rolling over his plump rosy cheeks and splashing onto his pinstriped lapels. "I don't know what to do, John. I know you're right. Father said you were too conservative, like a banker." He wiped his eyes and blew his nose. "Can you help me? Can we save the firm?"

I went around the desk and put my hand on his shoulder. "We can only try, Fredrik." His shoulder trembled beneath my hand. "But I think it might be too soon to talk about it now. I think it might be best if you went home. No. Go to my place." I gave him my key and pushed him out the side entrance, hoping the sharks would leave him alone.

I sat at Johansen's desk and punched the intercom.

"Norland." Lars Norland was chief of operations.

"Yes, John?" the tinny box responded.

"You've telexed the masters?"

"Yes. We put a tape on the machine to everyone, including the Norbulk offices. And I've talked to Lindstedt, who was on to you before, while you were with Frogh. I've also telexed Evgenides."

Ah yes, I thought, Evgenides. I'd forgotten about him and the *Rose.* Fredrik might know more.

Norland's voice came through again.

"I'm sorry, Lars?"

"I said, where are you?"

"Johansen's office."

"I'll be right around."

A moment later Lars Norland came into the office and closed the door quietly. He was a slight man, a little older than I, dressed that day in dark trousers and a white shirt, with a wine-colored tie and a very pale blue cardigan sweater. I had worked closely with Lars for many years. He was a good friend and a thoroughly professional shipping man, probably one of the best operations men for bulk carriers in Oslo, if not all of Norway. He was not prone to self-advertisement, and looked more like a schoolmaster, which is exactly what Johansen looked upon him as. If he ever resented that, I had never noticed. He simply went about his job very well indeed, and seemed to pay no attention to the way he was treated.

"Starting to snow," he said, looking through the window behind me. "Paul would have been delighted. John, whom are we working for?"

"I take it you mean, is Fredrik now the head of the firm?"

"Uncanny how you go right to the heart of the matter, John Henriksen."

"I assume Fredrik will be made chairman of the board, unless Johansen has willed the firm to the tax authorities or the Ministry of Shipping."

A smile went over Norland's lips like wind rippling through the grass.

"I was rather afraid you'd say that. I think it may be difficult to hold on to some of the younger people with the old man gone."

"Actually, we can't anticipate anything. I can't believe that Johansen would have left control in Fredrik's hands. I expect Borgensen will be calling an emergency meeting of the board momentarily. And if he doesn't I'll be ringing him."

Norland left the office shaking his head. Johansen had paid him well but had never made him a member of the board, although he had held out the possibility on many occasions that I had witnessed. I had never understood the game Johansen played with Norland, but then there was a great deal about Johansen I had never understood.

I placed a call to Frogh to let him know where he could find Fredrik and then called our lawyer Kjell Borgensen, Johansen's executor and the secretary of P. Johansens Rederi A/S.

Paul Johansen's father had died suddenly in 1955, and Paul had taken over. At first he had continued his father's conservative policy in operating a fleet of medium-size bulk carriers—vessels that carry iron ore, coal, wheat, and other commodities in bulk—on long-term charters or contracts of affreightment. Several things that had occurred in recent years had changed his thinking, however. He was intrigued by the experience of one of our Bergen colleagues, a tanker owner who never employed his ships long-term, who was on the verge of serious financial difficulty in 1967 when the Six-Day War closed the Suez Canal and he had five empty tankers in the Persian Gulf. That Bergen owner made a king's ransom the following year. The devaluation of the pound in 1967 and of the dollar in 1971 turned Johansen and the rest of us into foreign exchange traders, worried not only about earning our income, but having to hedge it as well, either through the banks or by putting more and more of our liquidity into ships. And inflation showed him the folly of locking himself into long-term fixed-rate charters. If one could not get charters with variable rates, then at least he could minimize the effect by keeping employment short.

But the thing that Johansen kept dwelling on was the experience of tanker owners, coupled with the growing need for oil around the world, a demand he felt would never diminish, at least until an alternate energy source as cheap and as abundant could be developed.

So in 1968, the same year we took delivery of our two Panamax bulk carriers from Kawasaki, we placed an order for one tanker of sixty thousand tons from Akers in Oslo, and another for one of a hundred thousand tons from Mitsubishi Heavy Industries.

Unfortunately, Shipowner Johansen underestimated the effect of greed, including his own, on the course of history.

At the time Johansen was killed, we had four medium-size bulkers comfortably chartered to Norbulk A/S, a company owned by a tough old Viking named Per Lindstedt, who couldn't give a damn about tankers. Our two Panamax bulk carriers—which is to say, the maximum size that can pass through the Panama Canal—were on long-term contract carrying coal from Norfolk to Yokohama for Nippon Steel. Of these six ships, only two had debt outstanding, and that wasn't much, so they were suppliers of surplus cash.

But we now had four tankers as well, and two of two hundred fifty thousand tons on order. All four tankers that were operating had mortgages, one of the two vessels under construction (newbuildings) would have, and the last we had not yet succeeded in financing.

Two of the tankers were employed and paying their way, but only barely. Two were unemployed and kicking around the Persian Gulf, looking for the odd cargo. They were eating into reserves. The two vessels on order would not even be delivered until the second half of 1977 and they had no employment to look forward to either. Together, they represented fourteen million dollars in equity. I remember how satisfied Johansen had been that he'd had the foresight to order the big ships before the market, and hence ship prices, started rising rapidly.

The problem was that everyone thought (as everyone does) that the world would go on being exactly what it was at the time. They could not have foreseen the Middle East war in the autumn of 1973 and the subsequent rise in oil prices, the oil embargo, the decline in energy consumption—the whole thing.

I had nearly forgotten the *Rose,* the fifteen-thousand-ton dry cargo carrier that flew the Liberian flag and tramped around Southeast Asia. Johansen had given it to the Greek Stratis Evgenides to manage. I knew very little about the vessel, because Johansen would not tell me anything about her. He knew I disapproved.

3

Kjell Borgensen did in fact call the board meeting for eleven that morning in his office on Haakon VII's gate 1. We met in his little conference room that looked down the street toward the harbor: myself; Borgensen as secretary of the board; Karl Wessel, our chartering manager; Atle Selmer, a fussy little man who was a deputy general manager from our Oslo bank; and Johansen's cousin Torvald, the owner of a cement company, who had yet to contribute anything to our meetings. Fredrik was also a member of the board, but of course was not there.

Borgensen, in his capacity as Johansen's executor as well as the board secretary, let us know that it was Paul's intention to name Fredrik and me joint managing directors of the firm until such time as the board determined that Fredrik could manage alone; he would then become chief executive officer. Selmer fussed a bit, as was his habit, and Torvald said nothing. We then voted on the disposition and found ourselves unanimously in favor, following which the board adjourned itself to lunch upstairs in the Shipping Club. I excused myself.

I stopped at the Theatercafe on the way to the office. I felt empty rather than hungry, and I wanted time to think alone about the arrangement that Johansen had made for running the firm if something happened to him.

It was clear he could not have left things in Fredrik's hands alone, and Torvald, his only close relative, knew nothing about shipping. He might have appointed anyone, including Wessel or Borgensen—or even Atle Selmer or someone else from the outside—but he had not. Despite our many disagreements, which had grown more and more frequent and bitter in the recent past, the old bastard had left the management of his firm and the tutelage of his son to me. I must say I was moved. And disturbed. There was a price to pay. Not the obvious one of trying to keep Johansens Rederi in business and turning a profit, but another. I now had to find out—which is to say, to participate actively in finding out—who had killed him, and why.

It was exactly the kind of difficulty Johansen himself might have thought up for someone's discomposure.

I had to talk to Fredrik. I knew the Norwegian fleet backward and forward, but I knew next to nothing about the *Rose.* Fredrik, with whom I knew his father had discussed the *Rose,* must be my first source before I contacted Evgenides.

The way out to my house was along Drammensveien, the road that as the E18 led to Kristiansand, among other places. It might have been along this very road, early that morning or last night, that the black Mercedes had come.

The snow was falling fast and sticking. It was only twelve-thirty, but it looked like twilight. I turned on the fog lights and was able to go no more than fifty kilometers an hour.

I lived then in a boxy-looking house in a district of no particular vice or virtue; but it was quiet. I needed nothing more since my wife from Bergen had left me and returned to the west coast, where there was more rain for her complexion. The house gave me room for my books and records and was easy to clean and cook in. The most important thing was that I could be alone—to read, to listen to Beethoven or Brahms on the record player, occasionally to feel sorry for myself. I could not live in a flat in town, which would have been more convenient, because I did not really want to be surrounded by other people's noise. Having the house outside the center of the city also forced me to leave the office. It is a great temptation for a solitary man to stay at work all evening as well as all day. On the other hand, it is true as well that a solitary man is not necessarily one who has no wife and children.

I left the car outside the garage next to Fredrik's yellow Porsche, pleased to note that my road had already been plowed once. I found Fredrik sitting in the dark, quite unable to do anything for himself, including turning on a light and reading a magazine. I felt quite sad for him then, and I began to wonder, for the first time, whether what I had taken as lack of intelligence was simply immaturity coupled with a personality that had been totally overwhelmed by that of his forceful father. There had been very few people in his life to mitigate that force—a nurse when he was very young, a housekeeper or two, perhaps a cook. His mother had died in childbirth, along with the second child, two years after Fredrik had been born, and other than his cousin Torvald, he had no relatives.

"Fredrik, for heaven's sake, turn on a light," I said, trying to be gentle.

He did so, slowly, saying, "The policeman Frogh was here. He didn't stay long."

"What did you talk about?"

"Nothing much. He asked me if I could think of any reason why my fa . . . why. . ." and he started to cry again quietly. "I told him no," he managed.

He'd had nothing to eat. I made him drink a weak whisky soda while I made him a sandwich, and while he ate we talked. I told him first about the board decision, at which he nodded listlessly. Then I asked about the *Rose.*

The *Rose* had a Greek master, highly recommended by Evgenides, and a mostly Hong Kong crew, which I knew could be a mixed blessing because of the frequent presence of Communist organizers among them; but Evgenides swore by them. The original intent had been to tramp from Korea and Japan up the east coast of Africa and through the Gulf as far as Khorramsharr in Iran, but with the port congestion that developed in the Gulf when OPEC started buying everything under the sun, it was decided to go no farther than East London and Durban (and later Mombasa and Dar es Salaam).

The first three voyages had produced an astounding profit, on which, of course, no taxes had to be paid, because there are no corporate taxes in Liberia. The vessel cost almost nothing to run, compared with a Norwegian ship, having been bought for cash and manned by that kind of crew. Fredrik said that his father had begun to get quite interested in the possibilities offered by a Liberian-flag cargo operation, perhaps Hong Kong based, with Evgenides or someone recommended by him as manager. He had been thoroughly impressed with Evgenides' professionalism. Fredrik said that his father had been sketching scheme after scheme at the dinner table—for expanding his service to the U.S. West Coast, for competing with the Chinese and the Japanese. He thought there might be room for a smallish, efficiently operated service with European management in the Far East market (this was before the Soviets started cutting rates on everyone). Johansen had even stopped talking about the headaches his tankers were giving him.

Then everything changed. Revenues dropped on the next three voyages, so that the *Rose* was barely breaking even. Evgenides claimed it was the absence of cargo for trampers, and he had performed so admirably in the past that Johansen was inclined not to press him on the issue. But then Paul began to get word from the agents—they were mostly agents for Norbulk who did not know that Johansen owned the vessel, only that he had an interest in it—not only that the *Rose* was not being maintained properly, which was bad enough, but that crew turnover was abnormally high and that the claim that there was no cargo was nonsense.

Johansen demanded a full explanation from Evgenides. The Greek conceded that there was cargo for Gulf ports or Nigeria, but he did not think that tying a vessel up for one hundred and fifty days in a queue waiting for a berth to discharge was very sensible. Then some crates of auto parts were stolen from the ship while she was anchored outside Port Kelang in Malaysia waiting for the tide. Paul had summoned Evgenides to Oslo.

"When was this, Fredrik?"

"Today."

"You mean Evgenides was supposed to be here today?"

"Yes."

"Had he in fact come, do you know?"

"Yes. My father talked to him last night on the phone. He was on his way to see him at the Grand this morning."

"He must be connected with your father's murder, Fredrik. Have you told Frogh any of this?"

"No. No, I don't believe it, John. Evgenides is a very nice man. He couldn't possibly." The boy was extremely upset, but I could understand that his distress had not allowed him to solve the simple equation. "I mean he could be dishonest, John, but not that other. He is so nice." Poor Fredrik. Anyone who was nice to him got full marks in his limited universe.

4

I called Frogh immediately and told him that Evgenides was—or had been—in Oslo that day and that I suspected he was connected with the murder. Frogh asked only that I keep him informed of my whereabouts, then rang off.

As I hung up, I could hear the boy in the toilet, vomiting. He came out looking extremely pale. I suggested he lie down; he acceded, saying nothing. I left him and returned to the office, telling Liv when I arrived to let Frogh know where I was.

Lars Norland looked up in the usual welcoming way he had as I stepped into his office.

"I seem to remember your mentioning that the *Rose* is in Singapore?" I asked.

"Yes, John."

"Please inform the vessel through Norbulk that they are not to move until they receive instructions direct from the owner. Anything from anyone else is to be ignored."

Norland nodded and reached for the intercom.

I went to my own office, where my desk was piled with telexes expressing sympathy. There were a dozen phone messages as well, including one from Per Lindstedt (timed two hours before) asking me to call him immediately, and the calling card of an American banker with a note of regret penned on it and the number of his room at the Grand. I'd missed an appointment with him.

I returned Lindstedt's call. He offered me dinner that night at home, which I accepted. I knew we'd have to discuss the situation with respect to Norbulk. While I was speaking with Lindstedt, Frogh called my secretary and requested a further interview.

By the time the policeman arrived, it was completely dark, which it becomes in midafternoon in Oslo in winter, and the snow was still falling.

Frogh wiped the condensation off his glasses and began his pipe operations: filling and tamping, filling and tamping, then three or four highly sulphuric matches whose reflections I could see in my office windows.

"The car was rented two evenings ago," he began, "from the Avis near the Hotel Caledonien in Kristiansand. The driver's license that was used is false. The clerk did not notice anything about the person who rented the car, except that he spoke English instead of Norwegian, despite the fact that he was Norwegian, which she knows because his driver's license was Norwegian."

"And of course, he was not Norwegian."

"Of course. She claims she was very busy."

"In Kristiansand?"

"I'm told it happens, Mr. Henriksen. It was the end of the day, and I'm sure she was not paying much attention." Frogh applied another match to his pipe. "Evgenides checked out of the hotel at midmorning, despite the fact that he had stayed for only one of the three nights he had booked. Did you know, by the way, that Johansens Rederi pays the bill? He took British Airways to London, which is the first plane he could have caught, so he was moving quickly. We have no idea what he did after that. We have asked Scotland Yard to assist, and we have contacted Interpol. I'm afraid that the three hours or so headstart he's had has put us at a considerable disadvantage. I am awaiting information now from the Greek authorities. How did Johansen meet Evgenides?"

"I have no idea. Fredrik might know."

"Is he still at your house?"

"Probably. I told him to try to sleep."

"He seemed to me to be quite fragile."

"Emotionally, you mean? Yes, I agree. A great deal of it could be guilt."

"Guilt, Mr. Henriksen? Ah, yes." He paused while he worried his pipe. "It was quite obvious that he didn't like his father."

"Precisely."

Frogh cleaned the pipe into an ashtray with a penknife. "Another bit of information. The shell casings we found in the car indicate the ammunition was of American manufacture."

To which I could say nothing. What vast terrible enterprise was it that found it necessary to plan and execute with such precision the murder of an unimportant shipowner in Oslo on a grim winter morning?

"What was Paul Johansen doing with a Liberian-flag vessel, Mr. Henriksen?"

"Evading taxes."

"And that's all?"

"I think he had a notion he was going to rescue the firm with a cargo liner fleet operating under flags of convenience. But he was not letting me in on his secrets concerning the *Rose*."

"And why was that?"

"Because I did not approve."

"For moral reasons or business reasons?"

"Inspector Frogh, I pay my taxes like a good citizen and begrudge the government every øre. Having said that, I would say that my objections to the *Rose* operation were mostly for business reasons. I did not think Johansen should involve himself in yet another area of shipping in which he had no special expertise. Particularly when the management was remote from him as well."

"What is the other area of shipping that he knew nothing about?"

"The tanker trade. Had Johansen not been so—the only word for it is greedy—this firm would be in sound financial shape, which it isn't now. Unfortunately, Paul in his last years considered himself infallible in matters of shipping."

"Where is the *Rose* now?"

"In Singapore, under instructions from this office through Norbulk's agents there. As I think you may know, Norbulk is a bulk carrier fleet owned and managed by Per Lindstedt, to whom we have chartered four vessels. We generally use his agents. I am about to go through *Rose*'s records, which are locked in Johansen's office. Would you care to look with me?"

"No thank you, Mr. Henriksen. You will bring anything of interest to our attention, I'm sure."

"Of course."

"Will you be going to Singapore, do you think?"

"On the way to Tokyo, yes."

Frogh formed the interrogative with his eyebrows.

"Inspector, this firm is in severe financial difficulty. What I know, and what I have been arguing about with Johansen for months, is that, in order to survive, radical surgery is necessary. We have two very large crude carriers—VLCCs—on order in Japan that will have to be canceled forthwith, something the Japanese will not at all care for. As a cancellation penalty, we may have to give up our entire equity, which amounts to approximately seventy million kroner."

"Now that Johansen is dead, who owns the firm?"

"He had ninety percent of the shares, which I think he has probably willed to Fredrik. You must ask his executor, Kjell Borgensen, about that. The rest are held by investors in the community, and each of the directors, of which I am one, owns one share. The board this morning elected Fredrik and me joint managing directors."

Frogh rested his eyes on mine. "Which in fact means that you, Mr. Henriksen, are running the show." It was more a statement than a question.

"That is correct."

Frogh said nothing, letting his eyes stare vacantly through the thick lenses into the middle distance. In a few moments, he looked up.

"*Ja,* well, Mr. Henriksen, I'll be off. When will you go to the Far East?"

"As soon after the funeral as possible. And as soon as you tell me I'm not needed here."

Frogh nodded and left, wishing me a good evening.

There was nothing unusual about the papers relating to the *Rose* that Johansen kept locked in a file cabinet: photocopies of the memorandum of agreement regarding the sale of the motor vessel *Achilleus*—she was purchased and renamed fourteen months before for one and a quarter million dollars (which sounded below market to me) from Aegean Maritime, Monrovia; the sales contract; the Liberian registration (Book X Page Y in the office of the Deputy Commissioner of Maritime Affairs of Liberia in New York); the bylaws and corporate resolutions of the owning corporation, Transoceanic Shipping Inc., located at 80 Broad Street, Monrovia (fortunately Lars Norland was one of the authorized signatories, Johansen and Evgenides being the other two, and each of them could sign singly—I would need power of attorney when I got to Singapore); and a small piece of plain bond with a man's name and the name and address of a bank in Geneva, where I assumed the original documents and the corporate account were. I called Norland on the intercom.

"Did you or Johansen have anything to do with the operation of the Geneva account for the *Rose*?"

"Practically nothing, John. That was handled almost entirely by Evgenides. I know very little about the operation. If Johansen was going on a trip, he would tell me what to sign if something came up, and I would sign. That's all."

"I bet I know what Evgenides did when he left Oslo."

"Are you speaking to me, John? I haven't a clue as to what you're talking about."

"Sorry, Lars. I was thinking out loud. Can you fire a telex off to this man Bauer in Geneva and tell him under no circumstances to release any funds? Will he pay attention to that?"

"Yes. There is an automatic twenty-four-hour delay on all instructions to the bank, if I remember correctly. If Bauer receives a contradictory telex in that time, then two of the three officers must agree and confirm the instruction."

"What if the contradictory telex is not on time?"

"Then it's simply too late. Bauer is not constrained to delay more than twenty-four hours."

I switched off the intercom and returned to the file on the *Rose*. The name of Evgenides' management company was Transoceanic Agencies S.A., which was in Akti Miaouli, Piraeus. There were also a few pages of handwritten cash flows. I could not believe my eyes at the low level of crew expense—poor pay may have been the reason for the high turnover of personnel. Each column of figures was more dismal than the last, so I assumed the cash flows represented actual results. It seemed also that Johansen had made some hasty projections preparatory to his meeting with Evgenides. And at the bottom of the last page in large letters was the name "Bechmann," underlined and followed by an exclamation point. The only Bechmann I knew of was a London merchant banker of extremely dubious reputation. If this were the same Bechmann, then I was afraid I knew how Johansen had met Evgenides.

The last item in the file was a clipping from *Lloyds List,* a newspaper that is read widely in shipping circles. The article was as follows:

THEFT OF CARGO FROM LIBERIAN VESSEL OFF KELANG

Singapore, Jan. 25—Armed bandits boarded Liberian motor vessel ROSE and stole six cases marked "car parts" while the vessel was anchored outside Port Kelang on Jan. 16 (Yokohama for Mombasa). "Straits Times."

I called the American banker at the Grand.

"Bill, do you know anyone named Bechmann?"

After a perceptible pause, he answered, "Yes. Raymond Bechmann. He's a director of Multicapital."

"That's the man I'm thinking of. Does he know anything about shipping?"

"He has shipping clients, John. Not any we'd want to deal with."

"Such as?"

"Fourth- and fifth-tier Greeks—faceless types running Cypriot-flag operations for German doctors and dentists who can take the depreciation against their incomes."

"Thank you, Bill. By the way, is your bank willing now to give us eighty percent ten-year financing for a two-hundred-fifty-thousand-ton newbuilding at Dai Ichi, delivery in October 1977?"

"You've got her fixed on charter then?"

"No, Bill. You know it's much too soon."

"We can't do it, John. No source of repayment. Mortgage isn't worth much either. Can you provide other security?"

"A couple of ten-year-old bulk carriers."

Another pause. "I know it's difficult right now, John, but I'd really like to get together with you and talk everything over."

"Let me ring you back on that, Bill. Everything is most confused right now. How long will you be in Oslo?"

"Until the end of the week."

"I'll be in touch."

"Thanks, John. I'm very sorry about Mr. Johansen." He had to ask. "Why did you ask about Bechmann?"

"Nothing important."

"That's good. Off the record, John, he's really a creepy guy."

5

I rang Frogh and described the bits and pieces I had unearthed about the *Rose,* including Bechmann's name among our papers and the banker's characterization.

"Did he elaborate, Mr. Henriksen?"

"No. He refused."

Frogh clucked once, thanked me in a distracted fashion, and hung up.

It was after six-thirty and the office was quiet. My night line—which does not come through the switchboard—rang. It was Fredrik to tell me that he was at home and would see me in the morning. My keys were in the garage. He also mumbled something about gratitude.

I slumped back in the chair, feeling utterly drained and exhausted. I was in no mood for the necessary dinner with Per Lindstedt, and I certainly did not feel up to the usual jousting with him that one always had to go through. He was relentless, but I supposed that's how he got where he was.

I returned to Johansen's office and looked around again before I turned out the lights. It was basically a bare room: nothing on the walls, a couple of chairs, a hard sofa, a small bookcase behind the desk holding *Lloyds Register,* some technical manuals, and a few newspapers. There was very little on the desk: a letter opener, some sharpened pencils in a cylinder, a calculator, folders with letters waiting for his signature, the day's copy of the *Norwegian Journal of Shipping and Commerce.* Paul Wilhelm, I thought, what were you about? I switched off the light.

I turned off the lights in the rest of the office as well, put on my coat and hat and boots, and walked down the stairs. I opened the frosted glass door and stepped out into the cold, clear night. The snow had stopped and the stars were shining. My car was parked in a garage just off Stortingsgata, toward which I turned. The neon thermometer on the Grundig sign said eight degrees of frost.

* * *

Like my own, Lindstedt's house was considerably out from the center; there the similarity ended. Lindstedt's house, where he lived alone as a widower—the children had grown and moved away—was large and comfortable, with a modest collection of original modern art on the walls and a photograph of himself looking formidable at a Norbulk shareholder meeting, taken by my friend Alice Nielsen. There was also a great deal of cosmopolitan bric-a-brac. Most people would have regarded the latter as souvenirs; but I knew they were really booty, all those perspex paperweights with commemorative coins inside, miniature models and photographs of ships, a glass vial with North Sea oil in it (he was on the board of the state oil company), a large chunk of bauxite mounted on mahogany. Had Lindstedt been born a thousand years before, he would have been ravaging the coast of Britain from a longboat, probably under long-term contract to the Danish king.

I was let into the house by the dumpy, severe woman who was his housekeeper and cook. She nodded peremptorily and disappeared into the kitchen.

Per Lindstedt was a tall and well-built man, a bit heavy, with dark hair just beginning to go gray, even though he was past sixty, and small, dark, penetrating eyes. He smiled easily, and the smile disappeared just as easily. He took me into his study, where a small bar had been set up on a table.

"You look very tired, my friend," he said.

I remember nodding, feeling a bit as if I'd just gotten off an overnight plane from New York.

"A sherry, or something stronger?"

I asked instead for a whisky soda with ice. He made it strong.

"Smoke?" Lindstedt said, offering me a tin of Schimmelpennincks. "Ah, no. You've given it up."

I then told him all the information that Frogh had given me, and the results of my own research about the *Rose.* Lindstedt simply nodded from time to time during my recitation, following which we moved into the dining room.

The housekeeper served us clear soup, followed by ptarmigan

that Lindstedt had shot and new potatoes. I discovered I was famished.

"But why this stupid playing about with flags of convenience?" Per asked.

"I think that he was frightened, Per, or perhaps I should say disturbed. He had been successful for so long, he had been right so many times, that he couldn't believe the decline in the tanker market was happening to him. It didn't matter that it was happening to everyone else, only that it was happening to him. It was almost a personal affront. I think it unbalanced him. And he certainly wasn't listening to any advice. Well, you know that yourself—you tried to talk him out of ordering the second two tankers."

Lindstedt looked depressed. He has always thought that P. Johansens Rederi should come in completely under the Norbulk umbrella, that is, charter all our ships to Norbulk. At least he thought that until we became tanker owners. Until then he'd liked our ships and our organization, and he'd respected Johansen as a shipowner, if not as a man. Johansen used to say that Lindstedt was power mad; he would charter to Norbulk, but that is as far as it would go. From my point of view, Lindstedt and Johansen were two mammoth and incompatible egos. Lindstedt was by far the more successful, even before we acquired the tankers, but Johansen somehow had acquired the reputation for success, and it used to infuriate Lindstedt.

Per poured me another glass of claret and looked at me with his eyes shining. "But surely Paul knew there is only one of us who is infallible in questions of shipping." The smile came and went quickly, too quickly to reach his eyes. This was the true Lindstedt; he really believed it, although there were some people in Oslo and Sandefjord, a bulk carrier pool operator, and, oddly enough, a couple of tanker owners, who might be said to share the honors with him.

"So Johansen, with no liner experience and no experience with flags of convenience, thought he was going to rescue P. Johansens Rederi from disaster by running a cargo liner service based on the other side of the world and run by a shadowy Greek who crews his ships with Malays and Lascars. The man had taken leave of his senses."

"And he would not admit the obvious things, Per. He would not think of canceling the two big ships, which we might have done a year ago far more easily than we will be able to now. Or of selling some of the others. And every day that goes by is a day wasted. It will be a very long time before the market improves."

"I agree," he said rising. "Let's have coffee in my study. Too much tonnage overhanging the market. Too much shipbuilding capacity. What a goddamn situation."

When we had gotten our coffee and settled into overstuffed chairs, he said, "What are your plans? I assume Fredrik inherits his father's shares. Johansens Rederi is under obligation to provide Norbulk with four bulk carriers of such and such size for so and so many years, and if it does not, I can sue—and win—and take virtually everything Fredrik owns."

I was taken aback by the harshness of his tone, but I supposed it was compounded of disappointment and anger that a man he respected should have proved such a fool. Whether his greatest disappointment lay in Johansen or in his own lack of judgment I couldn't say.

"The board, following what Borgensen suggested would have been Paul's wish, voted for Fredrik and me to become joint managing directors. The shares are obviously going to Fredrik. And the board has directed that our first order of business must be canceling the big ships in Japan."

"A large order."

"Yes. Perhaps to the point of forfeiting the fourteen million dollars that we paid down when we signed the contracts." I could see Lindstedt wince. "The next thing will be to get rid of the tankers, all four of them, as quickly as possible, chartered or not—and mostly not—before the market value gets below the debt outstanding."

"You will play havoc with the net worth of the firm."

"On paper only, Per. What will be left, I hope, will be solid value. And then I will feel that I have done my best by

Paul and by Fredrik. But it's going to be close."

Lindstedt nodded. "And then, of course, there is this ghastly *Rose* business." He gazed steadily at me. It was somewhat discomfiting.

"The object will be to get rid of her also, of course, and quickly. But let's face it, Per. Somehow the *Rose* is connected with Johansen's murder."

"You're convinced of that, are you?"

"Oh yes. So my hands are tied with respect to disposing of the *Rose*. Anything I do in that direction will have to be cleared by Frogh."

Lindstedt sighed heavily. "Why don't you—I mean the two of you, of course, the managing directors—sell P. Johansens Rederi to Norbulk? I want to keep those ships in the Norbulk fleet and I like the Panamax bulkers. All the rest is garbage. Would you like a long drink?"

I took a weak whisky soda, and while Lindstedt poured a Campari soda for himself, I thought about it. Despite the fact that we were fairly close and that he had known and, I thought, cared about Paul as a shipping man, Lindstedt was beginning to apply the same pressure techniques to me that he had used recently on a couple of other Oslo owners who had got into financial difficulty through imprudent investments, either in tankers or oil rigs. He held out their only hope of salvation, but they had to pay for it. His price was a discounted offer for their bulk carriers. In return he managed to get rid of their tankers or rigs and helped to rearrange the financing, making his own group the direct obligor or guarantor. The result was that his fleet had expanded rapidly in the past year, as had his liabilities, but every one of the vessels he had taken in was working and showing a surplus. To the owners who complained that his terms were too stiff, and said that they preferred to turn to the government Guarantee Institute, formed specifically to help owners in financial straits, he said only that they would lose their independence forever and that shipowners and bureaucrats made very strange bedfellows indeed.

"For net book value, I might be able to persuade Fredrik to sell," I said.

Lindstedt's eyes were shining again. He loved this kind of thing. "I was thinking of net market value, less a discount for the nuisance value of getting rid of the tankers."

"Per, my friend, there's at least a thirty-million dollar difference."

"Fredrik ought to be grateful that I will take everything off his hands for, I reckon, about nine million, rather than my insisting he pay me for working it out for him."

He meant me as well when he referred to Fredrik, and he was sounding waspish.

"Even on that basis," I said smiling, "I reckon closer to twelve million. You have to give some value to the Norbulk charters." Lindstedt laughed. "And the Hess charter," I added.

"The Hess charter is not worth anything, as far as I'm concerned. It expires next year. And by your own admission, the big ships are worth virtually nothing, and the fourteen million dollars is probably a dead loss."

"I think, Per, that we'll straighten out the firm first. Then we'll talk to you again, you old pirate. Or we might consider selling to Bulkhandling." Bulkhandling was Lindstedt's great rival, run by a man as tough and as smart as he.

Lindstedt laughed again, a short, barking, forced laugh, and slapped me on the knee. "Ah, you're a good man, Henriksen. I want you working for me."

"Thank you for the compliment, Per. I think the interests of Norbulk and Johansens Rederi, if not the same, are very close."

Lindstedt grunted and nodded. Then he grew quiet.

"I doubt very much if we can cancel the two VLCCs without losing our downpayment, Per, but I think we can save our equity by converting the order to bulk carriers."

"How many can you get away with, do you think?"

"No less than four. I think the Japanese would be willing even to take a modest reduction in the overall contract total as long as they keep the business. Three, perhaps, if one of them is Panamax."

"If I were negotiating with them," Lindstedt said, "I think I would end up with three open-hatch bulk carriers of about forty thousand tons with certain gearing, the specifications for which I have in the office." Lindstedt's eyes were positively flashing.

"You old fox," I said. "Are you getting into the timber trade now?"

"Perhaps. Let's say only that if Johansens Rederi were to acquire such vessels—with the gearing I've mentioned—it's possible that employment could readily be found."

"Thank you, Per," was all I could manage.

"Yes, yes. Well I'm sorry about Paul, and I like you, and, God help me, I even like that silly boy. We are getting maudlin. Let me ring you a taxi, John. I'll have your car driven in tomorrow."

"I'd appreciate that, old friend." I was feeling dreadfully tired suddenly, and Norwegian driving laws forbade my driving after the two whiskies and two glasses of wine I'd had.

I tried to think of nothing on the way home, and stared into the darkness through the window of the cab. But in my half-conscious state, disjointed thoughts came, whirling in my mind, and I could not prevent them from intruding.

After I had wiped the metaphoric tear from my eye, I was forced to remember that Norbulk was not a charitable institution, and Per Lindstedt was not, after all, a generous man. He had suggested open-hatch bulk carriers because Norbulk could use them. How fortunate that we would have to order them whether we wanted them or not.

I was troubled also because I did not think Per was acting as prudently as he had in the past. The expansion of his fleet in the past year, together with the expansion of his debt, seemed to me rather grandiose. Then again, perhaps he had merely seized on the opportunities of the moment. I certainly was not privy to his strategic thinking.

The house was bleak and cold. Before I went to bed, I went around and doublechecked that all the doors and windows were locked, something I'd never done before. When I finally lay back, I began to shiver, but not from the cold. The truth that I had been trying to avoid acknowledging all day, without realizing it, came flooding over me: Johansen's murder was not a blow against an individual; it was a strike against his company, and anyone connected with it was in danger. Whatever it was that Johansen had involved the firm in—and that Evgenides had not liked—had brought death to Johansen and could bring violence to the rest of us if it were to continue. But if we did not know what "it" was, how in heaven's name could we stop it? I had to call Frogh. I had to call him there and then. But the body raised one of its defenses against terror, and I fell into a dreamless sleep.

I was anxious to ring Frogh the next day, but there were a number of problems I had to deal with before I could get to it. One of these was a young man, very talented, from the chartering department. He was resigning.

I told him I was sorry to see him leave.

"Thank you, John. Nice of you to say so. I could stomach the old man because he was a tiptop shipping man. But I'm not going to work for that asshole Fredrik."

I looked at him coldly. "I think it would be best if you left now, Stein."

"John, I certainly didn't mean. . ."

"Now. We have a lot of problems to cope with. We don't need malcontents disturbing everyone as well."

The fool looked hurt. He was of a generation whose stock-in-trade is self-indulgence, a generation that has not yet learned to compromise its wants. And through the magic of modern communication, the sickness was everywhere.

The future looked black indeed that dismal February morning. I rang Alice Nielsen, who fortunately was in town, and asked if I could buy her dinner at Frascati. She said she thought buying dinner at any restaurant in Norway was a waste of money, but she agreed to meet me at seven.

I asked Frogh if he could come around to our office, since there was too much going on for me to leave. When he arrived, I had my secretary fetch him a cup of coffee, and while he filled my office with pipe smoke I told him my misgivings of the night before. He neither agreed nor disagreed immediately; he merely sat there, his watery eyes musing into the middle distance through his thick lenses. He seemed so far away that I started to look at the budgets for the year and note the points I wanted changed.

"There may be some truth in what you say," Frogh muttered finally. "I don't think they'll strike again yet, however. They'll wait to see if the warning they've delivered has been enough. Only trouble you'd be in at this point is if this were some act of really mindless terrorism—some mad environmentalist who has it in for tanker owners. Too many things against that. Number one, Johansen was not specially known as a tanker owner. Two, this thing was too well planned and too well financed for simple madness. And three, there were no calls to newspapers claiming responsibility and giving lists of nonnegotiable demands. We did get a crank call from one of your former officers shouting that it served the old bastard right, had it coming to him—that sort of thing—but he was just drunk. We let him dry out overnight and sent him back to his flophouse."

"What was his name?"

"Krogstadt."

"Ah, yes. He was dismissed for drunkenness about nine months ago. Used to be a good first officer. How the devil did you find him?"

"We asked him where he was calling from and he told us."

Frogh began to busy himself with his pipe in a way that I was coming to learn meant he had something on his mind.

"Evgenides' office in Piraeus—this Transocean, Transoceanic something—was bombed yesterday. A few passersby were cut with flying glass, but no one was in the office at the time. Curious that. We are told that it was very difficult to determine, given the extent of the destruction, but it looked as though the office had been vacated before the blast occurred. Although there was a telex machine—on which, by the way, the rent is in arrears—there was very little of the usual stuff one normally finds in offices, or even much to indicate occupancy. A bomb attack on his offices might suggest that Evgenides was not involved in Johansen's murder, after all. But it's a little too neat, this bomb going off in a nearly empty office."

I added information I'd received. "Even if Evgenides were innocent, we should have to account somehow for the fact that the

Swiss bank account of the *Rose* was nearly emptied out by Evgenides a week ago."

I showed Frogh the telex the bank had sent us that morning. It read:

> Urs 8th inst funds in amount dlrs 97000 trnfd 2nd inst b/o S. Evgenides to FNCB London a/c Aegean Shipping Monrovia stop Balance dlrs 823,07 Bauer

"B-slash-o is 'by order'?"

"Yes."

"S?"

"Stratis is Evgenides' Christian name."

"Who is Bauer?"

"An official of the bank in Geneva who handled the account. He was acting completely according to the corporate resolution."

"Does the amount of money that was in the account make sense to you?"

"No. It doesn't relate to any of the figures that I've seen, either historical or projected. But there is no reason to believe that this office—which is to say Johansen and Lars Norland—was fully informed. Evgenides had what amounted to complete discretion with both the account and the ship."

"Then why should he report poor earnings and thereby attract attention to how badly he was running the operation?"

"Perhaps to provide some explanation for the low balances in the account—and to cover his peculations."

Frogh sat back and began tapping his teeth with the stem of his pipe. He asked for a photocopy of the clipping from *Lloyds List*, and mentioned rather distractedly that he had asked Scotland Yard to interview Raymond Bechmann. I looked at my watch, unobtrusively I thought.

"I'm sorry if these interviews take so much time, Mr. Henriksen. Unfortunately, all of this is like putting together a puzzle when you don't know what it is supposed to look like at the end of the day. If, that is, it turns out to look like anything at all."

He tapped his teeth again. "We agree that Johansen's death was a warning, as well as a blow. The dynamiting of Evgenides' office in Greece was connected, but we do not know how. I think it pretty clear that what has been happening involves the *Rose.* Did it involve Evgenides? Almost certainly. Did it involve the master or the officers or crew of the *Rose*? Probably. This man Raymond Bechmann? Possibly. Did it involve any of the Norwegian staff or the Norwegian-flag operation? Probably not, from what I have learned from you and from Mr. Norland. How then do we find out about the *Rose*?"

When Frogh took off his glasses to wipe them, I was surprised to see that, without the magnification, his eyes were the same size as everyone else's. No doubt he could not see a thing without those glasses.

"How do we find out about the *Rose*?" he repeated. "Easily. I get on a plane—at taxpayers' expense, first class of course, every begrudged øre duly accepted with thanks—fly to Singapore, interview the crew, and return with the answers. Correct? I think not. Instead I ask one of Lee Kuan Yew's finest, Inspector Lee or Inspector Rahman or Inspector Singh, to interview the crew of the vessel at our behest, perhaps saving some of the taxpayers' money, and *he* finds the answers. Correct? I think not. All we might find by these methods is the teeth of the gears. Not the gears themselves, not the connecting rods, certainly not the engine." Frogh suddenly began patting his coat pockets as if he had forgotten his shopping list for the market.

"Mr. Henriksen," he continued, "the inquest is at four this afternoon, after which the body can be surrendered to the next of kin. Please have Mr. Fredrik Johansen call me with respect to whom we ought to release the body. I shall expect to see you at the inquest, following which I would like a word with you at my office. Again, I'm sorry to be taking up so much of your time, but there it is. Thanks very much."

The rest of the day was consumed by operating problems. One thing that was particularly irksome was the number of calls and telexes from suppliers whom we had always paid on the nail now gently reminding us of their payment terms. As a result, and as much as I hated dealing with the press—they were always misunderstanding what they were being told, and they didn't know enough to know they had misunderstood—I knew some kind of statement was in order to the effect that the firm of P. Johansens Rederi A/S, founded 1926, was continuing to operate normally under the joint management of Fredrik and myself. I drafted a statement very quickly and checked it over the phone with our lawyer, Borgensen, who suggested I add that Fredrik and I had been unanimously elected by the board. I made that addition and, to get the approval of another director, showed it as well to Karl Wessel, who thought it fine. I then had the statement hand delivered to the *Norges Handels og Sjofartstidene*; I also called a decent man I knew at *Lloyds List* and read it to him over the phone.

"Off the record, John, is Johansens going to make it?" Philip Stocks said. "Because it's not Johansen's death that's the problem."

"It's going to be tough, Philip, but I think we will."

And that, I thought, ought to be enough. I did not think at the time that this innocuous public statement was in effect flinging a glove into the faces of the murderers.

6

The inquest began at four and was over quickly. Fredrik was there in a dark suit, looking very sober. I'd not seen him since I'd left him at my house the preceding afternoon. He approached me in the hallway afterward while I was waiting to accompany Frogh back to his office.

"John, I've arranged for the funeral tomorrow afternoon. Just you and some of the others from the office and Cousin Torvald. And some people from the shipping community."

"Don't forget Per Lindstedt, Fredrik. He's a good friend."

"No, I haven't, John. And thank you for yesterday. Was it only yesterday?" He looked down at his shoes. "I shall have to sit down with you and Lars and Karl very soon and learn about shipping." Before he went off, I told him about the statement to the press. He nodded without expression and left.

Frogh's small office had been painted, none too recently, a cream color, with a pale green false dado. There were three dusty houseplants on the windowsill behind him, and a great cast-iron radiator that hissed and clanged whenever the heat came up. On Frogh's desk was an enormous orange glass ashtray with seven pipes resting around the edge.

"I asked you here, Mr. Henriksen, because I wanted what I had to say to be heard only by you and by no one else in your office. When we left off this morning—and I apologize for being a bit short—I was saying that the direct approach was not the way to get at the truth of the *Rose.* We would only be treating the symptoms, not the cause."

The phone rang. Frogh grunted briefly into it and hung up. "Someone you must meet," he said. "Should have been here already."

A tall thin man with pale skin and fine sandy hair came into the room and shut the door. "This," said Frogh, "is Mr. Jensen, from the government."

Jensen smiled—it was more a grimace—and shook my hand with his own cool one, saying, "Pleased." Then he sat behind me on my left. I faced Frogh across his desk.

"I was just telling Mr. Henriksen that we want to get at the truth of the *Rose*."

"Just so," Jensen said.

"Inspector, all of this business about the truth of the *Rose*; I begin to apprehend that you are talking about doing something other than finding Paul Johansen's murderer?"

"Not other than, but in addition to."

"What else is involved in the truth of the *Rose,* Inspector?" I was quite discomposed by Frogh's ominous tone; the question came out sounding peremptory.

I could see Frogh looking over my shoulder with a question in his eyes. It was not his customary vacant stare into the middle distance. He was, to my amazement, seeking permission to answer my question.

Having apparently received it, he said, "The weapon with which Shipowner Johansen was murdered was found this morning in the outskirts of Grimstad. It is an American automatic weapon, a so-called M-16, and we believe it to be one of a number that were stolen some months ago from an arsenal in Massachusetts, USA. Two of the same sort, and definitely from the same theft, were found last month in Northern Ireland. We have no idea what the connection is. Oslo is not Londonderry, and Johansen was not some alleged English oppressor. But, going back to our first conversation, Mr. Henriksen, you can see that it has international, and probably terrorist, implications—Black September, Red Army Faction, Red Brigades, Japanese Red Army, IRA, FALN . . . or something we've never heard of. We want you to help us make the connection between the *Rose* and the rest of it."

"We want you," Jensen said from behind my left shoulder, "to find out what it was that Evgenides was doing with the *Rose*, and to resume doing it."

I turned around and looked at Jensen, who returned my look mildly. "You want me to set myself up to be murdered like Johansen, is that it?"

"I think that's drawing the worst possible conclusion," Frogh said.

"In my position, I can't say I should work hard to draw any other."

"The world is a sad place, Mr. Henriksen," Jensen said, "and it becomes sadder every day. Sometimes civilized governments have to be unorthodox, particularly when dealing with mad dogs." Jensen came forward and leaned on the edge of Frogh's desk. His suit was impeccably pressed, and not a hair on his head was out of place. Frogh was looking into the darkness at the window. "If there were any other way, Mr. Henriksen—please believe me—we would not have suggested such a dangerous thing. And it is highly dangerous. But—fortunately or unfortunately—you are peculiarly well situated to look into things without arousing suspicion that you're working with the police. You've told Inspector Frogh that you must go to Singapore and Tokyo. Talk to the master of the *Rose.* Be completely businesslike. Find out what the *Rose* has been doing, and put her back to work." This last sounded a little like pleading—as much, that is, as someone like Jensen could manage. "We are convinced it is a matter of international security. There will be other nations besides Norway that will be grateful for your efforts."

"Please don't appeal to my better feelings, Mr. Jensen. After forty-eight years there are very few left, and those are reserved for individuals, not for gods, nations, or causes. Too many disgusting things have been done in their names. If I do this—*if* I do this—it will be for reasons you couldn't possibly think of." I looked from one to the other. Jensen allowed no emotion into his face, but he had become a bit flushed. Who was Jensen, come to think of it? Frogh looked a little upset. "I should very much like to get some air. I'm feeling nauseated."

Jensen said, "Please."

Frogh said nothing.

"Needless to say, this conversation is confidential," Jensen added.

"*Cela va sans dire,* Mr. Jensen."

I walked in the cold and darkness down to the brick pile of the Town Hall and looked out at the water, but there were no answers in the Oslo Fjord. The whole matter had gone beyond my comprehension, or at least I felt it could no longer be addressed on a conscious level. I was struggling to be released from the nightmare, to wake to find myself arguing with Johansen about the newbuildings, the tankers under construction. But I knew there would be no such thing as waking from this. Johansen was dead, machine-gunned in a street in Oslo, and what Jensen was proposing, once undertaken, would be irrevocable. And he had no better idea of what the consequences would be than I did.

The Jensens of this world frightened me: the mild-mannered, emotionless unknowns who set events in motion and could not envisage, would not admit the possibility of there being, an outcome other than the one they were seeking. Their glance took in continents, they talked confidently in global terms, but what they did, what they *did*, was at best shortsighted.

I returned to the office to see whether I could get any further with the budgets before I met Alice. I was hardly going to be ebullient company, but I had to have someone else understand what I was going through.

The office was empty. I threw my hat and coat on a chair and sat at my desk. The in-basket was piled high, and there was a note on the phone from Karl Wessel. He had fixed the *Zinnia* for a voyage, PG-West, at a rate that would pay the operating expenses for the voyage and make a small contribution toward interest; anything for principal was out of the question. The market was going to be that way for a long, long time. In the event, well done, Karl, I thought.

There was a plain envelope in the middle of my desk addressed to me and marked "Private and Confidential" in English. It had been hand delivered, because there was no stamp on it, and I suspected it was either from the American banker at the Grand or another resignation. My hands were shaking and my heart pounding when I picked up the envelope, and I knew I was getting close to the edge. I waited until my heart slowed before I opened the letter.

It was a threat.

7

I called Frogh immediately. He asked me to read it to him. "It's in English, made out of letters cut from magazines and so forth. Quote: Johansen's death is the first until you stop PLF. End quote. That's all."

"Not very good diction," Frogh grunted. "I'll be right over."

I called Alice to tell her I'd be delayed. "Forget the restaurant, John. Come to my flat, and I'll make something here."

"That would be lovely. You don't mind?"

"For heaven's sake, John. Have you ever heard me say anything I didn't mean?"

I certainly hadn't.

"It's very bad, isn't it?" she said.

"Worse than I could ever have imagined. I'll tell you about it. Say, between seven-thirty and eight?"

"Whenever," she said in English.

Frogh pondered the piece of paper for a long time.

"People's Liberation Front?" I asked.

"Could be."

"Someone with a shaky command of English."

Frogh looked at me over the bowl of his pipe. Out of deference to what he called his "scientists," he had not lit up. "Or with an excellent command of English trying to appear otherwise. I can't tell you why, Mr. Henriksen, but I think this is a fake."

"You mean we can disregard it? That it's the work of a crank?"

"No, no. I don't mean that, I think the threat is real enough. But I don't think it's from whom it purports to be. PLF indeed!" he snorted. "This message is too smooth, Mr. Henriksen. It's slightly garbled, but not so much that you won't get the point. And the point is very specific: Johansen's death is *only* the first *unless* you stop. It is, as you suspected early on, a threat against all of you. But it is not from any so-called liberation front. I'll show the message to Jensen. He'll be ecstatic." Frogh looked thoughtful. "I'm sorry about our conversation earlier. I realize the proposal Jensen made is a difficult one. I thought a long time about it myself. But I fear it really is the best way."

"Who is Jensen? Intelligence?"

"Something of the sort. By the by," he said hastily, "what Jensen did not say, and what you are not supposed to know, is that if you decide to go through with this, you will have some protection. Someone will be following you on your trip to the Far East. You are also to fly first class."

"And is the state going to pay for that?"

"Directly or indirectly, Mr. Henriksen, as you well know, *you'll* pay for it. The reason you fly first class is that if there is a difficulty, it is easier to control with fewer people around."

"I think it important that Fredrik Johansen come with me to renegotiate the contracts with the Japanese, Inspector Frogh. He is now the owner of the firm, as well as one of the joint managing directors, and it is time he got directly involved in the running of the company. Will this be possible if I undertake Jensen's mission?"

"I think Jensen would be absolutely delighted. Doubles the number of targets." His eyes twinkled. "Now do you have one of those plastic binder things I can slip this letter into? Thanks. The envelope too, please. Do you have a big manila folder or envelope? Thanks very much."

Frogh wound a hairy wool scarf around his throat and put on his coat. "There is no reason for you to do this thing if you don't want to, Mr. Henriksen. No one pays you to put your life in danger." He took out his gloves. "I don't want to make too big a thing of this," he continued, holding up the manila envelope, "so could you casually ask in your office tomorrow how this came to be here? Good. May I wish you a good evening?"

There could be no doubt that Alice Nielsen had an English mother. Her high color suggested Surrey or Suffolk, not Oslo. She was tall and slim, with blue eyes and black hair streaked with gray (she was five years younger than I). For the dozen years I had known her she had always looked the same, with the single exception of the graceful advance of gray in her hair.

She had always had many admirers, because she was a handsome woman, but she had never married and had no intention to. She valued what she called her freedom too much, at the same time freely conceding that everyone had his own definition of personal freedom. She did not look with disapproval on women who had children hanging onto their apron pockets and who waited by the door in the evenings with their husbands' slippers; but such a life was simply not for her.

Alice was an independent commercial photographer who spent a lot of time in places other than Oslo, to which she returned, she asserted, to rest. Oslo, she said, a little unkindly, made no demands on her, unlike the other places she went to on assignments for magazines for pictures of people (who mostly amused her) and things. Her pictures of people—diplomats, politicians, international society—were never vicious, but sometimes they were a little wicked. She was so graceful, so feminine, however, that no one ever thought the wickedness anything but innocent.

She had lovers, including myself from time to time, but she was such a complete human being and treated everyone with such warmth and honesty that she never seemed in danger of generating envy, rage, or jealousy in any of us. That was, at least, the way I felt, and if she talked about me in the way she used to talk about her friends in London or New York or Buenos Aires, treasuring the conversations that they'd had, and the people—*their* friends—that she had met, then everyone must have felt the same.

I liked to think I was one of the reasons Alice stayed in Oslo and tolerated the high cost of living and the taxes; but if that was the case, I was one of the minor reasons. She came back to Oslo, I think, because she had been happy here as a girl and had been very close to her parents. (She had a younger brother, whom I'd not met, of whom she was also very fond. He worked as an engineer for a large British firm in the Midlands.) And she was finding in her travels that happiness was coming to be an increasingly rare commodity that ought to be embraced wherever it occurred.

"You don't look as if you've been getting any sleep, John," she said, kissing me briefly.

"I've been getting sleep. I haven't been getting any rest." She put my hat and coat in the closet and told me to sit while she made me a whisky soda.

"There's a new phenomenon for the last quarter of the twentieth century," she said, handing me the drink. "The ugly Norwegian. You've not been to London recently? Very hard to get a place on a plane to London from here on Friday nights. Filled with our compatriots, John, in corduroy trousers and ski sweaters with little reindeer on them, and they've all checked empty suitcases. When they come back on Sunday evenings the suitcases are full of British goods, because the pound is cheap and everything is a bargain. I'm thinking of doing a 'before and after' series and calling it 'The Decline of the West.' Do you think *Pravda* would be interested?"

"I don't read *Pravda* with regularity, but I don't think they use many pictures. Perhaps they have a Sunday magazine."

She grew thoughtful. "Tell me about it," she said.

I found that once I'd got started I could not stop. I followed her into the kitchen while she made an omelette and a salad. I talked while I opened a bottle of white wine; I talked through dinner and over coffee. I told her all that Frogh had told me, and I told her also about Jensen and his proposal.

She said nothing for a while; then, "Jensen's proposal is ridiculous."

"But he *is* right, you know. The only solution to the problem is establishing the link between what happened here and what Evgenides was doing with the *Rose.*"

"No doubt he is correct. But let someone else establish the link."

"But, darling, I fear that I am the best person to do that because I can pursue it without raising the idea that I have other motives for doing so."

"The drinks have made you too mellow, John. You sound as if you are going to go through with it."

I put my hand over hers. "I think I will, Alice."

She looked at me steadily. "Whatever for?"

"Any number of reasons . . ."

"None of them any good."

"Please let me finish, Alice. Your concern for my well-being is not passing unnoticed. I want to do it for my old colleague, Paul—for my old school friend, then. The nice young man I saw off on the ferry to Tyneside when we were twenty and there was no possibility the world would ever end. I want to do it for the man I knew and respected—even though I would not say I liked him any longer—before he learned the secret of walking on water. I want to do it for Fredrik, who has never had a chance . . . and besides, I have no children of my own. I want to do it, Alice, because in my bones I think it's the right thing to do. Hush," I said, putting my finger to her lips when she was about to speak. "It was coming here to you tonight that helped me put my thoughts in order. You let me babble away and that cleared the cobwebs and the blockages to thinking clearly."

"Oh, Christ," she said, her eyes welling, "he's telling me I'm responsible."

We were sitting together on the sofa. I put my arms around her and felt her tears on my neck. "No, no, no, Alice. I and only I am responsible. You simply made it possible for me to think sensibly about it." I kissed her eyes. She pushed away from me and stood and crossed the room to the shelves on which she kept her photographic portfolios. She wiped her eyes and blew her nose and selected a portfolio. Flipping through it quickly, she said, "Do you remember this?" It was a picture she had taken of Johansen five years before in Athens at the Posidonia shipping conference. That was the time when the Japanese, having stockpiled raw materials on a massive scale and driven freight rates through the ceiling, had stopped stockpiling. The freight market was on its way through the floor. It was when Johansen could shake his head and commiserate with his colleagues who had kept their freight contracts short. Johansen, on the other hand, had those lovely long-term charters to Norbulk, and the contracts of affreightment with Nippon Steel, and was just starting out in tankers in a small way.

I looked at the photograph, which I had seen before but had not thought about for years. That was the old Johansen, before the adventures in tankers and dry cargo, before the financial worries;

the thin hair, the flat colorless eyes, the firm facial skin, the athletic body. Alice had taken the picture at a reception at the Athens Hilton, when Johansen was with some rather obvious Levantine types. He was looking, I thought, dreadfully Norwegian, with a dark, double-breasted blazer (no doubt blue) with light buttons (no doubt brass) and light gray trousers (no doubt light gray), and one could see the little light-colored anchors in his dark tie on a white shirt. His expression spoke at many levels: "Oh, you again, Miss Nielsen"; "Get out of my way"; "Will someone rid me of these troublesome Greeks?" That was the kind of man he was; but he knew his shipping. And it was one or two years before I had awakened to the mistake he had made in getting the tankers.

I'm not sure what Alice intended by bringing out the picture of Johansen. She was perhaps trying to force me to look through someone else's eyes at the person in memory of whom I was announcing I was going to undertake a most dangerous venture. But if that was it, Alice had gone astray. The photograph of Johansen—and it was one of her wicked ones—showed a man I knew, a man who held no surprises for me. As far as Paul was concerned, I knew exactly what I was doing.

But the week Alice had taken that picture had also been the happiest time she and I had ever had together, one during which we had reached such a physical and emotional peak that we each very nearly made a commitment, an avowal, a declaration, a what-have-you, from which we each had drawn back. I thought now of that time with sorrow.

I do not know what Alice was thinking at that moment. Her face said nothing.

"Yes, I remember this," I said. "This is the man I'm talking about."

She took the picture from me, slipped it back into the portfolio, and put the portfolio back on the shelf. While she still had her back to me, I could hear her breathe sharply, as if she were blowing off steam. When she turned, she said, "Is there any connection between Evgenides and Raymond Bechmann?"

"I'm sure there is, but Frogh hasn't yet heard from London. Or else, he hasn't told me."

"And what about this theft of auto parts? Is that significant?"

"It might be, but I doubt it. All that area is full of pirates still."

"But, John, they don't usually attack ocean-going vessels, do they?"

"I should think they'd attack anything that looked vulnerable and worth attacking."

"What would make the *Rose* look vulnerable?"

"I don't know."

"I think the auto parts are important. There are many odd things in this story right from the beginning. But the auto parts theft is one of the oddest."

She left that thought with me and after giving me a cognac, she went to do the washing up. We went to bed together but we did not make love. She was tense, I knew, and in her presence, my own nervous energy had drained away. She held me in her arms while I drifted to sleep. I remember—I don't think I dreamed this—that I asked her to marry me, and that she replied that I should not talk foolishness while I was vulnerable.

I woke at six-thirty, as is my habit, and listened to the unfamiliar sounds: the unidentifiable sounds in the apartment building, the odd car or truck passing in the street below, Alice's steady breathing. I stared into the darkness trying to recapture the words I had awakened with on my mind. And there they were. Aegean Maritime. I had missed a connection.

8

There was no need to get up. I was five minutes from the office. Plenty of time. I fell asleep again.

When I woke again, I felt a tremendous need for sexual release. I began to caress her body—gently, I supposed; clumsily and hastily, probably. Alice turned to me and, after a little, received me tenderly and without passion, which was just as well. In that place, at that time, my desire and my desperation were surely enough for both of us.

When I reached the office, I immediately went to the papers on the *Rose* to corroborate the connection I had made while I was half asleep. Aegean Maritime, to the account of which Evgenides had transferred the funds in the Geneva bank belonging to the *Rose,* was the company from which Johansen had bought the *Rose.* I called Wessel on the intercom.

"Karl, that million and a quarter that Johansen paid for the *Rose* was a bargain, wasn't it?"

"Absolute theft, unless she was in terrible shape, but I never heard there was any problem with her records or with the insurance. She'd just passed special survey, I think. You must ask Lars Norland. I think Johansen used an outside firm to do his own survey."

I called Frogh a little later to report that no one in the office seemed to know how the envelope had gotten onto my desk. I told him as well my conclusion that for some reason the ship had practically been given away to Johansen, priced so attractively that he could not have refused to buy. I began to get a sense then of how frightened Johansen must have become by the sudden reversal of the tanker market to have suspended his normally good judgment and to have become enmeshed in such schemes. He could have turned around on the same day he bought the *Rose* and made a two-million-dollar profit. Why hadn't he questioned the seller? In the event, he gambled instead on the longer term.

"Have you heard from London about this man Bechmann?"

"Not as yet—neither about Raymond Bechmann nor about where the money went after it got to London." Frogh faded away and I could tell he was conducting his pipe operation. "Your theory then," he continued, "is that the price of the vessel was bait for Johansen to buy."

"Absolutely."

"And that the reason was that Evgenides was using Johansen for something."

"Yes."

"Have you any reason to believe—or not to believe, for that matter—that Johansen was not allowing himself to be used at all, and in fact was using Evgenides?"

"I think that *was* happening, Inspector Frogh, but not in the way you mean. I think Johansen was terrified of bankrupting the firm—which fear, by the way, he never revealed to anyone here, as far as I know—and was grasping at straws. In that sense, yes, I think it was possible he was using Evgenides. He normally did not give people like Evgenides the time of day."

I could hear Frogh puffing in contemplation. "One more thing, Inspector. I have decided to comply with the suggestion that your friend made the other evening."

"Ah," said Frogh. "Can you join me here for lunch and we can talk about the arrangements? About twelve shall we say?"

It was becoming increasingly difficult to concentrate on the business of the firm, but one thing was very clear indeed and needed hardly any concentration at all. The conservative budgets I had asked for showed an extremely bleak picture.

I banged on the intercom again. "Wessel, you've been out of sale and purchase too long. Pick four to six of the best tanker brokers you know. I want you eventually to sell all of the tankers, but start with *Star Aster* and *Iris.* I'll send you the figures for the mortgage outstanding on each."

"I'm glad, John. I'll telex New York and ring London straight away. I think if we are willing to settle quickly at a fairly cheap price, we can generate interest in the Far East."

"Well, I hope. Let Norland know what you are doing."

* * *

The bilious decoration of Frogh's office was hardly conducive to an appetite, but when I arrived I found he had laid on a tray of sandwiches covered with a cloth, and a couple of bottles of Pilsner. We discussed the mechanics of our trip to the Far East for a bit: the flights we were to take, the hotel in which we were to stay. We were to make arrangements immediately and to leave as soon as possible. My impression during this conversation was that Frogh was preoccupied.

Frogh opened the beers and poured them into coffee mugs and uncovered the open-faced sandwiches. While we ate he talked, mostly about himself. He was married and had two children. I was surprised to discover that he was only forty-five. I fancied that he looked older than I, but after reflecting on what he must have experienced in his job, I realized he could not have helped looking older. His daughter was a delight; his son, who was fourteen, a worry—seemed to care only for rock music and film stars and hovered around the fringes of a tough crowd at school.

Frogh sighed heavily. "Would you like some coffee?" When I nodded assent he went to the door and gave an instruction.

"We have some more information," he began, returning to his chair. "The man Bechmann has disappeared. It has been established, however, that Aegean Maritime is a client of Multinational . . . mmmm," he opened a file in front of him, " . . . Capital Limited and that the account has at present a debit balance of three hundred seventy-seven thousand pounds sterling. Perfectly legitimate, I'm told. They have an overdraft facility for five hundred thousand. Mr. Bechmann was the Multinational director who handled the account. He was characterized by his general manager as a shrewd, aggressive banker. A check around the City at the behest of Scotland Yard characterizes Multinational Capital Limited itself as a quote fringe end quote bank—you perhaps appreciate what that means more than I—which is rather thinly capitalized and will perhaps be even more so when recent losses in the U.K. property market are recognized. We are also informed in confidence that the Bank of England is following the situation closely." He snorted and chuckled. "My contact in Scotland Yard has a very jaded view of the matter. He says that the general manager of Multinational is, as far as he can tell, regarded by no one—except the general manager—as either shrewd or aggressive. My contact says that he himself would be quite worried if the director on an account disappeared while the account was owing the bank three hundred seventy-seven thousand pounds. Ownership of the bank is evidently held by some quote shady end quote Arabs. Am I correct in thinking the word *wogs* is not one one would use in everyday polite conversation?"

"Yes."

There was a knock on the door, and a young blond woman brought a tray with cups and a pot of coffee into the room. Watching her, Frogh seemed to slip back into the somewhat depressed mood he had shown when discussing his son. The girl was certainly young enough to be a daughter of either of us.

"In any event . . ." Frogh resumed when she had left. "Please, help yourself. In any event, the Yard followed up and checked Bechmann's country house, which is in Oxfordshire." Here Frogh paused and seemed to be counting the number of pipes in his ashtray. "I'm giving it up," he said brightly. "Only two this morning." At which he proceeded to fill one of the pipes and lit up. "I have something very unpleasant to relate. If you want to change your mind about the Far East trip, let me know. You have only to say." His eyebrows made their interrogative mark. I nodded for him to continue. "A body was found in Bechmann's house. Had been shot several times. The face was mutilated beyond recognition, but based on identifying marks the police obtained from Greek records, it seems pretty clear that the dead man is Evgenides."

Frogh looked steadily at me. "I meant what I said, Mr. Henriksen. One word and the whole thing is off. You have done nothing irrevocable."

"You are very kind, Inspector, and I know that I can do that, but I won't." What, in fact, would I have said had Alice said the night before that she would marry me?

"I surmise, therefore," Frogh continued, "that Evgenides was doing something with the *Rose* on behalf of someone else, and that that someone else was Bechmann. That somehow Evgenides stumbled and had to be eliminated. But if Raymond Bechmann is the perpetrator—*if* he is the perpetrator—then we have him on the run, and everything will now go along swimmingly, and you won't have to do anything about the *Rose* when you go to the Far East. Except that I really don't believe any of it. It goes beyond Bechmann. Bechmann may be more than a pawn, but he's no more than a knight. I would be interested to know if Bechmann had an interest in Aegean Maritime. Can we find that out through the Liberian ship registry?"

"You'll get as far as the Swiss nominees and the bank references and no farther. Banking in Switzerland is sacred."

"I think we can get them to open the records if we can prove they are connected with a crime." He started to pack another pipe, then put it aside, looking somewhat sheepish. "Speaking of banking, the funds that went from the *Rose* account in Switzerland to the American bank in London were transferred internally to the account of a Brazilian bank branch in New York, for the account of someone called Amadeo da Silva. We are checking further." Frogh grew somber. "I am also somewhat troubled by your research into the origins of that letter you received last night. If no one remembers, that could mean no one noticed a messenger delivering a letter last evening, which hardly seems likely. What seems more likely, I'm afraid, is that there *was* no messenger."

"Meaning . . ."

"Meaning that the threat was made by someone inside your firm."

9

The service in the chapel attached to the crematorium was brief, and there were no eulogies. I saw several people I knew from the shipping community, including Per Lindstedt, but said nothing to them. Afterward each went to Fredrik and said a few words and went away.

He was looking very grim—older perhaps—and as if he'd lost weight the last three days. I drove him back to his father's house and went in with him. We sat and had a drink and talked of the trip to Singapore and Tokyo. Fredrik seemed quite composed by then. He seemed to have got over his grief, and perhaps his guilt, alone, and come through remarkably well.

I explained what I had undertaken to do with respect to the *Rose* and what I and Frogh thought the risks might be. I told him he was under no obligation to come with me, and in fact suggested forcefully that he join me in Tokyo for the negotiations with the shipyard and not bother going to Singapore at all.

"I hope you don't hold me in such low esteem, John," he said. "You have been very good to me these last few days, particularly allowing me time to sort things out without burdening me with office matters. I know you are—were—my father's friend, and perhaps you feel you ought to do something for me because of that; forgive my presumption. I don't know everything that you know about the situation concerning the *Rose,* but I know enough to recognize that what you are doing is very dangerous. I want to tell you there's no need for it. If anyone should undertake it, it should be me."

"Fredrik, I do what I do for my own reasons. That is enough. I strongly recommend against your coming with me. If you do, however, I'll be pleased to have your company."

"Thank you, John," he said and shook my hand. And began to weep.

I put my arms around him, and we stood there together, Fredrik crying on my shoulder. He was crying, I surmise, for many reasons, not least because of the end of childhood. And I felt that after all it was not a bad thing, this final purging.

In a few moments, he extricated himself, and laughed in an embarrassed way. "I'm sorry, John. I just . . ."

I said that no explanation was necessary. "Shall I arrange two air tickets and hotel rooms?"

"Yes."

"Good. Is your passport in order? We'll need shots. Smallpox, certainly, and cholera, I think. I'll have Marta check tomorrow and let you know. You are prepared to leave as soon as we can arrange things?"

"Yes, John. As quickly as possible."

"Goodnight then, Fredrik," I said. "Shall we meet in the office at seven-thirty? We have a good deal of work to get through before we leave." I wished him good evening and left to return to the office.

I could just make out someone standing in the entrance to the building in Ovre Slottsgate. I backed into the shadow and watched for a bit, my heart pounding in my ears. Then I saw him slump and put a hand against the wall to support himself, and I realized it was just a drunkard. Oslo has a lot of them that one can see at all times of day and night in the city center. They collect from all over the country, former sailors, most of them, whose last shred of pride will not allow them to wander drunkenly through their small home towns—Fevik, Haugesund, Lillesand—so they come to Oslo to hide and to lose themselves. The man leaning against our office door was another of these and I would have felt a lot more sympathy for him had he not given me such a fright.

"Get out of there," I shouted.

He looked up unconcerned, completely gone in an alcoholic fog.

I moved up to him and grabbed him by the shoulder. "I said, get out of here," and pushed, not very hard. I did not want him falling and hurting himself. He arranged his coat and started toward me.

"Do you want me to call the police, old man?"

The figure stopped and seemed to be peering through the

gloom. "I know you," he croaked. "Long time. Can't remember your name." He came forward a few steps. I involuntarily put my hand up. "Hope you can remember mine. Hard for me sometimes."

I strained my eyes in the feeble light from a street lamp. "Krogstad."

"Right first try. Win the bloody national lottery."

"Why don't you go away, Krogstad? I've already heard about you from the police."

"So they did in the old son of a bitch. Good riddance."

I turned away and tried to ignore him. "Good riddance," he said again. "That goddamn man ruined me, you hear?"

I unlocked the frosted glass door and turned on the hall light and began to close the door. He put his hand between the door and the jamb. He muttered in stinking breath through the opening. "I know who did it."

Had it been anyone but this disgusting spectacle I would have dragged him through the doorway. But in the light from the hall I could see Krogstad pretty clearly. He looked twenty years older than he was; what part of his face was not hidden in an unkempt beard was mottled. He was obviously missing teeth and he was dirty and wrapped against the winter in what seemed to be parts of coats. What could Krogstad know?

"How much it worth to you to know who did it? I'd like to go south for the winter."

"Krogstad, if you do know something and you haven't told the police, you're obstructing justice. You might as well have killed him yourself. Or maybe they'll consider you an accessory after the fact. I think I will call the police."

"No, no, no, no," he said. "I don't know who did it. I swear. Give me ten kroner. I can give you information."

"Goodnight, Krogstad." I pushed the door gently against his finger.

"No, please, let me sleep in the hall."

It was terrible to see the man quaking and trembling on the doorstep. I let him into the hall, which immediately filled with the stench of his body.

"You used to be a decent officer, Krogstad, but how could Johansen trust you anymore? I would have sacked you too if I'd been in his position." I was wondering if he was going to have a fit of some kind, and how long it had been since he'd been without a drink. "I want you to stop maligning the man. His funeral was this afternoon."

Krogstad started to wail. Tears poured down his face, and his nose ran. "Ah, poor old Johansen, poor old Johansen. You're right whoever your name is. Was a good officer. Not anymore. Demon rum. Too many empty nights on the empty sea. Poor old Johansen. Sorry. Sorry, sorry."

"I'm going to take you to the municipal hospital, Krogstad." He looked at me in terror. I was going to cut him off from his liquor. "Please no," he said. I had never in my life heard a plea like that. He tugged weakly at my sleeve. "Please no."

"Man, you're killing yourself. Is that what you want to do?"

By way of response, he opened the door and stumbled onto the pavement. I decided not to follow him. Even if I could get him to a hospital, I doubted that whatever they did for him would be permanent. Krogstad was doomed by whatever mixture of physical and emotional chemistry it was that led him to find the end of his loneliness in a bottle.

I locked the front door and went upstairs to the office and turned out the hall light. I rang Frogh, but he had already gone home, so I left word if he called in to have him phone me at his convenience, either at home or the following day at the office. Then I put the figures that the accounting staff had prepared for me into a briefcase, along with one of the pocket calculators, and started home.

Krogstad was lying senseless across the doorstep. I dragged him inside and rang for an ambulance, which came quickly. I was glad to see that somehow the man had accepted the fact that he needed help.

At home I ate some sausages and bread and drank a bottle of beer before I set to work on the numbers. I had had the accounting people make a number of projections using different assumptions with respect to cost inflation, revenues, layup of one or two tankers, cancellation of the big ships, sale of all the tankers, conversions to bulk carriers, interest rates, and general economic environments. They had done an excellent job. Depending on one's capacity for self-deception, one might be able to persuade oneself to a different conclusion; but in fact, no matter how rosy the assumptions, the course to follow was the one we had already set out on. Any other direction led to disaster, and the only question would be the timing.

While I was making coffee, Frogh called. I reported that I had told Fredrik virtually everything, to which he made no objection. I learned that the British were looking more closely at Bechmann's merchant bank; they had found that a number of people remembered Johansen calling on Bechmann there fairly frequently in the last several months.

So Johansen had been going to see Bechmann when he told me he was off to his tailor's, or to see the brokers, after we'd been to Hambros, or Kleinworts, or Citibank in a fruitless search for finance for the last VLCC. I did not like to recall those recent days when, against my judgment, I was directed by Johansen to devise scheme upon scheme whereby we might secure a loan. I kept telling Johansen how much I disagreed with what he was trying to do, but shipowners are a pigheaded lot. Toward the end, Johansen stopped listening entirely. Perhaps I ought to have resigned; I doubt that it would have made any difference.

I wondered what it was that kept Johansen returning to Bechmann. Paul was no fool about people. Surely he would detect that the man was something less than honorable. But if Bechmann had provided what Johansen had needed or needed to believe, then I suppose it didn't matter what the man was like.

I worked hard with Fredrik the following day, first making him completely current, if not conversant, with the state of our finances, the disposition of the fleet, and finally with the negotiating posture we ought to adopt with the Japanese. I felt we ought to insist on cancellation, full stop—no conversions, no penalties, pleading material adverse change, *force majeure,* threaten finally to refuse delivery if the ships were built, and so forth; all in order to wind up with three new open-hatch bulk carriers of about forty thousand tons with the gearing that Lindstedt wanted.

The morning was nearly exhausted by the time I asked my secretary, Marta, to get started on the arrangements for the trip. We were to fly to London and pick up the flight to Bahrain and Singapore. We were to stay at the Mandarin Hotel in Singapore. I was surprised to have everything confirmed within two hours. The hotel, it seemed, was already holding bookings in our names. I detected a whiff of the government.

We met again after lunch in the small conference room with the photographs of P. Johansen's first ships, a couple of eight-hundred-ton colliers. We discussed the trip in a general way since we were off in four days.

"You must make a will, Fredrik. It's one thing to leave the operations temporarily with Norland and Karl Wessel; it's quite another to leave the firm virtually with no owner."

"I know you are quite right, John, and I have been thinking about it, but I don't know what I want or can do."

"If I may?" To which Fredrik nodded. "I suggest you get Borgensen to work a little harder for that fat retainer we pay him and set up a trust for the benefit of whomever. You should leave the firm to the trust, and I suggest you make Per Lindstedt and Atle Selmer's bank the joint trustees. I can't think of a better way to protect your capital, particularly if you intend to leave your estate for the benefit of someone who is not in shipping."

"I should very much prefer to make you the trustee, John," he said. "But I can't very well do that, can I, if you come with me. Can't I persuade you to cancel your trip?"

I could only smile at the very young man speaking in Fredrik. He sighed. "I suppose I shall make Cousin Torvald the beneficiary. He knows even less about shipping than I do. Although he knows a great deal about cement."

"Don't underestimate yourself, my boy. You have breathed the atmosphere of shipping all your life. You have learned a great deal subconsciously."

He seemed to shudder. "And rejected much of it consciously."

He began to tap the table with an index finger, as if he were wondering whether to continue. He looked very drawn. "Shipping has been poison in my life. Father was in England taking delivery of a ship the day my mother died in childbirth. From that moment on the family ceased to be a part of my father's life; he cared only for this place." He stopped tapping and looked at the symbols that surrounded us and then very directly at me. "I must be honest with you, my good friend. My feelings about the firm are very mixed. I need time to sort them out." He looked again at the old photographs on the walls. "I think now, if you don't mind, I'll go see Borgensen."

10

That evening, Lars Norland and I had a drink with Bill Clark, the American banker who had called me earlier in the week, at the bar in the Grand Hotel. The bar was crowded and the noise level was high, but Clark fired question after question at us. We responded on the optimistic side of candor, but it was a depressing exercise even so, and when we left him in the lobby, he looked a worried young man indeed.

Lars and I walked together down to the garage where I kept my car. The night was clear and very cold, but it felt good to be breathing fresh air after spending the day in hermetically sealed overheated rooms of one sort or another.

"Lindstedt has offered to buy the firm, hasn't he?" Lars said.

"Well he has and he hasn't," I responded. "He offered a knockdown price of nine million dollars, which I can't believe he expected to be taken seriously."

Norland blew air forcefully. "What did you say?"

"I told him we'd sort out our difficulties first; then we might entertain a proposal."

Lars was silent for a time. Our feet squeaked in unison on the packed snow. "The man's prescience is uncanny," he said, without particular relevance.

"I'm not sure his expansion recently has been all that wise."

"Don't you indeed?" Norland said, sounding rather more surprised than I thought he might.

"But I must admit," I added, "that his crystal ball does seem clearer than most other people's."

"I hope we don't regret that nine-million-dollar offer someday," Norland said.

The remaining days slipped by quickly. The Norbulk offices had been informed, the Japanese had been informed, the master of the *Rose* had been informed. There were loose ends to tie up, a hundred directions to give. I saw Alice once more before I left; in the night, we clung to each other like two children in a cave during a thunderstorm. Alice was very nearly sick with fear, and my own state of mind was not the best. I was more unnerved by Frogh's idea of the source of the letter threat than I cared to admit. Negotiating with the Japanese, if we ever got to that point, would come as a relief.

In the morning Alice said to me, in rather a matter of fact way, that it was possible we might see each other in the East, as she had been asked by a French magazine to do a photo essay on Vietnam.

"Have you accepted yet?" I asked.

"Not yet."

"Then please don't. Or if you do, please go sometime later."

"I don't recall," Alice began in her most lady-of-the-manor accent, *and* in English, "any arrangement in which I promised to obey you, John." At which I protested. To which she protested. And we started bickering over the breakfast table as if we had been married years and years. It was lovely.

At the office on the day before we left, I received a call from the hospital that Krogstad was asking to see me. It was an incredible bore; but at the same time, I was too preoccupied to be of much use in the office. And I was annoyed, although I cannot say surprised, that there had not yet been a single indication of interest in either *Star Aster* or *Iris*; perhaps Wessel was losing his touch—or didn't care. In the event, I went to the hospital, telling myself I might do the poor man some good.

Krogstad's bed was in a quiet ward. He was a lot cleaner than the last time I had seen him, but among the white sheets in his white hospital gown he looked very shrunken and old, despite the fact that he was probably no more than fifty-two or three. He was very sick, and he took a long time between thoughts to get his breath, but it seemed that something had fallen into place for him, perhaps for the first time in years.

He thanked me for what I'd done, which was embarrassing, because it had been precious little. Then, without of course knowing the extent of my involvement, he told me a most extraordinary story. It was painful for him to speak, so it took a long time to tell.

"I never liked the old man. Plastic bastard. No heart at all as far as I could tell. But nobody should die like that. Good Christ, in Oslo? I don't know if it has anything to do with anything, but maybe it does. About a year ago, maybe more, maybe less, I was on *Celandine*—my last trip before that son of a bitch sacked me. We were at anchor in Hong Kong, down by Causeway Bay. That little Freedom the old man had an interest in, the *Rose*, was next to us for a day or so. Looked terrible. If I'd been mate on that tub I would have shot the master and kicked the ass of everybody else on board from there to Kobe. I was leaning over the rail one night, wondering where my next drink and my next piece of ass, in that order, would be coming from, when I see this long, low powerboat draw up alongside *Rose*. Christ that thing growled like it could go forty knots without even trying. Kind of thing pirates use. Well goddamn me if they didn't offload eight big crates, using the cranes, mind you. It was all very quick, like they had a train to catch. I thought it was goddamn strange. Never saw the like before. Middle of the night, goddamn powerboat, no running lights. What the hell were they doing? Smuggling, no question of that. But not hit or miss. This was organized. Told the old man. Master of the *Celandine,* that is. He told me to get below and sleep it off. Wouldn't believe me. Johansen didn't either. Fuck 'em both. I didn't imagine it. I see the drainpipes in Oslo turning into snakes and all that shit, but what I saw in Causeway Bay happened just like I said." The poor man sank back exhausted and paid no attention when I left.

I rang Frogh immediately when I returned to the office. He listened but said nothing, thanked me, and rang off. I was a bit disappointed in his reaction. Krogstad's story reminded me of the cases of auto parts that were stolen from the *Rose* in Port Kelang. It might have happened in almost the same way, but what Krogstad had seen in Hong Kong had obviously been arranged.

The next morning, early, Karl Wessel picked me and my two suitcases up in his capacious Volvo. Fredrik, who lived in the center of town, was already in the car. We drove to Fornebu to catch the first BE flight to London. Almost everyone checking in for the flight was a businessman going to London for the day and had nothing with him but a briefcase and a newspaper. We checked our own bags through to Singapore.

Karl wished us a good trip and went off to work. Fredrik and I sat in the black vinyl chairs in the waiting room. We did not speak, each occupied with his own thoughts. Whatever Fredrik was thinking he never said; I thought mostly of Alice Nielsen and deeply regretted what we were about to do.

The morning was black through the plate glass, which had begun to gather streaks of water. It was raining or sleeting, and the only things we could see beyond the glow from the windows were the blue runway lights.

The flight was announced, in Norwegian and English, and we gathered our briefcases and coats. There would be a security check in the underground passage on the way to the plane.

As we approached the hostess in dark blue at the gate, I saw Frogh to one side. His coat was open. He had an unlit pipe in his right hand and his hat in his left. A wisp of a smile passed his lips, and he nodded encouragingly. Beyond Frogh, perhaps three or four meters, in a dark suit and tie and a white shirt, hands behind his back, and even at that distance looking paler than death, was Jensen, his head bobbing almost imperceptibly, as if from some chronic condition. Then the underground passage received us, and Frogh and Jensen disappeared from view.

11

We rose steeply through the dark gray mist, water and sleet streaming horizontally across the windows. When we broke above the clouds into the smooth air, the sky above was very deep blue, fading lighter and lighter toward the east, where the sun was low on the horizon. It was the first sunlight we had seen in two weeks.

As we leveled off the steward began to pull down the tables for breakfast. A heavy man sitting alone across the aisle from us asked for a copy of *Die Welt* and a glass of champagne. His face was very pink, and he looked as though he might be sweating.

We were given a reasonable semblance of an English breakfast, but Fredrik only picked at his food, his mind obviously elsewhere. I thought it best to leave him alone with his thoughts, and began to turn the problem over and over, seeking a new perspective.

Two men, a Norwegian and a Greek, who had been associated in life, were dead, both murdered. The other major things they had in common were the *Rose,* which one owned and the other managed, and a London merchant banker, Raymond Bechmann, through whom they had been linked, certainly initially, and probably up to the end. One was murdered on his way to see the other. Their meeting would have had to do with the *Rose.* Johansen was dissatisfied with Evgenides and was about to dismiss him. Evgenides certainly must have suspected that the relationship was about to end, and he probably knew also what was going to happen to Johansen, but perhaps not when. In the event, he was ready. He had stolen most of the funds from the current account of Johansen's shell company, Transoceanic Shipping. As soon as Johansen was murdered, Evgenides, had left Oslo; had run to London; and as we now knew, had then gone to Bechmann, where he in turn was killed. And Bechmann had disappeared.

What of the *Rose*? A good earner for the first few trips, dismal thereafter. Rumors about her not being maintained. Theft of a cargo. And the strange story that Krogstad had told me about the offloading of crates at night in Hong Kong, which had happened early on in Johansen's ownership of the vessel.

There was a great deal that we knew, but it did not lead anywhere yet. It was clear to me that the *Rose* had been engaged in smuggling. It is true also that smuggling is a dangerous game and gets people killed, usually by rival smugglers.

But Paul Johansen was killed in Oslo with an American army weapon stolen from an arsenal in the States. And he was killed halfway round the world from where, presumably, the smuggling was taking place. It all seemed a bit too significant for a smuggling operation. The goods being smuggled must have been very special indeed. But what in heaven's name could be that special?

Did Johansen know the *Rose* was being used in such a manner? Did he condone it? Did he actively encourage the operation? I simply could not believe Johansen's doing anything of the sort. He was extremely upset about the financial situation of the firm, it was true, but he could not have been that desperate. Or could he? It was true that toward the end I felt I could no longer say I knew the man. He seemed to have suspended his judgment in the matters of Bechmann, Evgenides, and the *Rose.* Could he not have gone further? What finally would have led him to do so?

I was surprised by the announcement that we would be landing shortly at Heathrow. We dipped into a pearl-gray cloud, losing the sun, and became suspended in time and space. We did not come out of the clouds until we were very low. It was very dismal beneath the clouds, and I could see the orange lights of the M-4 leading east toward London and west toward Bath and Bristol. The whole area beneath us was sprinkled with lights. The plane whined and screeched as we came closer and closer to earth and the air brakes were applied; the landing gear thudded open, the landing lights came on, and we could see it was pouring rain.

We taxied slowly toward the terminal, which looked bright and cheerful in the gray morning. As we stepped from the plane, one of the ground people was saying to the man in front of us, "Message for Mr. Henriksen from Oslo." The man shook his head and went on.

"I am Henriksen," I said, stepping up to him. It was then that I noticed a man in a tan raincoat standing behind him. The raincoat moved toward us.

"Mr. Henriksen? And Mr. Johansen? Will you come with me please, gentlemen?" When I hesitated, he opened his wallet and showed us an identification card for Criminal Investigation Division, Metropolitan Police. We followed him through long glassed-in corridors leading toward the immigration hall. "I hope you don't mind, gentlemen," he said, looking back over his shoulder. "And please don't worry yourselves. We'll get you to your connection in plenty of time. Shouldn't be surprised if your plane is late. Filthy weather."

We walked briskly toward the passport control, but when we arrived we were waved through. No entry stamps were put in our passports. I was becoming so on edge and suspicious that I wondered whether this was significant or might prove so later. Fredrik followed along behind me.

We were taken to a small room between immigration and baggage claim and asked to wait. There were a few straight-backed chairs and a worn table.

"Constable Shadwell will be outside if you require anything, gentlemen," said the policeman in the raincoat before he closed the door. "Can't recommend Heathrow tea. Disgusting stuff." He closed the door.

"Do you want anything, Fredrik?"

He shook his head. "What the hell do you suppose this is about, John?"

I shrugged. The door opened and a man in a rumpled brown suit came in. He was of medium height. His hair was dark, and he had blue eyes and a dark complexion, almost Mediterranean-looking. He introduced himself as Inspector Lloyd.

"I hope this is not inconveniencing you," he said. "There are a few recent bits and pieces that my opposite number Frogh thinks would be useful for you to know before you go on your way to Singapore. By the way, your outbound aircraft has only just landed, so your departure will be delayed. Please sit down.

"Now as to the odd bits. The first is that this chap Raymond

Bechmann, we have learned through the kind cooperation of our Swiss counterparts, was the silent owner of Aegean Maritime. He was, in other words, using his bank's money to support a personal little adventure in shipping. I am told that the general manager of this Multinational Capital Limited has been invited to the Bank of England to discuss matters, and that the Arab shareholders are quite beside themselves. You're sure you wouldn't like some tea? No?

"To continue. Raymond Bechmann has quite disappeared off the face of the earth. We can find absolutely no trace of him whatever, so it appears that Mr. Bechmann had a passport with a false—well perhaps not false, but at least different—name in a safety deposit box somewhere, put aside for a rainy day, and that he has skipped the country. It is possible, of course, that he is hiding out somewhere, but we tend to doubt it. Or he could be lying undetected in a field or at the bottom of a well. That's the theory your compatriot Frogh has been working on. He sounds an interesting chap, Frogh.

"Lastly, when you arrive in Singapore, you will be contacted by a Sergeant Ng—that's en-gee, but you must pronounce it as if you have sinus trouble. He's from their own C.I.D. When you decided to go to Singapore, we contacted him and put him in the picture. Sergeant Ng will not meet you at the airport or anything pleasant like that."

"In any event, we are being met by people from the Norbulk office," I interjected.

"Just so. We—he—have decided that you must not be obvious in your contacts with the police after you get on the plane. After all, Mr. Henriksen, you are about to become a criminal of a kind."

"Indeed," I said. "Smuggling is what has occurred to me." Fredrik looked quite startled.

"I suspected something of the sort," Inspector Lloyd said. "But it is not simple smuggling, Mr. Henriksen. It's something very big indeed. Our friend Ng has already been at work and has unearthed something. Most extraordinary. Several village bazaars on the west coast of Malaysia have turned up with brand new parts for Japanese automobiles—piston heads, silencers, crankshafts and the like. When friend Ng learned this through the ASEAN—that is, Association of Southeast Asian Nations—clearinghouse of odd bits, he sent an enquiry. There was a short investigation, and in the rubber trees upcountry they found the remains of six cases of auto parts—Nissan, I think. The crates were marked with the words *auto parts,* along with the name of a consignee, a freight forwarder in Mombasa, and the name of the vessel, *Rose.* The scavengers—the ones with two legs—had been at work and all the crates were empty. We don't know what it adds up to. Either the thieves who picked the crates from the *Rose* got what they had come for and left the rest, or they didn't get what they'd come for at all. I think it is quite certain they were not looking for auto parts."

He looked at his watch. "That's all I have for you gentlemen. Questions? Sergeant Cook—he's the chap in the mysterious mackintosh who met you at the jetway—will take you over to Terminal Three. I hope you won't have too long a wait." He opened the door, called Cook's name, and turned back to us. "I'll wish you a safe flight and good hunting, gentlemen." He shook our hands. "Off you go now."

We followed Cook down a narrow, scruffy flight of stairs and into an unmarked Ford Cortina with a waiting driver.

"Quite a character, Inspector Lloyd," said Cook. The rain pelted against the windshield. "Not a drop of Welsh blood in him, despite his appearance and his name. Gets furious whenever anybody suggests he give us a song. It happens rather a lot."

A short ride through the rain and gloom brought us to a narrow doorway, through which Cook led us. At the top of the stairs beyond, he had a word with a uniformed policeman, and we were allowed through. We found ourselves in an obscure corner leading to the departure lounge of Terminal Three. Fredrik and I turned to say good-bye to Sergeant Cook, and found not only that he had gone, but that we were being pointedly ignored by the constable to whom he had spoken. We hurried along to the departure lounge.

We checked in at the transfer desk and walked once through the duty-free shops and the bookstall, where we bought newspapers and paperback mysteries. For the next hour and a half, surrounded by large Indian families and crying children, we read the papers and talked in a desultory way, interrupted by flight announcements. Our own departure was delayed until twelve-thirty. When at last we were going through the security check—I had by now almost forgotten that one used simply to go to the airport and get on the plane when the flight was announced—I recalled the exchange I had had with Frogh about terrorism. He agreed with me, he said. Terrorism had assumed a life of its own. I thought of those little brown children playing hide-and-go-seek amongst their parents' belongings in the lounge, of the straight, healthy bodies of the peripatetic young with their knapsacks and jeans, and of how indiscriminate a terrorist bullet or hand grenade was—how purposely, pointlessly indiscriminate—and how nothing truly or lastingly good would ever come out of any of it, no matter what specious arguments were put forth by or for this or that national liberation front.

We walked down the sloping jetway to the entrance of the aircraft and were shown seats two rows forward of the door on the left. The first-class section appeared to be nearly full, and there were any number of possible policemen, agents, or assassins. I decided to stop toying with my imagination, which was becoming bizarre, before I began to be consumed by my fantasies. I refused the champagne, which Fredrik accepted, and settled into one of the mysteries, paying no attention while we were pushed away from the gate, while we taxied, and while we were instructed in the use of the oxygen mask and the life jacket. It was only when I felt the tremendous thrust of the engines and the gigantic machine started thumping down the runway that I lifted my eyes from the page (Sir Antony Bayes-Lawless having just been discovered garroted in his locked library) to watch the airport hotels across the Bath Road bounding by the plane. We rose over Windsor Castle, which disappeared quickly beneath the clouds, climbing and circling to the left, and finally breaking out into full sunlight again.

Fredrik continued to drink champagne; I had two sherries before lunch. We both ate a good deal more than was necessary—

I suspect because we were both tense—and Fredrik had an appreciable amount of wine.

While we were musing over the coffee, with which he was taking a cognac, he said, "I'm frightened, John."

I responded that I was as well.

"I understand. Of course you are. But I'm scared in a different way. You see, I don't see what any of this has to do with me. I have been thinking a good deal since we last talked, and I'm beginning to realize that I don't care anything at all about P. Johansens Rederi."

I could not help remarking the change that had occurred in Fredrik these past days, certainly physically, and, I supposed I was about to discover, emotionally also. He still weighed more than he ought, but a good deal less than he had, and he no longer looked like a child. There were deep hollows around his eyes, and his face was drawn.

"Don't say anything you might come to regret, Fredrik."

"No, John, you must understand. I'm being completely honest. I know perfectly well what I'm saying." He paused and sipped the cognac. "You can't know how terrible it's been. All those tributes, all those people saying those nice things about him. I didn't like him, John. I hated him."

"Fredrik, Fredrik," I began, but knew as soon as I had that I should not be able to stop the purgation that the young man sought.

"Please, let me go on. I have had to wrestle with feeling guilty, too, because you don't know how often I have wished him dead. Him or myself. He was never physically cruel. I can't remember his ever raising his hand to me, in fact. But he was cruel in other ways. He was never there, John. Even if he was physically there, he wasn't present. He never paid attention. He was always thinking of the firm, of the ships. The ships were his children, not me. Oh, I always had nurses when I was young, to wipe my nose and feed me, and some I loved. But it's not the same thing as having a father who cares whether you're alive or dead." He pulled the call button for the steward. "And later on, of course, the schools took care of me. Middling schools in which I gave a middling performance. I hated him even more then, because he seemed so good at what he did, and I was so poor at what I did. I know my mother was not strong after I was born, and I have the feeling my father blamed me when she died. He could not blame the new baby because it—she—was dead, too. And of course, he could not possibly blame himself for again impregnating a woman still weak from bearing the first child. I don't know how I know this. I was only two when my mother died, so how could I remember that. Was I told? By whom? Did my father tell me?" The steward poured another cognac for him. "Did you know my mother, John?"

"Hardly at all. Your father and I went our separate ways after he went to Durham. I was working in New York when you were born. So I only met your mother a year or so before she died. Neither of your parents thought much of my wife."

"So you really can't say what my mother was like."

"No, I'm afraid I can't." In fact, I could recall that Fredrik's mother was always quite sickly and was totally dominated by her husband. What was the point in telling him that? I could not even remember what she had looked like.

He looked depressed. "Fredrik, have you ever considered that your mother's death may have made your father realize that he had insisted on having his way once too often? Perhaps all that time when you thought he was blaming you he was blaming himself."

"It took a strange form, John." But he looked pensive indeed, and his second cognac was quite untouched.

"Such things often do," I said. I do not know if I believed my supposition entirely myself. It was possible on an unconscious level. But Johansen never gave the impression of caring a damn about anyone. Fredrik was certainly correct in saying that his father was always thinking about the firm, about the ships. But if the ships were, in fact, his children, how far would he have gone to protect them?

"I'm sorry?" I said to him. He had been talking to me as I wandered down the corridors of my own mind looking for Paul Johansen.

"I said, so you think it possible that all the time he was seeming to be indifferent to me he was really disliking or even hating himself?"

"Entirely possible."

Fredrik fell silent and looked out the window at the clear, pure blue sky. Perhaps it was my imagination, but the way he was sitting seemed to be a bit more relaxed. I eased my own chair back and picked up the mystery novel again; but before I got into it, I reflected on how little I knew of the man with whom I had spent a good deal of my adolescence and for whom I had worked for thirteen years. I wanted to ask Fredrik whether he thought his father could have been involved in illegal activity of this sort, but I could not—at least not yet. On one level, it was too soon to ask something like that when he was in the midst of coming to terms with how matters stood between himself and his father. On another, more primitive level, I had forced myself to recognize, with as much disinterest as I could muster, that Fredrik had the brains and the motive to have had his father murdered.

12

During the hour or so we spent on our stopover at Bahrain I overheard someone talking in American English about Christmas trees and moon pools, both of which related to oil rigs. I was reminded of our colleagues in Oslo who were talking with nearly equal ease in 1972 and '73 and '74 about the semisubmersible oil rigs in which they had invested, or of which they were about to take delivery for use in the North Sea. Now, with a glut of rigs on the market, and world petroleum demand in decline, the sundry governments concerned, including Norway, had slowed their exploration programs, and these same colleagues avoided talking about their unemployed rigs about to come out of the shipyards, except to negotiate with their bankers about restructuring their loans. I could not gloat—Johansen had made enough mistakes, but one thing he did not do was to order an oil rig—because too many of our friends were wondering where their next krone was coming from, and Oslo was full of gray-faced young men from the foreign banks that had lent them money. Oil dominated our lives; I mused how, since the autumn of 1973, the world would never be the same.

We left Bahrain as uneventfully as we landed, climbing into the clear Arabian night full of stars. We had reached that part of a long flight at which I began to feel worn and used up. I slept fitfully for the next two or three hours, waking whenever there seemed to be a change in the sound of the engines or when we hit a patch of turbulence. Images from the past ten days revolved through my mind without order or direction, but if there were any connections to be made, my subconscious was unable to make them.

By the time we started our approach into Singapore, it was after one o'clock in the afternoon. I had no thought for the *Rose,* only for a warm bath and a long nap. We were surrounded by blue sky full of mountainous cloud formations of the purest white, such as I'd never seen before. As the angle of descent increased and we banked for the final run, a moment of pure panic gripped my intestines. It left quickly, but I realized it had had nothing to do with the landing.

We had been following a green coast which I assumed was Malaysia. Now, as we descended below the level of the clouds, we came over lush, deep green tropical vegetation and occasional pink slashes between the trees where land had been cleared for roads or building sites.

We thumped down onto the runway. The steward told us the temperature was eighty-nine degrees Fahrenheit, or thirty-two degrees Celsius. The heat and humidity enveloped us as we left the plane and got into a bus for the short run to the terminal. When we had collected our bags and were at last outside the terminal, we saw a young Chinese man holding up a sign roughly lettered with the word *Norbulk*.

"Mr. Henriksen? So happy to meet you," said the Chinese. "I am Hector Lau."

It was a name I knew well. He was Norbulk's chief accountant in Singapore, and a man for whom Lindstedt had a great deal of respect. "I'm glad to see you, Mr. Lau," I answered, also in English, "but you should not have put yourself to this trouble."

"No trouble at all, sir. Mr. Ritter is very sorry he could not come himself."

"Do you know Fredrik Johansen?"

They shook hands. "I'm so sorry about your father, sir."

"Thank you, Mr. Lau."

There was a moment of awkwardness; then Lau turned around and motioned to an East Indian or Pakistani who was dressed in a gray, short-sleeved shirt worn outside uniform trousers of the same color. The Indian nodded and disappeared into the crowd at the front of the terminal.

"Omar will fetch the car. Are these all your bags? Was it a good flight?" We nodded our assent.

"How cold is it in Oslo now?"

"It sometimes gets up to zero."

"Zero. My goodness. I've only been once, to Mr. Lindstedt's office, and I was quite chilly, and that was May." Mr. Lau chuckled and shook his head and chuckled again. He probably resented the time he was wasting at the airport.

"Ah," he said, "here is the car."

A white Volvo drew up and the man named Omar got out. "This is Mr. Henriksen and Mr. Johansen, Omar," Lau said.

"Very happy," Omar answered, rolling his *r* slightly. "Welcome to Singapore, sirs," and he flashed white teeth in a very dark face. He put the bags quickly into the trunk and Lau took the passenger seat in front while we got into the back. The air conditioning in the car was a relief. Omar turned off the tape deck so that we could speak, and Lau turned in his seat to face us as we drove off.

"As to your immediate schedule, Haakon—I mean Mr. Ritter—would like to give you dinner this evening if you are up to it."

I looked at Fredrik, who nodded. "We'd be delighted. And please call me John."

"Thank you, John. We have contacted the master of the *Rose* according to your instructions, but he is quite insistent on seeing you in the city and has very obviously neglected to invite you aboard. In any event, you will have a conference room at your disposal to interview him. He is called," and he consulted a manila folder, "Captain Pappas, and he can be reached at this number." Lau gave me a sheet of typed paper. "He is very charming and pleasant, John. Said your wish is his command, or something of the sort." He glanced from me to Fredrik and back to me. "But it is very obvious that he does not want you on board the *Rose,* and from what we've heard about the condition of the vessel, I'm not surprised. I *am* sorry, are you dreadfully tired?"

We both demurred, of course, but it was a relief when we were at last checked into our rooms. Through the window, the sky grew dark gray, and within minutes it began to rain harder than I had ever seen it rain before. I took a hot bath and then went to bed, falling asleep with the sound of the rain.

At eight-fifteen I collected Fredrik from his room and we went down to the lobby. Haakon Ritter was waiting for us, and, as was his fashion, greeted us both warmly, although to my knowledge, he had never met Fredrik before.

Haakon was one of the most capable people in the Norbulk

organization. Norbulk operated with a mixture of contracts of affreightment that covered as little as one year to as many as ten, for the carriage of specific amounts of such cargo as iron ore, coal, cement, bauxite, and alumina. Lindstedt insured that at no time did the company have more obligations in respect of its bulk carriers than the long-term contracts covered. That was what Per Lindstedt—and a lot of other people—considered competent management. It was in the management of the short-term employment (still on contract, almost never tramping) that Lindstedt, who depended heavily on people like Ritter, was spectacularly successful.

Two elements in particular were needed: the tonnage to be able to accommodate any request, and an intelligence system that would reveal not where the cargoes were, but where they would be six, twelve, even eighteen months hence. All companies that operated like Norbulk aimed at something of the sort, but Norbulk did it better than any group I knew, with the exception of the Bulkhandling pool, which is also based in Oslo. It was the beautifully orchestrated earnings from Norbulk accumulating over the years that had caused Johansen's downfall, but which were also the source of the firm's salvation, for a while, at least. The reserves he had built through his earnings from Norbulk gave him the wherewithal for speculation; what was left of them was for the time being preventing our collapse. Ritter was a genius at managing the intelligence network for the pool in the Far East.

Haakon was tall and thin. I doubted very much whether his rapidly disappearing dark hair ("Neither age nor worry, John," he once informed me soberly. "Genetic.") had ever experienced a comb. He dressed with anonymity. He had spent twenty years in the East and had no desire to go anywhere else, particularly not back to Oslo. If he had, I had no doubt that Lindstedt would eventually have made him his managing director. His wife was a handsome Chinese woman with a superb mind who spoke with zest the American English learned from Methodist missionaries in Ningpo when she was a child. They always spoke English at home, because Haakon could not imagine why anyone but a

Norwegian would want to learn the language. As a result he was beginning to forget his mother tongue.

He took Fredrik aside and said a few words to him in sympathy, which he could not possibly have known made the young man distinctly uncomfortable. But when they turned back together, Fredrik was smiling.

"Now then," said Haakon, "nothing exhausting tonight. A quiet drink, some good food, a little chat, and off to bed with you. Joan is expecting you tomorrow evening at home. She's not with us tonight because she's begun a new art course—she's bored with the kids away at school—and she's so good, it's frightening. She's derivative still—but, my God, she's only just started."

It was Ritter's old way of talking, but there was something a little different about it, something not quite up to the mark. Not nervous. Not disturbed even. Preoccupied?

"Now then, my friends, Singapore is a lovely place to eat, even in restaurants—Chinese, Indian, Malay, Indonesian, although it is reputed by all that despite the fact that you can nearly hit Indonesia with a rock from here, the best rijstafel is in Amsterdam. There is also the European stuff, but why come to the East and eat that? What would you like? Up to me? Then I suggest we go to a North Indian place just up the road a bit. It changes cooks regularly and goes through peaks and valleys. At the moment, it's at a peak."

We went first to the bar at the top of the hotel.

"There's a batch of telexes from Oslo, John, but they can wait. Let me get unpleasant things out of the way first. When do you want to see Captain Pappas?"

"Eleven?"

"Good." He slapped the table. "I'll ring him when I get to the office tomorrow, and you can come in when you like."

"Hector Lau told us that Pappas seems quite pleasant," Fredrik said, sipping a glass of beer.

"Absolutely true as far as it goes. But when you deal with him, sit with your back to the wall, and if he shakes your hand, count your fingers afterward. God knows I am not a bigot, but Pappas is the sort of Greek who fits all the clichés about Greeks. Fredrik, will you have another?"

He nodded affirmatively. He was the most relaxed I'd seen him, at least since this whole matter had begun, and perhaps longer than that. I think he relished being treated as a human being and as an adult.

"I had an interesting conversation with Lindstedt on the phone just before I left the office tonight. It is, by the way, snowing again in Oslo. The man bubbles with ideas, most of which I like. I used to like all of them, but that's another story and of no moment. He told me about your mission in Japan. I think the Japanese will buy the bulker scheme. They see the handwriting on the wall. The people I worry about are the European shipyards, the Akers and the Gotaverkens and the Swan Hunters of this world. Anyway, just by way of background, we've found some superb sources of timber supply here who are willing to do the transportation exclusively with us in return for a small equity stake—I think less than one percent, actually—in Norbulk. They're not shipowners, and they have no interest in being shipowners. They are first-class overseas Chinese, based in Kuala Lumpur, but they have properties in Thailand and Indonesia as well. Suggested to me by an accountant I knew. Like all Chinese, they like to see black ink at the bottom of the profit and loss statement, and they see the advantage of dealing with an organization like Norbulk, which has contacts and can provide the transportation. They have good Japanese customers, but we set them thinking long-term not only about their Japanese, but also about a dozen Americans and Europeans. They had never thought beyond Asia before. So this venture into the timber trade is not as speculative as it may have sounded at first. We reckon we can take a few timber carriers in on short-term charters until you take delivery of the new bulkers, if you manage to get that sorted out. By that time the trade will be booming, because Lindstedt says it will; besides, by then, the long-term contracts will be in place."

"And if they're not?"

"If Per Lindstedt suggested you ought to order open-hatch bulk carriers because Norbulk can use them, Norbulk will use them.

In any event, Lindstedt is putting another kettle on the fire. He thinks some of the owners we charter-in from ought to sell out to decent Hong Kong owners and charter the ships back and fix them to Norbulk. He thinks Norwegian flag is a luxury that only the best owners can afford, and it's absurdly expensive even so. Norwegian seamen—good and bad—are getting harder and harder to find. The Japanese have been selling ships to the Hong Kong owners and chartering them back for years and years; why not the Europeans? Let's go to dinner."

We drove in the white Volvo to a squat building whose ground and first floors contained arcades of shops. The restaurant was on the second floor. As the lift crept upward, Ritter said, "Lindstedt also told me he wants to persuade Fredrik to sell P. Johansens to Norbulk."

"We've already talked about it," I replied. "Fredrik and I have agreed that we would clear up one or two problems before we sold—if we sold—so that we could maximize the return."

Haakon did the ordering, mixing mild and hot dishes, liquid and dry. Fredrik took his first experience with Indian food very well, taking copious draughts of beer while his eyes streamed with tears.

"P. Johansens I can understand," Ritter said over the coffee. "Lindstedt knows the ships, and most of them are employed by Norbulk anyway. But I don't understand his interest in some of these small companies he's picked up, particularly ones with vessels of a size and type we've never used."

I thought he was looking a little wistful. "But they're employed?"

"Every goddamn one of them, but we had to hustle in some cases. I'd like to put a boot to Lygren, and I think sometime soon I will. Are you going to Hong Kong?"

"No," I said, thoroughly puzzled. Sven Lygren was head of the Norbulk office in Hong Kong.

"Just as well. What I was saying, getting back to Lindstedt, is that he is acting his most Christlike recently, and I think he might bite off more than he can chew. I wish the man *would* make a mistake, for once. A small and inexpensive one."

"But he always has been right, hasn't he?" I said.

"Absolutely. No denying it."

"Given his record then, old friend, I should say the odds run strongly in his favor."

"Right again."

"But, old friend, I have to tell you the same thought has occurred to me."

Much to my surprise, Haakon looked relieved, as if someone had finally understood what he was talking about.

13

Haakon watched us and watched the time, and when he thought we had been up long enough, he told us it was time to go back to the hotel. It was just about eleven when I got back to my room, and I was looking forward to a decent sleep. When the phone rang, I swore aloud.

"John. Sorry. It's Haakon here." He was speaking in Norwegian. "I have been instructed by a Sergeant Ng to ask you to go to room 1209." Before I could respond, he rang off. In the last couple of hours, seeing Haakon Ritter, talking about Norbulk and the market, I had almost managed to forget why we were in Singapore. But it came to me at once that knowledge of this imminent phone call must have been the reason for Ritter's earlier lack of ease.

It was early, so there were still people in the halls of the hotel, but no one paid the slightest attention to me. I knocked at the door of 1209. It was opened by a short, slight Chinese man, who might have been any age between thirty and fifty. His hair had been cut recently. He was wearing a short-sleeved white shirt, open at the neck, dark blue trousers, and what looked like canvas shoes. There were deep wrinkles at the corners of his eyes. He smiled and asked me to come in.

"I am Ng," he said, "at your service. We can speak openly. The room has been checked for bugs."

I was startled by his remark. "To tell you the truth, Mr. Ng, the thought had not occurred to me until now."

"Yes, quite. But one must be careful. It's Sergeant Ng, actually. Friends, enemies, acquaintances, and family call me Y.C., and I hope you will do the same. May I call you John?"

"Please."

"Tea?"

"Thank you."

He poured yellow-green liquid along with large dark green leaves into two glasses. He perched on the edge of the bed and motioned me to an upholstered armchair.

"You will see Captain Pappas soon?"

"Tomorrow at eleven."

"Where?"

"At Norbulk's office." I looked at my diary. "The U.I.C. Building. Shenton Way."

"Yes. Nice view of the harbor. You'll be able to see the *Rose,* if they have a good pair of binoculars." He sipped tea noisily. "I wanted to tell you a little about Pappas. He is an adventurer. He is always close to the edge of the law, and his name, at least, is known to police in Vancouver, New Orleans, London, Marseille—well-known there—Piraeus, and points east. He—or one ought to say, vessels he has been connected with—have from time to time been linked with the carriage of drugs. A culprit is always apprehended, but it is curious that Pappas is always connected with a ship as well when these things happen—as third officer, second, first, finally as master. As far as we know, up to now his technical record is okay. As a ship's officer, he knows what he's doing. No problem there, although the *Rose,* we are told, looks a mess. It's Pappas' outside activities that concern us. Although nothing has ever been proven against him, it can be assumed that Pappas not only skirts the law but breaks it. He is a criminal, John, and may be a bad one. So you must be careful. If at any stage you think he suspects anything—and I am thinking of the future beyond just your interview tomorrow—break off as quickly and unsuspiciously as you can and report to me at this number and this address." He handed me a card. "That will be the end of your involvement. More tea?"

I nodded. The tea was remarkably refreshing and invigorating. Just the thing after a night ski at Holmenkollen. With Alice.

"Do you intend to involve young Johansen?" Ng said.

"He wants to be involved."

"Invent some reason for him not to be. It's too dangerous. And under no circumstances are you to go aboard the *Rose.*"

"Have you any idea what I'm looking for?"

Y.C. shrugged. "Drug smuggling is big business in Southeast Asia, and market prices have shot up since the Americans left Vietnam and took their drug cooperatives with them. It may be just drugs—in a big way, of course. I should like to have a dollar for every body we have fished out of the harbor that was connected with the drug trade—all, by the way, on the selling side. But the Johansen and Evgenides murders happened far away from here. These were not the typical Asian entrepreneur expressing displeasure at a competitor. This is bigger than that and very, very professional. What else? Ah, yes . . . Raymond Bechmann, the banker from London. He has not yet turned up. Now, one other thing and I'll let you go to bed—I do apologize for keeping you up and for these ad hoc arrangements, but I did want to ensure you know whom you are dealing with. On both sides." Ng smiled. Then the smile vanished.

"There has been a suicide of an Englishman here in Singapore that seems to have caused more than the usual flap in the British embassy. I have dealt with the British and I have a sixth sense about it. The man was simply an unmarried accountant—partner in one of the big firms in Shenton Way. He'd been here for years.

"The rest is between us, John. In dealing with the *Rose* matter, you might be able to make a connection that we would never be in a position to make. We—or I ought to say, my compatriots in intelligence—had been watching this chap Tomlinson for some time because we thought he was a British agent. In fact, he killed himself with a cyanide capsule. My instinct is that he stumbled onto something, and that the something concerned the *Rose*. Nor do I think he committed suicide. I think he was forced to bite that capsule."

By this time, I was so tired that, while I heard and understood Ng's words and the horror they contained, I had no reaction, other than to nod numbly.

"Come, my friend," said Ng. "Time you got to bed. I'm terribly sorry to have kept you awake so long." He put his hand on my arm as I rose from the chair, and we went to the door together. I was at least a head taller. "You are a courageous man, John," he said, "but please don't be foolhardy."

I would have agreed with anything he said at that point. We bid each other goodnight, and I was out in the hallway with the door closing softly behind me. I looked down the hall, which was completely empty. In my state of exhaustion, it was like looking into the wrong end of a telescope, and despite the fact that it was reasonably well lit, it looked somehow sinister. I traversed the hall as swiftly as I could and had what seemed an endless wait for the lift. When I reached my floor, I had again to walk down one of those treacherous hallways to my room. My heart was pounding rapidly. And it was only when I'd gotten inside the room that I realized I'd been holding my breath, for I don't know how long. I still had to inspect the room, however; I turned on all the lights, looked into the bathroom and out onto the balcony. I slipped the chain onto the door and tugged the door several times to insure that it was double-locked. Walking toward the bed I began tugging off my shirt and shoes and trousers; by the time I reached the bed, I was already asleep.

There was a great banging and instantly I awoke, my heart in my mouth, alert, but seemingly paralyzed. The lights were still burning in the room, which seemed somehow inappropriate, but I could not reason why, and as it seemed the banging didn't have anything to do with me, I didn't care either. I fell asleep again.

I awoke again with my heart racing. I had been dreaming I was racing down the hall outside my room, but it went on forever. There was something behind me, breathing hard, the breath cold on the back of my neck. I knew I must get away from it somehow, but the hallway went on for ever and ever and I knew that I would never get away from it—I was getting more and more tired and slower and slower. When I recognized that the dream was only a dream, I fell asleep again, noting only the pale glow of light behind the balcony curtains.

When I awoke in the morning, it was after eight, and I must say I did not feel tremendously rested. I showered and shaved and tried to wake up, then called down for a small breakfast. I read the *Straits Times,* which had been slipped under my door while I slept, and, once breakfast came, I ate slowly and looked out the window at the skyscrapers rising from the bougainvillea and the frangipani.

Just before I was ready to leave, I rang up Fredrik to make sure he was ready for me to come collect him. The phone rang a long time before he answered, and I was terrified because I did not recognize the voice on the other end until he addressed me.

"John, I am so sorry. I am very, very sick. I'm sure it was the food." There was a muffled sound, as though he put his hand over the phone. "The food was fine I'm just not used to it, that's all."

"Well go back to bed, Fredrik, and come into the office when you can. And if not, I'll see you, say, about six-thirty?"

"Thank you for understanding, John," he said and rang off quickly.

I was absolutely delighted. Even before Ng issued his warning, I had determined to suggest to Fredrik that his time in Singapore could be better spent studying Ritter's operation than mucking about with the *Rose,* but obviously I had no way of making him follow my suggestion. Now I could not only deal with Pappas alone, but because of that I could keep Fredrik away from it in the future as well.

When I stepped through the front doors of the hotel into the sticky heat, Omar appeared at my elbow, saying that Mr. Ritter had sent him and were we waiting for Mr. Johansen? I shook my head and followed him to the white Volvo. He held the rear door for me as I got in, and he switched the air conditioning on full when he got into the driver's seat.

We went into the city along the length of Orchard Road, through automobile, truck, and motorcycle traffic, by blocks of shops, enormous hotels, people, noise, energy. Singapore pulsed with life, despite the heat. Presently we passed the massive white buildings of the Supreme Court and City Hall, the exquisite greensward in front of the Cricket Club, and the cathedral, built of soft, mellow stone. We were soon in Shenton Way, a broad road lined on both sides with office blocks. Omar turned into the garage for the U.I.C. Building and let me out before he drove up the ramp.

When I left the lift on the thirteenth floor, I was greeted with the enormous word NORBULK in blue bas relief covering perhaps five meters of the wall opposite the elevator bank. I turned into the reception area. A young Chinese woman took me back to Haakon's office. He took me around, introduced me to the staff, and showed me the offices, which were comfortable but austere, indicating Lindstedt's influence: Spend only what you must.

"Let's look at Johansen's orphan," Haakon said, and we returned to his office. He opened the curtains. Nearby, the harbor was full of sampans and lighters. Farther out, the vessels became larger. "Here," Ritter said, adjusting the telescope that he kept on a tripod. He peered once more and said, "Take a look."

Although she was small, I could clearly make out a white T on the dark blue funnel. Johansen had ordered the T, for Trans-oceanic, in the same style lettering as that used for P. Johansens Rederi. It was his idea of a little joke, a little act of defiance. The upper part of the hull and the superstructure, except for the funnel, were white. She was riding high in the water, so that one could see that she was dark blue beneath the Plimsol line. At that distance she looked clean and trim, but I knew otherwise.

Haakon's intercom spoke. "Mr. Ritter, Captain Pappas to see Mr. Henriksen."

Haakon looked at me and smiled encouragement. He knew nothing of my intentions, although he thought he knew. I selfishly wanted to tell him all of it, but it was too dangerous to involve him.

He put his hand on my shoulder and squeezed lightly.

I went out to the reception area. A dark man with a large black mustache and very dark eyes was sitting easily in one of the armchairs, and regarding the receptionist intensely. She was making an effort to ignore what must have been nearly a palpable stare. When he saw me approach, however, he bobbed to his feet. He was of medium height and looked very heavy in the chest and shoulders. He was neatly dressed, in a white uniform shirt with blue shoulder boards and white trousers and deck shoes. He smiled broadly, displaying even white teeth.

"Mr. Henriksen, I assume?" He extended a large hand. "I am Pappas. Captain Andrew Pappas at your service." His English was heavily accented. He gripped my hand and shook it vigorously, holding it a bit longer than necessary. "Call me Andy."

PART 2
Voyage

14

I took Pappas to a small conference room that Ritter had showed me, and closed the door. He circled the room in an offhand manner, inspecting the nautical prints on the walls.

"I've already looked it over," I said. "There's nothing to worry about."

Pappas managed to look shocked at my implication and reassured at the same time. I sat down and motioned him to a chair across the table from me.

"The *Rose* has been on holiday long enough, Captain. Time to put her back to work."

He shrugged and raised his hands as if to say, "Well, of course, but . . ."

Instead, he said, "Please understand, John, this is not by our choice."

"Understood."

"But we are used to taking our instructions from Transoceanic Maritime Agencies. When an instruction comes direct from the owner, we pay attention. That instruction was to do nothing. Accordingly, we do nothing. May I say I was surprised to receive that instruction through Norbulk." He looked around the conference room as if he had just detected a bad smell. He was being offended and defensive at the same time. "By the way, I have heard nothing from Stratis—Evgenides, that is—in two weeks. More than two weeks." His large brown eyes widened with concern and perplexity.

"He is *hors de combat* at the moment."

"Yes, yes, I understand. All is understood. Otherwise he would be giving instructions. But what is it you want the *Rose* to do?"

I had cleared the harbor; now there were no more charts.

"I want the *Rose* to continue tramping in her special way."

Pappas smiled with irony and shook his head sadly. "Have I been misinformed? Has Mr. Johansen not been murdered? And what has happened to Mr. Evgenides? Is it true you want the *Rose* to continue doing God knows what that has offended someone and caused these terrible things?" He took a set of amethyst-colored worry beads from his pocket and began running them through his fingers. He had said "things." He knew that Evgenides was dead.

"What makes you think these terrible things are connected with the *Rose*?"

Pappas rolled his eyes to the ceiling. "John, why else are you in Singapore? Why else did we get those peremptory—if I may say so—instructions through Norbulk? Why else are we talking? I am at your service. Tell me please what to do. But please tell me something sensible." Pappas folded his hands, the beads falling decorously over them like a rosary. And he waited, patient, sensitive, long-suffering but stoic, looking slightly pained—like a man who had received a blow to his professional pride, willing, nonetheless, to forbear and to forgive all. I would have been deeply moved had I not been warned that he was a fraud of the first water.

"Let us stop fencing. Our interests are mutual."

He slapped his hands together and again rolled his eyes to heaven. "My God, my God," he said. "Mutual interests. Yes, they are mutual. As mutual as any of servant and master."

I had truly entered into a nightmare. The image of the long corridor with neither beginning nor end passed through my mind again. None of this would do. I had to take a chance. If it did not work, we would never know the answer. But if the *Rose* were got rid of, then perhaps everyone would be safe and we could return quietly to rescuing the firm. Perhaps.

I looked directly at Pappas. "When I said our interests are mutual, I meant it. I meant yours and mine. And Raymond Bechmann's."

I had struck home. The interest flickered in Pappas' eyes before he could prevent it. I had to press the advantage.

"Evgenides was in the way. He is no longer."

It was a lucky coup. Pappas grimaced briefly. "I knew that Bechmann had gotten to someone in Oslo," he said, "but I didn't know who. He didn't want anyone to know anyone else. He thought there was safety in putting everyone in boxes. I thought it was awkward. You see what it has gotten us. Bechmann told me about Stratis. 'In the way' is a very delicate way of saying selling out. He did not have long to enjoy his thirty pieces of silver, did old Stratis?"

"But why go running to the man you betrayed?"

"I can only guess he panicked when he realized he had outlived his usefulness to them and that he was next on their list. And he took a chance that Bechmann did not know or would not have guessed. Poor Stratis was stupid as well as greedy."

"And Bechmann told you to wait here to find out what we had in mind?"

Pappas suddenly became wary again. "Yes."

There were too many revelations crashing in on me. I needed time to sort them out. Whom had Bechmann gotten to in Oslo? Who were those who were after Evgenides—they to whom he had sold out?

I smiled with reassurance. "Good. As arranged."

"And what *do* you have in mind, John?"

"We continue to trade as before."

Pappas threw his hands in the air. "I thought I was talking to a man of reason. What you suggest is mad."

"Bechmann is prepared to recognize an increased level of risk."

"Not for fifty percent would I take this on."

"We were thinking of twenty, actually."

"That is an insult to the intelligence, and preposterous, considering the risk."

"No one of us ever thought this a riskless venture, Captain. But as you know, risk increases as the level of reward increases. In addition, I realize that I am not talking to an old woman who stays at home with her knitting. Bechmann and I admired your resourcefulness in keeping the hardware away from the pirates."

"How the devil do you know about that?" His eyes kept dancing back and forth and avoiding mine.

"The police told me." This time Pappas was truly shocked. "Captain, Captain," I said hurriedly, "of course I am in contact with them. I am now managing the firm. They *must* talk to me. I am finding it very useful to our little enterprise."

"Forgive me, John. You quite startled me. But their missing the arms was no virtue of mine. Somehow they were misinformed. Probably our friend Evgenides. They must have been furious when they opened cases of auto parts and found auto parts."

And, no doubt, my dear Captain Pappas, I thought, you shifted the weapons without instruction because you also were cheating your employers.

"Nonetheless," I said, "perhaps we ought to stay with soft goods for a time."

"You mean passengers as well as medicines?"

What on earth does he mean? "Yes," I said.

"Impossible. That will make them even more furious. The fares provide a very high return—and even bonuses, as the sponsors are often very grateful. I could not possibly undertake such risks for any less than fifty percent."

"Bechmann indicated willingness to consider twenty-five percent."

"I could not possibly agree."

"Then I am sorry, Captain Pappas. It appears as if our association must come to an end."

"However, because I value that association, I would be willing to continue in my capacity and to assume additional responsibilities for forty-five percent."

"We also appreciate the association, Captain. Thirty percent."

"Absolutely not."

"Then I really must bid you good-bye. There are others . . ."

"Fools."

"Perhaps. But they will do it for twenty percent."

"Out of the question."

"Of course, my friend. The extra ten percent is to compensate for the risk and recognizes your professional skill in general and your knowledge of the *Rose* in particular."

"I cannot conceive of any less than forty percent."

"Ah, but we can. And, you know, we shall all have extra expenses in the next days."

"Forty percent is the absolute minimum."

I raised my voice. "The meeting is at an end." I was barely civil, my voice quaking with the effort to restrain my rage. "I shall thank you to leave this office instantly."

"Thirty-five percent."

"One third."

"Of everything?"

"Of course," I said, calmer now, wondering what "everything" meant.

"Done," Pappas said, sitting back and smiling broadly. "I knew we could come to an accommodation."

"How quickly can you get away from Singapore?"

"Within twenty hours."

"Make it twelve. The *Rose* is costing us all money."

"It shall be done, John."

"I also want to be kept informed through this office. Where you load, where bound, with what cargo. The last should be a word beginning with *A* for hardware; *B* for medicines; *C* for passengers; *D*, the first two; *E*, the last two; *F*, the first and third; *G*, all of them. Very simple. No one here will understand except myself. What would you tell me now?"

Pappas was at once on guard. "I have already discussed it with Bechmann."

"Bechmann is in transit now, as you know. So am I. It has been difficult for us to keep in contact."

Pappas seemed to be weighing the matter. Then he said, "Bangkok, Yemen, coconuts."

"Who are they?"

He spoke solemnly. "There is a rumor that there are some high-spirited young Germans in Bangkok who had to leave the Federal Republic in haste and who require transportation to a more healthful climate."

"Excellent," I said, wanting to reach out and take Pappas by the throat. He may as well have kicked me in the stomach. So the *Rose* carried terrorists quietly and safely where they wanted to go, with no formalities or annoying requirements such as passports.

She carried stolen weapons for terrorists and whomever else wanted them. She carried drugs on behalf of the world's gangsters. She was a plague ship, carrying late twentieth-century forms of epidemic. I thought, how fortunate it is that you are dead, Shipowner Johansen.

"Do you anticipate any difficulty, Captain?"

"Not on this trip, perhaps. After all, our Judas is dead, isn't he? But their intelligence is astounding, and their operation is very big. They will catch on eventually. But by then we may be in a different line of work. In any event, we shall take more than our usual precautions. And who knows," he continued, with a smile, "we might even decide to cooperate."

He stood. "The *Rose* will weigh anchor by zero one hundred hours, John. You have my word." He again gripped my hand vigorously. "This has been a most rewarding meeting."

I walked with Pappas through the reception area to the elevator; again with his eyes he stripped the woman at the desk. She shifted uncomfortably in her chair as we passed. When he had gone, I felt enormous relief. I had been in the presence of great evil. But the information could now be passed on to Ng; the vessel would be off soon, and the killers would be smoked out. And perhaps the whole filthy business would be brought to a close.

For the next half hour I sat alone in the windowless conference room, the hum of the air-conditioning machinery low in the background, and made detailed notes of the conversation. I read them over several times to insure I had forgotten nothing. Time and time again, I returned to one particular thing that Pappas had said: "I knew that Bechmann had gotten to someone in Oslo." The someone might have been Johansen himself, but I doubted it. There were a dozen people in Oslo, including Fredrik, whom Bechmann might have involved. Especially Fredrik. I should not have been so open with him. If he were involved, I was in great danger, and probably the only thing that had saved me was Bechmann's compartmentalization. Fredrik would not have known Pappas, but was Fredrik really ill?

I told myself that I could not possibly believe such a thing as Fredrik's criminal involvement. The chill that went through me was not caused by jet lag and air conditioning. Again I thought of Pappas' words: "I knew that Bechmann had gotten to someone in Oslo."

Haakon Ritter took me to lunch on *dim sum* at a vast, dark restaurant across Collyer Quay from the Ocean Building. The room we were in had terraces of tables, a stage and a dance floor, and dozens of tiny lights in the ceiling scattered as if to resemble a night sky. It was spectacularly gaudy.

In response to my inquiry, Haakon confirmed the place was a night club. "The *dim sum* are good. The variety acts are not. Joan and I came to see them once. That was the last time." He picked a meat-stuffed dumpling up in his chop sticks, dipped it into chili oil, and popped it into his mouth. "Actually the place was well on its way to bankruptcy when it got a new lease on life with a bit of romantic—dreadful, really—notoriety. Fellow named Tomlinson killed himself over a cold shoulder he got from a little Australian strumpet who used to sing here. Same man actually who put us on to the Chinese timber suppliers."

Tomlinson was the man who Ng thought was connected with the *Rose*. I asked Haakon to continue.

"Tomlinson had been out here for years. He was a partner in one of the accountancy firms in Shenton Way. He had been alone for a long time and lived quite an eventless life. I knew him, more or less, because he was the treasurer of my club; he did a bangup job of managing the finances—only club I've ever heard of with a surplus year after year. Suitably small, of course. At Christmas every year there was a free party for members and guests.

"Poor old Tomlinson. I can still see him—mid-fifties perhaps. A tall, sandy-haired, stooped-over Englishman with gray eyes that never told you a thing. Most forgetful man I've ever known. He'd ask you for a match and find he had forgotten his pipe. Or if he'd remembered his pipe, he would have forgotten his tobacco. One would have to remind him to button this or that. He was forgetful about everything except numbers—and bridge, which is the same thing. He was a positive terror at the bridge table. He knew what you had in your hand almost before you had finished counting your points. I think he sometimes played through some hands just to be accommodating to the other players. The only players he couldn't cope with were bad ones, because they were unpredictable.

"He was so good with numbers that early on, before we found Hector Lau, I recommended to Lindstedt that we should go after him. So one time when Lindstedt was out here, I introduced them. That was when Lindstedt was still fallible; he said simply that he didn't care much for the man. Frankly, I don't think Tomlinson was interested anyway.

"Picture this, then. This gracelessly aging ex-pat accountant, fussy, somewhat effeminate, has lived and worked here for years, now and again flying to Jakarta or Kuala Lumpur or Bangkok on auditing trips, I suppose, playing bridge at the Bukit Timah Club, occasionally—very occasionally—dining out, always eating and drinking in moderation. Suddenly he stops showing up at the club. He seems distracted whenever one meets him. He takes to coming to this place—actually the newspapers did not disclose either the nightclub or the girl, but you could put two and two together if you'd lived here long enough. So he starts spending all his nights here, mooning over this not very attractive and not very talented singer like a love-sick adolescent. He started sending her flowers or perfume—things like that—which she never acknowledged. Finally he sent her a declaration of love. They printed it in the paper later, along with the rest of the story. Awful. The note was very silly. Told her he was a widower and lonely and had put a good bit aside, so he was well-fixed, and would she consider . . . and so forth. Just dreadful. She did acknowledge the note. She told him to stop annoying her with flowers and mash notes. That pushed him over the edge. He went home to his dreary flat and blew his brains out."

"Shot himself, did you say?"

"Yes. The papers went into detail on how messy it was. The reading public loves it."

I nodded. Ng had told me that Tomlinson had taken poison. So that part of the story the papers had was untrue. I wondered if the whole thing was.

"Was there a suicide note?"

"No. But that didn't seem to bother the police."

"But where did all the information come from?"

"The girl. She was so horrified when the story came out in the paper about the body being found—no one knew any of this at the time, of course—that she called the police straight away. Her motive was interesting. She wasn't sorry about Tomlinson. She just wanted to make sure she wasn't going to be blamed somehow. She thought it might hurt her career."

Ritter shook his head. "Really a terrible thing it was. I rather liked old Tomlinson, although God knows he was no one you could get close to. I was surprised to find he was a widower. I had never heard him talk about a wife. In fact, I would have thought he was homosexual. Or at least asexual."

"What happened to the girl?"

"I have no idea. She's certainly not performing in Singapore—unless she's changed vocations. The way the world is, I wouldn't be surprised to find she's a rock star making millions. The poor man."

While we were waiting for change from the bill, Ritter asked what was going to happen with the *Rose.*

I was tempted to tell him, but I said only, "I beg you not to ask, old friend."

Haakon looked at me without comprehension but said nothing further. What did he suspect? What did he *know*? My sense of proportion was being eroded, and I was suspecting everyone.

I spent the balance of the afternoon responding to the telexes, most of which were from Lars Norland or Karl Wessel. The latter had received an indication of interest in the *Iris* at five and a half million dollars, bang on book value, which was four million less than she ought to have fetched in normal times, and a million and a half less than I hoped we could get for her now.

I also called Fredrik, who was feeling better but was still somewhat under the weather; he thought he would be able to dine later. He asked nothing about the morning's interview.

Sergeant Ng and I had worked out an automatic arrangement for meeting in room 1209. Starting at ten-forty in the morning and again at six-ten in the evening, he would be in the room for one hour. If I did not appear, he would repeat the process at the next fixed time. It was past six when I asked Ritter if I could borrow Omar and the car.

"Of course," he said, somewhat coolly, I thought. "I'll pick you both up for dinner at eight."

Ng opened the door immediately when I knocked at about six-thirty. Referring now and again to my notes, I told him in detail about my conversation with Pappas. I also gave him the notes. He was silent for a while, absorbing what I had told him.

"You've done extremely well, John. Pandora's box is now open. I must be frank with you; you are not quit of this matter yet. From the moment the *Rose* sails until the moment we or our counterparts elsewhere catch the perpetrators, you and those with whom you are connected are in danger. I do not think I'm telling you anything surprising. We have been watching the vessel. Others have been watching her also. We can follow her in ASEAN and international waters, but we cannot follow her where we are not welcome. They can and will. When they discover that the warnings have not been heeded, they will strike." Ng paused a moment and then said, almost to himself, "Which is, of course, exactly what we want them to do."

"Have you any idea what this is all about?"

"Specifically, no. We know that the criminals are not the usual Chinese smuggling operation." He smiled briefly. "There seems to be a kind of occidental expertise here. We Asians have difficulty comprehending these things."

What a shame, I thought, that Frogh and Ng would never meet.

"It has been a pleasure working with you, John. I know that you have a bodyguard who is unknown to yourself. Nonetheless, if you feel you require assistance, please ring the number I gave you. And exercise the utmost caution. You will go to Tokyo?"

"Yes. It is imperative."

"And how have you planned to return?"

"The polar flight from Tokyo to London, by way of Anchorage, with a connection to Oslo."

"I think it may be a good idea to return by way of Singapore instead. There are a number of people in your Oslo office who know your plans. Change them. Remember what Pappas said."

"Yes. 'I knew that Bechmann had gotten to someone in Oslo.' "

"Just so."

"You need not convince me, Y.C." I was badly frightened.

"By the way, John, we have word from Oslo that your friend Miss Nielsen is on her way to Singapore, ultimate destination Hanoi."

I was appalled. They knew everything about me. I felt totally naked. Once, when I was doing my military service, my battalion was conducting winter exercises near the Russian border. At the worst possible time, as we were crossing on foot an area that was flat and almost without cover, we were caught a kilometer or so beyond our vehicles by a freakish storm. We could move neither forward nor back. The twilight that passed for day that far north turned pitch black. We burrowed into the snow like moles and covered ourselves with shelter halves. Sometimes in the night I can still hear that wind shrieking and feel that cold that is beyond cold. The storm lasted less than half an hour, but I had never since felt so helpless and so exposed—until Ng's last words.

My reaction was obvious, because he said then, "I did not mean to shock you. We know a great deal about you. We had to. We had no idea whether or not *you* were connected with this ugly affair." It was the first time I recognized that I might have been under suspicion, might be under suspicion still. In fact, Frogh's candor with me had led me to believe otherwise. Yet all these things that were being told me might be lies or half-truths, fed to me to see how I might react. I ought to have been more cautious with Frogh, more cautious with Ng. I ought not to have revealed myself, been so open. Who knew in whose employ they were? Who knew how these things might be used against me?

"In the event," Ng continued, "I suggest you avoid Miss Nielsen's company. I see you are upset, John. I understand. But you must understand that sometimes we are required to give up cherished freedoms like privacy to protect the rest of our liberties. It has been going on for years and will no doubt go on for more years. Heaven grant that we can strike a balance." Even in my paranoia, I sensed that Ng was genuinely moved. But I could imagine Jensen saying the same things just as sincerely.

The suggestion that Alice might become involved was terrifying. She had clearly ignored me. Whether that was because she genuinely wanted to go to Vietnam, or whether she thought she wanted to be near me, I could not begin to fathom. I was both troubled and flattered.

"How long should I stay away from Miss Nielsen?"

"For as long as there is danger."

I nodded numbly.

"Thank you again, John. May I say good evening, and I hope you have a pleasant dinner with Mr. and Mrs. Ritter."

Fredrik and I went to the lobby to meet Haakon at eight. The young man looked pale and unwell, and he was very quiet. It was incredible to me that I thought him capable of the cynical dissembling that permeated this matter.

We drove north from the hotel in the white Volvo, away from the city, for ten or fifteen minutes, turning finally into the driveway of a brightly lit bungalow with a tile roof, surrounded by palm trees and enormous flowering shrubs that perfumed the night air.

Haakon's Chinese wife, Joan, slimmer, taller, more elegant than my years-old memory of her, greeted us warmly and at once took Fredrik under her wing. After weighing his condition, she gave him a drink, brownish red in color, that brought some blood into his cheeks almost immediately.

"Old Chinese formula," she said, looking simple and sophisticated at the same time, "available from the chemists."

We were joined shortly by the Laus (she smiled and nodded pleasantly through the entire evening, but said not one word) and an old friend of mine from Oslo, Erik Hovdesven, and his second wife, Marta, whom I'd never met—tall, blond, striking, slightly mad, like all Danes.

We sat on the screened porch for drinks, the light coming from citronella candles, and a chorus of tree frogs forming a background to our conversation. Erik and I talked a little about mutual friends in Oslo. He even asked me about his former wife, which I thought extraordinary, but I almost never met her anymore and could plead ignorance in good conscience.

"The bottom of the tanker market is beginning to look like the Mindinao Trench," Erik said. "What about bulk carriers, Ritter?"

"They will shortly be in oversupply," Haakon replied. "With all the conversions from tanker orders, and with all that capacity in Japanese shipyards, there's no hope for it. A man would be mad to take on a bulk carrier without long-term employment."

"The voice of Per Lindstedt heard round the world," Hovdesven said, and Ritter laughed.

"But he has done well for himself, you must admit."

"Up to now, yes. He does seem to be rather on a shopping spree now, doesn't he?"

Ritter mumbled assent.

"He is not endearing himself to some of his old friends either."

"But then he never did."

"I would not want to be working for a shipyard just now," Hector Lau said. "The overcapacity is absolute, not relative. If the market turns around, it doesn't matter. There's still too much capacity. And whenever the Japanese turn their attention to something, it's in oversupply the next year. In six months it will be bulkers. In twelve, supply vessels or car carriers."

"Quite right, Hector," Haakon said. "But I understand that if we can hold on until 1985, everything will be tickety-boo."

"Ships, ships, ships," Marta Hovdesven muttered into her glass.

The subject of oil always overshadowed any discussion among shipping people of the market and the world in general. We were now supposed to order new tankers or rebuild the ones we had, so that our ships would all have double hulls and segregated ballast tanks. No environmentalist was offering advice, however, on how we were to pay for all of this, with our reserves depleted in the face of the worldwide drop in demand, a hundred million tons of excess tanker capacity, and the price of oil four or five times what it was in 1973. That is not to say anyone was right or wrong—certainly it was wrong for tanker owners to think the market for oil was never going to change and to order all those ships; it was wrong of the banks to pander to that foolishness by providing the financing; and it was certainly wrong for all of us to rely so unthinkingly so long on a wasting asset subject to cartelization. But how in heaven's name was the independent shipowner going to move oil from point A to point B, observing all the restrictions and requirements, and maintain a price the end user could afford? Slowly but inexorably, we concluded, the independent shipping companies were going to go out of business or merge with the stronger firms, which might last a few years more.

We all held similar views, except for Mrs. Lau, who said nothing, and Mrs. Hovdesven, sitting on my right at dinner, who said merely, "Ships, oil, money," and under her breath, so that only I could hear, "Bugger all of it," accompanied by a hard squeeze of my thigh. It was clear she was bored with us, bored with her husband, bored with Singapore. I tried to concentrate on the Shanghai-style dinner that Joan had prepared and was very glad when the Hovdesvens left soon after coffee. They were followed shortly thereafter by the Laus, who must have thought the entire occidental pack of us barbarians.

Haakon poured us another brandy. "I would appreciate your keeping me informed on your negotiations with the yard."

"Absolutely." And to Joan's questioning look, I said, "Some of those conversions from tankers to bulk carriers we were talking about earlier."

"Norwegians puzzle me," she said. "You know, before I knew anything about this business you are all involved in . . . when I was young and even more foolish than I am now, I always had the idea that the round eyes were the prudent ones and that we Chinese were the wild men. A good product of my Methodist education, I was. Now I am fifty years old, and suddenly I realize, and Haakon confirms it, that my compatriots—hell, my fellow citizens from Shanghai Province—are printing money up in Hong Kong, when the Bank and Jardines let them, while dear old Haakon's friends don't know where their next meal is coming from. Greed is an easy accusation to make. But you also fail to recognize the long-term consequences of what you are doing in favor of the short-term advantage. Not all of you, but most of you. I used to think Lindstedt was different—so different, in fact, I was convinced he was Chinese."

"Have you changed your mind?"

"The shopping spree that Erik Hovdesven mentioned. Haakon has said the same. Success is not an unmixed blessing. Genghis Khan went out to steal horses one day and ended up in Vienna."

The next morning went too quickly for my taste. I looked through the telescope in Ritter's office; the *Rose* was gone. Haakon's secretary confirmed seats on Cathay Pacific to Tokyo at three that afternoon. There were some telexes from Oslo to answer. Haakon gave me a bulky envelope of documents to deliver to Bob Mori at Norbulk, Tokyo. Fredrik had bounced back from his illness and was full of apologies for letting me down. He was also maddeningly verbose. I did not want to dampen his enthusiasm, but I would soon have to make him aware of the danger we were in. The closer we came to having to leave the more exposed I felt. I had come by this time to doubt the existence of the protection that was to be provided us. I had become suspicious of everyone, including Ritter, as irrational as it might be. But what if "getting to someone in Oslo" were figurative, not literal, and meant getting to someone in the organization? Why did it have to be the firm, rather than someone with whom we worked closely? Why couldn't it be Norbulk, which, after all, acted as our agents in most ports? Why couldn't it be Ritter?

Hector Lau took us for lunch to one of the old streets behind Shenton Way, where we got noodles with bits of fried vegetables and meat from one food cart and *satay* with a hot peanut sauce from another. We then said our farewells in the office to everyone. Ritter took me aside and said he was sorry about his reaction the day before when I had said I could not tell him anything about the *Rose*. "If I had any brains, old friend, I should have known there is something about this situation that is sticky.

Particularly when you are dealing with the police. I hadn't connected the two."

"Thank you, Haakon. I wanted to tell you, but I couldn't."

"Enough said." He turned around. "Omar. Time to get the car."

Ritter took us to the lift. "Give my love to Joan," I said as the lift door closed between us and Haakon.

During the flight, I outlined to Fredrik what the *Rose* had been involved in, how there was nothing further we could do in the matter, but how we must be extremely cautious. I let him know the name and telephone number of the Tokyo police inspector, Watanabe, that Ng had given me in case of difficulties. Watanabe had been fully briefed. As the *Rose* had made a business of carrying terrorists, it seemed likely that members of the Japanese Red Army had been among their number.

Bob Mori met us when we emerged from the crowded customs hall at Haneda into the chilly March night. It was nearly nine-thirty—we had stopped in Hong Kong, and we had lost an hour and a half through time zone changes. The long road into the center of Tokyo to the Palace Hotel was still full of traffic. Mori left us alone for the most part, leafing through the papers I had brought him from Ritter and touching only briefly on the negotiations with Dai Ichi Zosen that we were to start in the morning.

I was exhausted by the time I got to my room. I unpacked as quickly as I could, getting some laundry ready to send out the following day. I got ready for bed, and it was only when I was sitting in pajamas on the edge of the bed about to turn out the light that I noticed the small vase with a single red rose sitting on the end table next to the small sofa. So tired was I that my first thought was merely that it was a strange thing for a hotel to put in a male guest's room. A Japanese custom, perhaps. It didn't really make sense. Rose . . . rose . . . *Rose*! The meaning became all too clear, and a sliver of ice went through my vitals. With my eyes on the rose, I rang the front desk.

"Can you tell me who left this very nice flower in my room?" I said, identifying myself.

"One moment." The phone seemed to go dead. There was a small envelope in front of the vase, but I could not reach it from where I was sitting. "Sorry to keep you waiting, sir," the phone said. "It was the florist shop in the arcade on floor A."

"But you don't know *who* it was?"

"Sorry, sir. That is not in our record. Is there not a card?"

"Yes. But it's not signed," I added, knowing that it wouldn't be.

"I see. You will have to ask at the shop, sir."

"Is the shop open?"

"No, sir. It opens at nine-thirty and closes at seven."

My hands were trembling so badly that I could hardly get the small envelope open. Inside was a card on which had been typewritten in English, "We are watching."

15

I rang the number Ng had given me for Inspector Watanabe. It was not Watanabe to whom I spoke, but the message was relayed quickly, and he arrived in less than ten minutes. He was a small man in a dark suit and greeted me with a smile and a bow. He observed the rose and the card with a sharp intake of breath and a shake of the head. He looked around the room carefully.

"We'll talk to the florist tomorrow first thing. In the meantime, don't worry. We'll take care of you."

While Watanabe waited, I called Fredrik to find whether anything untoward had happened. I then asked the policeman to place a guard on Fredrik's room as well, which he immediately agreed to do. Then he wished me goodnight.

Ten or fifteen minutes later, an enormous argument in Japanese erupted in front of my door. I looked through the peephole to see two bellboys, several people in dark suits, and what I took to be a very angry guest whom they were trying to placate but who was being removed from his room nonetheless. Watanabe was posting his guard.

Fredrik and I met for breakfast at eight to review our position. We would not involve the engineers from Norbulk until we had reached agreement with the yard on the principle of conversion, because it might be construed as arrogance on our part and that we had taken it for granted they would agree to conversion. Every fact one knew about the shipping market led to the conclusion that they would agree ultimately, but neither of us must lose face in the process.

At nine-thirty, following directions that Norland had given us, we walked in the cold sunlight three short blocks to the headquarters building for the shipyard, near the Long Term Credit Bank. The shipbuilding docks themselves were in Nagasaki.

The Ship Export Sales Department, Section Two, was on the sixth floor. It was an enormous room beyond frosted glass doors, a sea of green linoleum and gray metal desks beneath cold fluorescent lights. At each of the desks, each of which was piled high with papers, sat a man in a white shirt and dark tie, or a young woman in a blue jumper. We asked one of the women for Mr. Hiroshi, and she slalomed through the desks to a man who sat with his back to a window. He immediately rose, putting on his jacket, as did two others. One disappeared, and one joined the man I assumed was Hiroshi. They bowed and we exchanged cards and shook hands with him and with his colleague, Mr. Ito. He asked us to follow him. We went back through the frosted glass doors and along the dimly lit corridor to the lift bank. When we got into the lift, Hiroshi pushed the indicator for the ninth floor.

The lighting was soft, the floor thickly carpeted in beige, and the walls were paneled in light-colored wood decorated with simply framed examples of calligraphy and brush painting. A receptionist in a beige jumper led us to a conference room, also paneled in wood. It was furnished with a large sofa and four or five overstuffed chairs, all of which had lace doilies on the arms and lace antimacassars; all were grouped around a long, low, wood table. Mr. Hiroshi offered us cigarettes, which we refused, but which he and Mr. Ito took and lit with great satisfaction. Mr. Hiroshi asked when we had arrived in Japan and whether we had come direct from Norway and how we found the weather. Before we could answer, we were joined by two other men, one of whom was from Technical Section Number One and the other from the Finance Section. They all expressed dismay at Johansen's death. The four Japanese then had a brief conversation among themselves, following which we were asked how the weather was in Norway. Before we could answer this question, we were joined by two more men, the first of whom was an assistant managing director, Mr. Kunio. His companion, a young man with a leather-bound notebook, was his interpreter. A conversation ensued among the six, following which we were asked how we had found the weather in Singapore, and if we had visited their new yard in Jurong Township, which is an industrial area in Singapore. As we were answering these questions, two women in beige jumpers came in and poured us green tea from dark red ceramic pots into small dark red cups.

Mr. Kunio looked at us without expression and began speaking. The interpreter wrote in his notebook. When Kunio finished, the interpreter said, "Mr. Kunio expresses his deep sorrow at the death of Mr. Johansen."

Fredrik thanked him for his kindness.

"Mr. Kunio wishes to know how he can be of service."

This was simple politeness. Everyone in the room knew that we had come to talk about canceling the big tankers, which were worth a great deal of money to Dai Ichi Zosen.

"As Mr. Kunio knows," I began, "the firm of P. Johansens Rederi is under great pressure owing to the death of the major shareholder and chairman. He has expressed that knowledge in the kindest possible way. However, Mr. Kunio may not be aware that the firm is also under pressure due to the regrettable decline in the tanker market. We wish this were not so, but wishing has nothing to do with reality. Accordingly, it is with deep dismay that I tell you we must cancel our order with you for the two VLCCs that are scheduled for delivery in October and November next year. I refer to hull numbers 841 and 842."

There were sharp intakes of breath all around as this was translated. Kunio breathed deeply on his cigarette, and answered briefly.

"Mr. Kunio says it is impossible."

"I understand Mr. Kunio's position completely and sympathize with it. I sympathize with all our friends in the shipbuilding industry. But I ask that Mr. Kunio understand and appreciate our position also. Our bulk carriers are trading well. Our tankers are not trading well or not trading at all. Our reserves are rapidly being depleted."

"Mr. Kunio says he is sorry, but it is impossible."

"We have no employment for one of the big ships, and for the other we have neither employment nor finance."

"Mr. Kunio says he is sorry, but it is impossible."

"Can you arrange financing for us?"

"Mr. Kunio says it can be done—in yen, for seven years, with a bank guarantee for the first six installments."

"We need financing in dollars for ten years. Our revenue is in dollars, and we refuse to take the exchange risk."

"Mr. Kunio asks if you have a cargo guarantee?"

"We do not. If we had, we could get financing elsewhere. As it is, the bank that has committed to us on the first ship is getting nervous."

"Mr. Kunio says he is so sorry."

"Well then, we must cancel."

"Mr. Kunio says he is sorry, but it is impossible."

We had this conversation, in various permutations, for the next two hours, during which we all drank a great deal of green tea and they smoked a great many cigarettes. The room was overheated as well, and Mr. Ito in particular had difficulty staying awake. The conversation was not heated, but Mr. Kunio and his colleagues, they following his lead, were being immovable in the nicest possible way. When it became obvious we were getting nowhere, we agreed to meet again the following day, which belied the intractable position we were being shown.

At the end of our discussion, the interpreter said, "Mr. Kunio hopes you are free for dinner this evening and would be most honored if you would join him."

"We are grateful to Mr. Kunio and accept with great pleasure."

"A car will come to collect you at the Palace Hotel at six-thirty. Mr. Kunio says, 'until this evening.' "

On our way back to the hotel, I told Fredrik about the rose and the card.

"What can we possibly do about it, John?"

"Not much more than we are already doing. Exercise caution and hope to God the protection is there when it is needed. I don't know why, but I somehow felt that this thing wouldn't follow us to Japan. Wishful thinking. I don't want to have to put up with it while we have this negotiating to do. One thing that we ought to do right after lunch is change our tickets. You and I, old man, are going to have to split up on our way home."

We did not know, of course, when we would be able to leave Tokyo, but we picked the itineraries and the flights, if not the days. Fredrik was to go to Honolulu and San Francisco, change for a domestic flight to New York, change again for Paris, and connect for Oslo. I chose instead to return more or less the way we'd come, by way of Hong Kong and Singapore, but on different carriers and going only as far west as Frankfurt before connecting for Oslo. Both flight plans were far longer than the one by which we had come to the East, but neither of us was inclined to second-guess Sergeant Ng.

Fredrik took a bus tour of Tokyo that afternoon, accompanied discreetly, Inspector Watanabe assured me, by a plainclothes policeman, while I made notes about the negotiations and worried and slept. I could not remember a time when I had not had that hideous pressure upon me, nor could I imagine its ever not being there in the future. Things were moving too slowly. I resented the fact that the negotiations were going to take so long, that we were going to have a social evening that would advance nothing, that we were not in discussions round the clock until we solved the problem. I no longer doubted where we were going to end up. The question was how . . . and for how much?

Dinner, as it happened, was a pleasant respite from our problems. A comfortable car appeared for us at precisely six-thirty. We drove probably for forty minutes without ever leaving traffic or getting out of the city. It was cold outside, and there were large neon lights all around, advertising God knows what. We were greeted in the vestibule of an inn by Kunio, Hiroshi, Ito, and the interpreter. We removed our shoes and were led by a tiny, smiling woman in kimono and obi and wooden sandals to a warm tatami room, with walls of wood and rice paper. We sat crosslegged at the low table, drank whisky, and talked. Fredrik described his father's death and told how puzzled the police were about the motive. He managed by his straightforward presentation to convey that he was beyond his grief, and that it was acceptable to go on to other matters. While we were served a number of courses, all of them fish, we talked about the market, and Kunio questioned us closely about the condition of a number of Scandinavian and Greek owners, indicating what essentially was their customer list.

Fredrik and I drank warm sake and beer, while all the Japanese continued to drink whisky, and we talked a good deal about shipping, present and future, and the economic state of the world—and never once mentioned the issue that had brought us together. At a quarter past ten we all rose. Mr. Ito was the only one of us who was obviously drunk, and they saw us out to the car. Along with all the women who had served us, they stood waving while we were driven off.

"It was a great dinner, John," Fredrik said, "but I think I drank rather too much."

"Perils of travel, my boy. You don't show it, in any event. Not like Mr. Ito."

"Quite sloshed he was. Oh dear, why do I do such stupid things?"

As the car wound back through the city in the darkness, I wondered how Fredrik had managed under the pressure to have held up so long without taking to the bottle or otherwise crumbling. As it was, he was showing a good deal more mettle than his father had in his last year of life.

Before I was allowed to enter my room, the guard from across the hall rapped once on the door. It opened straight away and there emerged another guard who had stayed in the room while I was out. I slept very soundly that night.

The next day we went on the offensive. We demanded not only that they accept our cancellation of 841 and 842, but that they return our entire downpayment. At that point the conversation became very intense, but it remained below the level of emotion. If anything, Mr. Kunio's eyes became even more hooded. We drank a good deal more green tea. The subject of a cancellation penalty was mooted. It appeared that it would amount to the entire fourteen-million-dollar downpayment, even if they were to agree to cancellation, which they would not do.

"Absurd," I said.

"Mr. Kunio says he is so sorry, but it is impossible."

We agreed to meet at the same time the following morning. It was at this meeting, our third in that windowless conference room, that Ito, who seemed to have been asleep during most of each of the previous meetings, broached the subject of conversion in a most offhand manner. He was leaning over for another cigarette and said the word *conversion* in English, to the table or to himself, not to any of us. There was a moment's pause. Then we spent the rest of that meeting talking around the possibilities, including smaller tankers or product carriers, all of which we rejected out of hand. Then Hiroshi mentioned the magic words *bulk carrier.* We promised to think about that and arranged to meet them the following morning at the same time.

At the fourth meeting, they agreed to have their engineers meet with ours to discuss the specifications for three forty-thousand-ton open-hatch bulk carriers with special gearing. The technical people then had two all-day meetings. At the final meeting, Kunio, Fredrik, and I signed a contract for the vessels at a cost of eighteen million dollars each, to be delivered at quarterly intervals beginning in March 1977. They agreed that the funds already paid in represented the twenty-five percent required upon contract signing; in fact, it exceeded the required amount by five hundred thousand dollars, which Kunio astonished me by agreeing to reimburse immediately, a measure, I fear, of their desperation to keep their order book intact and their people at work.

We were positively ecstatic in our telexes to Lars Norland—particularly when we could tell him to expect five hundred thousand dollars into our main London account—and to Lindstedt and to Ritter. I asked Norland also to begin talking informally with Bill Clark about financing for the three bulkers, with payout based on firm Norbulk charters, the details of which we had not worked out yet.

In the excitement I forgot that Inspector Watanabe had told me they'd reached a complete dead end on finding the sender of the flower. As it was a cash transaction, the florist had noticed nothing about the person who ordered the flower sent to my room except that he was a young Japanese. End of search. There was no reason why the florist ought to have noticed anything more.

16

We returned to the hotel from the Norbulk office and agreed to meet later for dinner. I left Fredrik in the elevator and was on my way to my room, feeling tired but immensely satisfied with the outcome of our negotiations. A major stumbling block to returning the firm to financial health had been gotten rid of. Then Watanabe fell in behind me and followed me the short distance to the door. I had not had many dealings with him, but whether on the phone or in person, he had always been polite and unfailingly cheerful. I just caught a glimpse of him as he came up behind me, and he looked very grim indeed.

As usual, a guard came out of my room and held the door for us as we entered. The inspector began speaking as soon as the door had closed.

"Please excuse this intrusion, Mr. Henriksen. I wanted to tell you some days ago, but felt I should wait, as you were in important negotiations. These are concluded, yes?"

I answered in the affirmative, wondering how in heaven's name he knew, unless it showed or unless he had an informant in the Dai Ichi Zosen office.

"Then, sir, I must tell you the *Rose* has disappeared."

I motioned him to a chair. He sat, with his raincoat still on, kneading a cap in his hands while he spoke.

"The vessel went to Bangkok, as you said. It arrived in Bangkok, loaded general cargo—crates, boxes, bales. And five passengers, late at night, from a small boat. The immigration officials didn't see; our agents saw them: three men, two women. The vessel started south. Four days ago she disappeared in the Gulf of Siam. We have not been able to find her since."

Four days before had been Friday. I wondered if she'd been hijacked or blasted to the bottom by whoever "they" were.

"What can we do?"

"Leave quickly," Watanabe said, and he looked heartbroken. He looked as if he felt personally responsible for someone's having lost track of the vessel. As if he had been reading my thoughts, he said, "They are strange waters, the Indonesian Archipelago, Cambodia, Vietnam. Anything can happen. Sorry." That the last word did not in any way convey the pain he was feeling was obvious in his face.

"We can try to have our tickets written for tomorrow."

"I would advise that, Mr. Henriksen. We do not like this development. Sergeant Ng is very displeased. Please tell the guard when you wish to leave for Haneda. We will send a car. I apologize for our discourtesy." Watanabe bowed and left the room.

Followed by a plainclothesman, Fredrik and I had a tempura dinner on the lowest basement level of the hotel. I am certain every Japanese in the restaurant knew we were being watched by a policeman; they eyed us curiously. If the other "they," in fact, were watching, they must realize that the voyage of the *Rose* was a ruse. Perhaps. On the other hand, we might be under surveillance by the Tokyo police simply because, while we had legitimate business in Japan, we were nonetheless unsavory characters who would be allowed to do their business and then to leave. The possibilities were endless.

Covered by the noise around us, I told Fredrik what had happened. He followed the bits and snatches of information given mostly in Norwegian, although occasionally I threw in a few Swedish words. He understood immediately what I was doing and listened attentively. I asked him to get to work on his ticket as soon as the airline office opened in the morning.

I lay for a long time that night staring into the darkness and listening to the susurration of the traffic in the broad road that ran between the hotel and the grounds of the Imperial Palace. I had just begun to fall asleep when the phone rang.

It was a call from Norway. There was a great deal of acknowledging that I was indeed John Henriksen—in English to the Japanese operator, in Norwegian to a compatriot, and finally to Liv, who had placed the call for Karl Wessel. When he came on, the connection was as clear as if he were in the next room.

"John, congratulations on the bulk carriers. We are all of us very excited here."

"No need to shout, Karl, I can hear you perfectly. Thank you very much. But you're not calling about the bulk carriers, are you?"

"No, no. I wanted to tell you as soon as I could. T. T. Lee, in Hong Kong, has expressed great interest in the *Star Aster*, *Iris*, and *Ivy*, and would like to see someone from our office as soon as possible. I know you must be exhausted, John, but can you handle it, do you think?"

"How real do you think this is?"

"Very. Lee has a first-class reputation, good banks behind him, and works with all the majors. As far as I can tell from the Olsen report, he is not overcommitted in big ships and is not overly cozy with any of the Japanese—either the Big Six or Sanko. Very real indeed. I think we could talk to him about the *Zinnia* also. He came on by telephone, John."

"This is excellent news, Karl. And just as you said. The interest would be in the Far East. I'll leave today."

"When is that?"

"Today. It's two o'clock in the morning here."

"Oh God. Sorry."

"Nothing, old man. I'll take Cathay Pacific direct from Tokyo to Hong Kong."

"Fine. I'll send details on the telex to Norbulk Asia."

"Good. Remember, Karl, I'll be going direct from Tokyo to Hong Kong."

"Yes, yes. Good, John. As you said, the connection is excellent."

I had, of course, no intention of flying direct from Tokyo to Hong Kong and perhaps overdid it with poor Wessel, who must have thought I was quite mad. In the morning after breakfast, in fact, I booked my ticket on All Nippon from Tokyo to Osaka, China Airlines from Osaka to Taipei, and Thai International from Taipei to Hong Kong.

A cable had been slipped beneath my door when I got back to the room. It was from Alice, and read, "Simply love to see you anywhere stop Reply Mandarin HKG." Convenient, I thought. I'll just ring her up when I arrive.

It was a troublesome message. Alice was neither frivolous nor imprecise, and the cable was both. She was counting on my knowledge of her to realize the text had been carefully composed to appear that way. It told me she had something on her mind that was important, and she had decided not to be open about it in a public communication. Despite Ng's advice, I would have to see her now.

Fredrik was leaving an hour before me, so I rang Watanabe and arranged for two cars. I went round to Fredrik's room to give him one of the signed copies of the contract with Dai Ichi Zosen (one was already in the mail to Oslo; the third I kept).

"I must tell you, John, that this has been a great experience for me. I learned more on this trip than I ever would have sitting in the office in Oslo. I'm only sorry that I failed you in Singapore." We shook hands and I wished him a good flight home.

"And for God's sake, Fredrik, do be careful."

"Don't worry, John. I've been looking behind me ever since we started out."

I was driven at high speed in a black, unmarked Datsun to the airport by a man who nodded when I entered the car and nodded when I left—that was the sum of our communication. There followed a series of irritating delays, slow boarding procedures, dull transit lounges, and a general sense of ennui until we began circling over Hong Kong in preparation for our final approach. The night was crystal clear, and the city a carpet of lights beneath.

When we emerged from the plane, the sky was full of stars and the air warm and heavy with humidity. I was back in the subtropics, out of the early spring chill in Japan.

Sven Lygren was waiting as I came out of customs, and I followed him out to his car.

"I'm afraid you have to make do with our place tonight and tomorrow, John. We couldn't get you into a hotel on such short notice until Saturday. It's the Furama, right next to the office."

"It's kind of you to take me in, Sven. By the by, I was wondering if you've got a telex for me from Karl Wessel? He said he was sending one."

"Not yet, John. I suspect there'll be something on the machine in the morning. Congratulations on that neat bit of negotiating with the Japanese."

"Thanks very much, but I was lucky. The Japanese yards, just like everybody else, are being hit with all kinds of cancellations and conversion demands, and a lot of jobs are being threatened in Japan. That made the yard amenable. And second, we're lucky that old Lindstedt has a use for those bulkers. We could have found ourselves converting from tankers no one needs to bulk carriers no one needs. I'm not deluding myself."

We went through the Harbour Tunnel and started up past Midlevels on our way to the other side of the island. Lygren did not acknowledge my comment, but seemed to be concentrating on the road. There was a certain distracted quality about Sven that I'd never noticed before. I thought back to Haakon Ritter's remarks in Singapore and wondered why he had begun to find Sven tiresome in some way.

Lygren lived in a flat in a tall apartment block on Repulse Bay Road, looking out toward the South China Sea. By the time we arrived, his wife Elisabeth was already in bed. He showed me my room, and I rang Alice at the Mandarin. She was not in. I left a message that I would call her in the morning, then went to bed and fell asleep wondering absurdly why Alice had not been there to receive my call.

Sven woke me at seven-thirty, and we were on the winding road back to Central, with a roll and coffee in our stomachs, by eight-fifteen. The traffic was heavy and grew heavier. We left the car in a car park next to Connaught Centre and walked the short distance to Norbulk's crowded office in Sutherland House.

"The offices are not much to look at," Lygren said as we entered, "and we've outgrown them. I've persuaded Lindstedt to let us move down to Gammon House, which is a bit further east. Whole of Central is moving that way really. Say, John, I hope you won't mind, but I've got rather a lot on my plate just now, so can I leave you to your own devices? There's an office and a desk you can use, and a delectable morsel named Susie, who along with everything else is a good secretary." I looked to see if Sven was smiling, but he was not. "The telex room is this way. Let's see if you have the message you were looking for. All we got yesterday was your cable saying you were on your way." He picked up the long yellow-and-white sheets of paper that were hanging from the machine and had begun to pile up on the floor and went through them quickly. "Sorry, old man. Not here yet."

"That's damned strange. I'll have to ring them up."

"Hang the cost, John. We'll send you a bill. Wait until after three, and you'll get them just as they're opening." A young Chinese man entered the room. "There you are, Sammy, you lazy bugger. These telexes should be separated and distributed by now."

"Yes, sir," Sammy said evenly.

"And when you go through them, make sure there is none for Mr. Henriksen. This is Mr. Henriksen. If you find one or if you get one during the day, make sure he gets it *chop chop*. Understand? He'll be in Mr. Baker's office."

"Yes, sir," Sammy said.

Lygren took me to the office I was to use. "I'm hamstrung without that telex, Sven," I said, "because I have to know what has passed already between T. T. Lee and Oslo. Do you know anything at all about the deal concerning our tankers?"

"Nothing whatever. Must rush now, old man. You remember Mike Price? Good. He's in the last hovel on the right," pointing down the corridor. "See him if you need anything. This is Susie," pointing to a small, perfectly formed, beautiful young Chinese woman, who stood up at her desk and smiled with her dark, dark eyes and her mouth in a way that made my knees feel a bit weak. "This is Mr. Henriksen, Susie. Please help him in any way he requires."

"I shall be pleased to help you with any secretarial tasks you may have for me, Mr. Henriksen." Her voice was like the tinkling of wind chimes.

"Thank you, Susie," I said, but she was watching Lygren walking—stalking really—down the corridor to his office. It was an icy look. She turned back to me and said, "You're welcome. Would you like some tea now, or coffee?"

"Coffee, thanks. White please."

I woke Alice, who talked in warm, sleepy tones.

"John, how perfectly divine that you're in Hong Kong. Yes, I got your message. Can't wait to see you. I hope you don't have a lunch. Wonderful. Come to my room. I'll lay on some sandwiches. There's lots to drink here, too. We've so much to talk about." Nattering away, as if she hadn't a care in the world.

I took the coffee that Susie brought and went down the corridor to Mike Price's office. Price was another old Asia hand, like Ritter. I think he'd started life as a banker, first working with one of the large clearers like National Provincial. He spent the war in the Far East, and when he was demobbed, elected to live in Hong Kong and went to work for a John Swire shipping subsidiary, then Wallem, and a couple of other companies until he joined Norbulk Asia. He was a round, jolly Englishman, with small, twinkling blue eyes and only a fringe of sandy hair around his head, with none at all on top. He was Lindstedt's chief finance man for East Asia, including Japan.

He smiled broadly and stood when I entered his office.

"John Henriksen, you old reprobate, how nice to see you. How are you getting on?"

"Pretty well, Mike. How are you?"

"Couldn't be better, old chum. How long are you in town for?"

"Have no idea. I'm trying to sell some of our tankers to T. T. Lee."

"I think then we'd better—for heaven's sake do sit down—I think we'd better find you some permanent office space. And you'll need a flat, of course."

"Is he as tough as that?"

"Tougher. Absolutely fair, totally honorable, and hard as nails. But you can bet that if he's interested in the tankers, there's a reason. I don't think it's just that he's taking advantage of a messy situation." The phone rang. He pushed a button on the intercom and ignored the phone. "John, for God's sake, what happened in Oslo? The papers here carried a pretty big story about Johansen. No information, of course, just a lot of smoke and mumbo-jumbo. He was machine-gunned in the street. Have they found out why?"

"No, Mike, they haven't. I think they've got some things they're working on. I know a little more, but I can't tell you. Mostly for your own sake." Price's eyes widened slightly at that. "I don't mean to sound mysterious, but it's a complicated situation."

"Not just a senseless act of violence then?"

I nodded.

"Well, it was a hell of a shock, let me say." Price shook his head. "So you're doing your damnedest to rescue P. Johansens for the son and heir? Lovely job on the bulk carriers. Even Lygren almost smiled."

"Perhaps you can tell me something."

"Shoot."

"First of all, will you throw me out of the office if I'm bothering you? I don't have a thing to do until I talk to Oslo. They were going to telex me, but the telex hasn't come yet, and I need their information."

"Good Lord, man, don't tell me you've nothing to do. I'll find you something in five seconds flat. Don't worry, John. I'll throw you out if necessary. By the way, lunch? Dinner then? Well let me know. I'd like to tie on the feedbag with you while you're here. What was it you were asking?"

"What's wrong with Lygren?"

"Why do you ask?" He rose and walked to the door. "Any more of whatever it is you're drinking? No?" He closed the door.

I said, "He was treating the telex operator very roughly this morning. And he said some things . . . well, one about and one to this lovely girl Susie that implied she's a whore."

"Won't give him the time of day, that one."

"And then Haakon Ritter seems annoyed with him. Implied that he is not pulling his oar."

"Indeed he isn't. Can't quite put my finger on why. He seems to be falling apart. His marriage is threadbare. He once made a play for the girl—Susie is not her name, by the way, it's Mei Lin—and she cut him dead. 'Susie' is Lygren's little joke, because it's a typical name a Wanchai prostitute would use. He can't fire her because she's too good, and her boss, Tony Baker, would be mighty annoyed. So Lygren's putting on the pressure and trying to make it intolerable for her. He also comes on like the worst British colonial types, thumping the table and referring to all Chinese males as 'boy.' I used to think that a combination of pressures got to him. It isn't the job by itself, because he did quite well when he first came out. Even so, if you combine a job to which he is not particularly suited with a foundering marriage in a strange setting, with all the additional pressures that entails—getting used to a new life, getting kids into a proper school, which isn't all that easy here—you might have an answer to the riddle of Mr. Sven Lygren. But I don't think you do. I think there's more there than I see. He's nervous and distracted. He makes mistakes, horrendous ones sometimes, but Ritter has very quietly put in some controls. Lygren knows about them, but he doesn't connect them with his own performance. He's also begun to drink rather more at lunchtime than he ought. He's not making any friends for us around here, and I'm afraid he may lose us some expensively trained people."

"Why does Lindstedt keep him on?"

"I'm not sure how much Ritter has kept Lindstedt insulated from this in hopes he can turn Lygren around. On the other hand, the old man is a savvy bastard, as you know, and sees through walls. He probably knows all about it. But Per is a very loyal man. Lygren probably did him a small favor once, so he keeps him round. Never mind. If the present trend continues, Mr. Sven will soon be back in the snow and sleet."

Price yawned and stretched. "Say, have you heard Lindstedt's latest idea? He wants to expand the Norbulk to include one solid-bulker owner—independent—from the U.K., Greece, and Hong Kong. He thinks that will make the company even stronger than it is now in terms of tonnage and intelligence and contacts. And, incidentally, stronger than our friendly competitors. I know what's on his mind. He thinks that this stuff the Soviets are pulling in the liner trades—cutting rates to the bone, operating at a loss, running boxes to Europe on the Transsiberian Railway—is just the beginning, and that it's only a matter of time before they're going to be pulling the same stunts in the dry bulk trades. So he wants to be ready, with superb tonnage and the cream of the business all locked up on long-term contract."

That was so like Lindstedt. He was always ten steps ahead of most everyone else. But what a drain on the people in the Norbulk organization. Such an expansion would more than double the amount of traffic they had to manage. I mentioned as much to Mike.

"I quite agree. On the other hand, while the old man always thinks of the ideal situation, he always executes in practical terms."

"His expanding the fleet doesn't bother you then? The acquisition of these little companies in Oslo? He's after us too, by the way."

"Doesn't bother me at all. Every ship he's bought is profitably employed, isn't it?"

"Yes."

"Well then? As for buying P. Johansens, what could be more natural?"

The pavement was crowded with people moving at a variety of paces, and cars and trucks and doubledecker buses roared along Chater Road.

I came in out of the hot sun through the rear door of the Mandarin and went up to Alice's room immediately. She had never looked better, I thought. Her eyes shone and her color was high, and her smile was wide and welcoming. I took her into my arms and held her tightly.

"Oh, God, John, I have been worried about you."

I ran my hand through that wonderful black hair streaked with gray and kissed her.

We were in the sitting room of a suite that overlooked as much of the harbor as could be seen beyond the Connaught Centre.

"Your Parisian magazine does not seem to mind expenses," I said.

"I've long known that, in your heart, John, you are just an accountant. Actually, this is even more astonishing when you realize that this is supposed to be for me what the American military calls R and R. However, I am working. I was at a very chic ball last night."

"How do you explain all this luxury?"

"I can explain it, John, but it's not rational. In this very silly world, magazine photographers, fashion photographers, are becoming as, quote, important, end quote, as the people they photograph. Since image has become everything, and reality is of no importance at all, it is the image makers who are rising to the top of the dung heap. Like marsh gas bubbling to the surface. I don't suppose you see enough high fashion advertising to tell, but it's remarkable how many photographs now contain a model who is holding a camera, or how many adverts are made up of multiexposure contact sheets. I think it is *amour propre* raised to the level of consuming passion."

"I have, Miss Nielsen, a consuming passion for you."

"Such a barbarian, John. There are some sandwiches. Can I give you a drink? I have almost everything."

"Dry sherry."

"And I have something to show you." She handed me a generous measure of sherry.

"I thought you had something on your mind. Or was that postdebutante telex you sent just an indication that your mind has turned to jelly?"

Alice looked a bit somber. "I was counting on your knowing me well enough to know that I thought I was onto something important. I did not say more, because I did not want to get you into any trouble." She poured white wine for herself. "I want to show you some photographs. I don't *know* that they will come as any surprise, but they might."

We sat together on the sofa and began to nibble on the sandwiches. She pulled a manila folder on the coffee table toward us.

"First look at this," she said.

It was a picture of a harbor, with perhaps a half dozen ocean-going vessels in it and numerous smaller craft. It was obviously taken in Asia, because of the style of some of the smaller vessels. I thought I could distinguish a hammer and sickle on the funnel of one of the bigger ships. The foreground contained a pile of wreckage. I guessed it was a large, second-class harbor.

"Where is this?"

Alice shook her head. "In a minute. Now look at this."

It was an extremely grainy enlargement, taken probably from the picture that Alice had first shown me, a kind of half view of the stern of one of the vessels. There were dark letters on a light background that read, ". . . SE" and ". . . OVIA." It could have been "ROSE, MONROVIA."

"May I see the first photograph again? Ah." Without its having been pointed out, one might never have noticed, but even in the original photograph, one could discern the white *T* on the dark funnel.

Alice said, "Haiphong, five days ago."

"What made you make the enlargement?"

"The question should really be, what made me take the picture? I'm half Norwegian, and I'm a photographer. I not only look at ships, I *see* them. I've been particularly sensitive to them since you told me about the *Rose*. I was being taken on a tour of the harbor area to observe the triumph of socialism in rebuilding after the war. I saw the whole name, by the way, but they would only let me take photographs from this angle. We were closer than this looks by the way. This shot was done with rather a wide-angle lens."

"Fantastic, Alice. The *Rose* disappeared about a week ago."

"Disappeared?"

"She was being followed by the police in some manner and they lost contact. Let me use your phone, will you?"

I rang a number that Inspector Watanabe had given me and asked for Lieutenant Goldsmith. When Goldsmith came on the wire, I identified myself and told him that the *Rose* had been in Haiphong five days before.

"How the devil do you know that?"

"A friend of mine was there and took a photograph of it."

"You're quite sure it's the *Rose*?"

"Quite."

"Good-o. I'll let all the chaps know. Say, old man, we ought to meet, you know. Where are you staying?"

"With a colleague in Repulse Bay."

"Ah, no good. Perhaps I could nip round to your office?"

We arranged that he should come to Sutherland House at four.

Before I left, Alice asked that we have dinner together.

"If I can. I don't know whether Sven has arranged anything."

"Bother the firm."

"Alice, I'm the man's guest."

"Well you ought to be mine. See you at eight?"

My call to Wessel went straight through at three.

"You don't have the telex?" he said incredulously. "One moment, John."

I could hear him talking on the intercom. While I sat looking out the window at what remained of the grounds of the Hong Kong Cricket Club, I visualized Wessel's office: small, cramped, stacks of paper on every surface, the lights burning because it was still dark in Oslo, his old porcelain coffee mug, stained brown, which he had had since he was a third officer for Wilhelmsen, perhaps snow pelting against the windows, the heat coming up in the pipes. . . He came back to the telephone.

"John, I am sorry. I don't know what happened. I tried to send it myself, right after I talked to you in Tokyo, but for some reason I couldn't get an answerback from Hong Kong. I typed it out and left it for Kurt with a note to send it immediately when he arrived in the morning. But he says now he never saw it. Look. I'll stand over him this time. You will certainly have it by your opening tomorrow."

I let Sammy know that the telex I'd been expecting would be in the morning's traffic and told Sven that the message I'd been looking for had never been sent at all.

"I'm also having a visit here in a few moments from a policeman."

"I hope you have plenty of cash," he said sourly. "I understand they don't take checks."

"I'm afraid I don't . . ."

"The Hong Kong Constabulary are famous for supplementing their incomes."

Goldsmith was a solidly built man, in his mid-forties I judged, and tall, with light blue expressionless eyes. He was wearing a tan lightweight suit, as was the man with him.

"I'm Lieutenant Goldsmith of the Constabulary, and this is Mr. Potter." Mr. Potter was small and thin, with small black eyes, and a few strands of dark hair lying across a freckled scalp.

We sat behind a closed door in the office I was using.

"Quite a looker you've got out there, Mr. Henriksen," Goldsmith said, referring to Mei Lin. "Now then, do you have this photograph with you?"

I took the two pictures out of the large envelope that Alice had given me.

They both looked at them for a few moments and then at me.

"Could get sticky," Potter mumbled to Goldsmith, who simply nodded.

"How were these pictures obtained?"

"An acquaintance of mine was in Vietnam on assignment for a French magazine. She knows ships and knows a little about the *Rose.* She saw it when she was being taken on a tour of the harbor at Haiphong."

"How much have you told your acquaintance about the *Rose*?"

"Only that it is somehow connected with Johansen's death."

"And this person is what nationality?"

"She carries a Norwegian passport."

"And you've known her for some time, have you?"

"Many years. Not nearly long enough."

Goldsmith smiled broadly; Potter did not react at all.

"Have you heard of a man called Herbert Tomlinson?"

"If that is the same man who committed suicide in Singapore recently, the answer is yes."

"And how have you heard of him?"

"In two ways. Sergeant Ng told me about him and his suspicion that Tomlinson's death was somehow connected with the *Rose*. And my friend and colleague in Singapore, Haakon Ritter, told me the story about Tomlinson that appeared in the newspapers."

"How did his name come up?"

"Ritter and I were having lunch together in the place where the girl involved used to sing. We were talking about this and that, and the name came up."

"Do you know of any way in which Herbert Tomlinson's death might be connected with the *Rose*?"

"I do not."

"Well, thank you very much indeed, Mr. Henriksen. If you require any assistance, just give me a tinkle on the blower. The Hong Kong Constabulary never rest." And Lieutenant Goldsmith and Mr. Potter left. Who on earth was Mr. Potter?

I rang T. T. Lee's office and made an appointment to see him at eleven the following morning. Sven and I left together at six. He'd not said a word to me about dining, so I simply informed him I was eating back in Central.

"Why don't you take the car, John?" he said. "We won't be using it tonight."

"I've never driven a right-hand-drive car before, Sven. And I don't know Hong Kong at all. I think you're mad to trust me with it."

"First of all, it isn't mine. It belongs to Lindstedt, just like I do. Secondly, driving here is a piece of cake. Thirdly, right-hand-drive is very simple. Only thing different is where the gear shift is; clutch is left and brake is right, just like left-hand drive. No problem. And you'll have a tough time finding a cab to take you all the way to Repulse Bay at that time of night. They hate it. Take the goddamn thing."

Elisabeth, whom I'd never met before, greeted Lygren with a peck on the cheek and called him darling. She had a glass in her hand that was almost empty.

"So sorry to have missed you until now, John. I was simply too exhausted to stay up last night." At which Lygren snorted, which she ignored.

She had been a good-looking woman once. Now her ash-blond hair was more ash than blond. Her skin was pasty, and her ample figure was running to fat. She smelled very strongly of gin.

"Are you joining us for dinner, or do you have other plans?"

I told her that I was dining in Central with a friend. I also said that Sven had offered the car, which I hoped did not interfere with anything she'd been planning.

"Oh no, no," she said, more to the wall than to me, "we never need the car at night anymore, because we don't go anywhere anymore at night—at least, not together. Whenever the press of business keeps Sven in Central, he just keeps the car with him. That's becoming more and more frequent, isn't it, darling?"

"Do shut up, Elisabeth."

I excused myself to bathe and change. "Would you like a little drinkie while you dress, John?"

"Very kind, Elisabeth, but I think not."

I got out of the flat as quickly as I could. My heart was in my mouth at the beginning of the drive, but after a few minutes, I was beginning to get the feel of it. The right-hand drive, as Sven had promised, was not at all difficult, but I had to remind myself not to end up in the right lane after making a right turn. The narrow, curving road and the speed were things that took more getting used to.

I put the car into the same car park Sven had used in the morning, as it was nearly directly across the road from the Mandarin. Alice was wearing a plain dark blue sleeveless dress with a single strand of pearls and some low heels. She told the cab driver to take us to a Szechuan restaurant in Causeway Bay, where we had a great deal to eat that was spicy hot to our bland old Norwegian taste buds, and we drank a lot of Tsingtao beer from the mainland. It was one of those lovely evenings when one forgets everything but the moment; it may be that everything that had been happening was subconsciously making each minute especially bittersweet in the best possible way. After dinner we returned to the Mandarin, had a drink in her suite, and made love with nearly adolescent abandon the first time, with more deliberation and more satisfaction the next.

As she lay cradled against my chest, I said, "I can't possibly imagine your not marrying me, Alice."

"Oh, but I can, darling," she answered.

"I like talking with you, drinking with you, eating with you, making love with you, walking with you, going to the theater with you, running with you, singing with you . . ."

"Singing with me?"

"You know what I mean. Being with you."

"I feel the same about you, John . . . dear John." She smoothed my eyebrows with an index finger.

"Then why?"

"Independence."

"An illusion. A rationalization for loneliness."

"But I'm never lonely."

"Never?"

"Almost never."

"And the rest of the time?"

She did not answer.

I said, "If we were together more often, think how much more marvelous it would be."

"It may be marvelous because we're not together more often."

"Promise you'll think about it, Alice."

"I promise."

"I love you very much."

For a long time she didn't answer. Then she said, "I'm truly a lucky woman."

I left her reluctantly and with the taste of irresolution dry in my mouth. But I thought it wiser to get the car back to Lygren. A small twinge of apprehension began as I descended in the lift. The lobby of the Mandarin was full of people, men in black tie and women in long dresses, and there was an avalanche of amplified sound coming from the Captain's Bar, where a Filipino group was performing. The traffic in Connaught Road was still roaring, but there was less of it. I stepped from the air conditioning into the sultry air of the South China Sea.

The underpass by the Mandarin to the Star Ferry and the car

park was well lit, but there were relatively few people about, and voices and footsteps echoed in the passage. Someone followed me up the steps in the car park, but when I looked over the edge of the stairwell, I could see nothing, not even a hand gripping a bannister.

Lygren's white Mercedes was standing fairly isolated at the harbor end of the second level. The overhead fluorescent lights threw a bluish glare across the concrete floor. There were two figures standing beside an automobile not far from the Mercedes, but at that distance, all I could see was their silhouettes. Behind me I heard the soft scrape of shoes on the cement.

I glanced over my shoulder. About fifteen feet behind me was a man in a dark suit, an Occidental of medium height, following slowly and carefully, looking straight ahead, and deliberately avoiding looking at me.

I began to walk faster and looked back again. He had not changed his pace at all, but kept coming steadily after me. Had he had a gun he surely would have fired by now. I could assume only that it was a knife—at any rate, something that required close range. I walked even faster, half ran really, and reached the car. On and on he came. I unlocked the car, fumbling with the key, found I was on the wrong side, but slipped in anyway, locking the door behind me, for whatever good that would do. I wedged myself over the gear shift and slammed the key into the ignition. The car burst into life.

The silhouettes near the Mercedes became two middle-aged Chinese men who were engaged in a rapid conversation and paid no attention, either to me or to the man behind me.

I eased the car across the floor, cutting across lanes and parking docks. The man I thought was following me again paid no attention, but while I watched, he began to stagger and stumble from side to side. I realized that what I had interpreted as single-minded purpose was his fight against drunkenness, which he had just lost.

I shouted with joy and relief and drove down the ramp two levels and into the street, which was, I was happy to observe, comfortably full of vehicles boiling past.

I had taken reasonable care to memorize Sven's instructions. They were not difficult in terms of direction, only with respect to traffic patterns. I passed along the harbor and began the ascent toward Midlevels without difficulty, although I still had to mind being in a right-hand-drive automobile.

The Mercedes purred contentedly, however, and took the climb and the curves without effort. The traffic around, behind, and ahead of me began to thin appreciably, dropping away into this side road and that.

Two or three cars seemed stuck behind me, but I forced myself to think nothing of it other than to be aware that they were there. I had not relished my reaction to the man behind me in the car park. I had, in fact, been close to panicking, and that would have done me no good at all.

A Mitsubishi Colt in front of me turned right. I continued straight on. There were now no cars in front of me, at least as far as I could see, and none coming toward me. One car behind was very close, but I couldn't blame him, because I was not maintaining a very even speed, being unacquainted with the road.

I thought briefly of slowing down enough to let him pass, if he were foolish enough to do that on a curve or a hill, and started to do so. However, something made me change my mind.

As soon as I slowed down, the car behind pulled out and started to draw abreast in the process of passing me. Knowing full well that the driver would curse me, and for no reason of which I was aware, I put the accelerator to the floor and roared ahead. Simultaneously, I heard a noise like a truck backfiring. All of the glass from the rear windows of the Mercedes disappeared with the sound of shattering crystal. I felt a searing pain in the back of my neck and my right ear went deaf.

I kept the accelerator on the floor and fought to control the car on a road of which I had almost no knowledge. The car behind me stayed close, but we were twisting through a series of curves. I was driving as fast as I could, and I was sick with fear. My palms were sweating and my shirt felt damp through my jacket. My collar was also wet, but God knew what that was. The air screamed through the openings where the windows had been.

I heard another sound, different from the first, more like a cough; and quite suddenly the car swerved toward the left retaining wall, over the edge of which I could see a great deal of Hong Kong spread out below. I fought the wheel, twisting hard to the right. The car hit the retaining wall and bounced off, skidding into the opposite lane. I stamped on the brakes and slid almost broadside into the wall on the right, hitting first with the right front fender. Something hit me hard in the lower ribs on the right, and I couldn't breathe. A car speeded past, exploded in a ball of orange flame, and cascaded over the retaining wall. Another car went past me and stopped. The lights went out. I tried to move, but I couldn't. My ribs seared, and I was still having difficulty breathing. When I tried to lift myself out of the seat with just my arms, I found I could hardly move my arms, much less anything else. I felt broken all over.

The night was still, although I seemed to hear a police hooter far away. There was a sound of steps on gravel. A featureless face looked in the window on the left of the car.

"Can you reach the ignition, Henriksen?" the face said in English, in an accent I did not immediately recognize.

"Yes," I whispered. It hurt to speak.

"Turn it off. How are you feeling?"

"Can't tell. Ribs. Neck."

A torch flicked on and off. "Looks a bit bloody back there. Could be the glass. Here." I could see his arm reach in and very gently press a cloth against the back of my neck. "I won't move you, because there's no telling. Ambulance will be here soon. I'll wait until they've come. Might still be some vermin around."

"You're American, aren't you?" I said stupidly in Norwegian.

"Goodnight, Mr. Henriksen."

The police hooter was quite close now.

17

My ribs were bruised, not broken, and after the x-rays, they put a kind of corset around me to insure that I would move stiffly and not strain them. They patched the cut at the back of my neck that I had received from the flying glass. And they insisted I remain in the hospital for twenty-four hours. In the end I felt as if I had had the ultimate fight with the school bully—and bested him. Lieutenant Goldsmith—it must have been he—put a police guard on the door of my room, and I slept like a baby for what remained of the night.

In the morning I felt very unwell indeed, and I was assaulted by waves of nausea until midmorning. I dozed for a bit, and woke to see Goldsmith and Potter coming into the room.

Goldsmith drew up a chair by the bedside and sat down. Potter stood at the window, hands behind his back, and looked out.

"Now, Mr. Henriksen, we'll try not to keep you long. Do you feel up to telling us what happened?"

When I'd finished the story, Goldsmith said, "Did you get a look at the car? My chaps tell me there's not much left."

"I saw nothing but the headlights, I'm afraid."

"And the car driven by this fellow with the American accent?"

"Nothing at all. I didn't even know he was there."

"You're quite sure you'd recognize an American accent?"

"Quite."

Goldsmith turned to Potter. "Lovely view, isn't it? What do you make of all this, Stanley?"

Potter said, "Bloody meddling fools. I'm having a word with my opposite number, I should say." Potter turned away from the window.

"Stanley, don't you think you may be being a tiny bit rigid? After all, Mr. Henriksen might not have survived if that bloody fool had not been meddling."

"Don't belabor the obvious, Goldsmith. I realize that. But it's a matter of principle."

"Exactly my point, Stanley. Couldn't have put it better myself."

After lunch, of which I ate practically nothing, I slept again, awaking to find Alice sitting next to me. The room was in twilight behind drawn curtains.

"Aren't you bored sitting there in the dark?" In her face was a mixture of tenderness and anxiety.

"Never," she said.

I lay for a few moments looking at the high ceiling, watching the shifting patterns of light that crept around the edges of the curtains.

"Alice, darling, please place a call for me. I want to speak with Sven Lygren at Norbulk Asia."

Lygren came right on. When I started to apologize, he said, "For heaven's sake, forget the car, John. Are you okay? Are you calling from the hospital? It's in all the papers. 'Prominent Norwegian businessman attacked viciously' and so forth."

"Except for the 'prominent' that sounds accurate."

"But why?"

"That, my friend, I can't begin to say."

"It can't have been without motive."

"I agree."

"Then what . . ."

"Sven, I hate to be a bore, but I was supposed to have seen T. T. Lee this morning."

"Say no more, John. He saw the paper, too, and was on first thing this morning wondering how you are and if there is anything he could do, and of course he realized the meeting would have to be deferred. For a Chinaman, he's first class, is old T. T."

It was left that I would contact Lee as soon as I felt able. Alice left me then, after insuring that I needed nothing. I slept heavily until late afternoon, then had a sponge bath and took some dinner. Alice returned at six, with her camera bag over one shoulder, and a parcel with shaving things, a pair of corduroy trousers, a shirt, and underwear.

"You look breathtaking," I said to her when she came into the room. She was wearing a beige blouse with a gold-toned necklace and straight, brown trousers that caressed her figure.

"Oh, John, do shut up. You sound much better."

"Just sore all over."

"I thought these things would be useful. I can't imagine you can wear what you were brought here in."

"Thanks very much, darling. The doctor has suggested I stay the night to make doubly sure. I felt bad this morning, he says, because I was coming out of shock." She sat on the edge of the bed and held my hand. "Alice, how long will you be in Hong Kong?"

"Another two or three days. I have a verrrry important reception at the Hong Kong Club tomorrow."

"You can't make it sooner?"

"You want to get rid of me, do you?"

"No. I am afraid for you."

"I don't think you need be, John. A policeman is following me everywhere."

I was not at all mollified by that information, but I kept my own counsel, because I saw no point in worrying her further. We had all been lucky up to now. There was no reason at all to believe that the luck would hold.

The evening passed slowly after Alice left. I was too well rested to sleep, and my ribs were still painful. I read the newspapers with impatience and threw them aside. Night came on. The hospital grew quiet.

There was a tap on the door and it opened. A Chinese constable came in, followed by two Chinese doctors. I thought they would poke around a bit, give me pill, and turn out the lights. Sleep would be a relief.

The two men in white coats approached the bed, while the constable remained with his back to the closed door and looked toward the window. Something was not right. I began to sit up. One of the doctors shoved me back roughly against the bed, one hand across my mouth, and fell across my chest. The force knocked the wind out of me, and the weight on my ribs was agonizing. I felt the sharp jab of a needle in my left arm, and everything went black.

* * *

I woke to total darkness, surrounded by a horrid stink. My head pounded, and successive waves of nausea swept over me. From the bottom of a well came a babble of voices, indecipherable, incomprehensible. The top of my head came off and I fainted.

There were dreams: bits of brightly colored glass whirling in a vortex, trees and mountains going swiftly by as if I were in a fast moving car.

When I woke again, the room was striped with gray light that came through cracks in the walls. It was quiet now, and the air was warm and fetid. I was lying on a straw pallet on the floor, covered with a greasy sheet and, except for the bandage around my middle, I was naked. It took a long time to assemble these facts.

The room was becoming clearer as the light filtering in grew stronger and my eyes began to focus. I pushed myself upright with difficulty. My head began to swim, and I lay back down and rested a moment. When I sat up again, the vertigo was a little less. I got unsteadily to my feet, feeling very unwell.

Except for the pallet and scraps of paper and dirt on the floor, the room was bare. The walls were made of rough wood and the ceiling was very low. The door was bolted on the outside. My stumbling around precipitated sounds of movement outside the room.

After a bit, the door opened and a bowl was pushed in along the floor. The door slammed and was bolted again. The bowl held a cold rice gruel, the sight of which made me realize I needed to eat something. I sat crosslegged on the pallet and ate the gruel with my fingers. It smelled of nothing and tasted of nothing. It had the texture of an overripe banana and took no time at all to finish.

I stared at the wall opposite, but I saw nothing. "They" had caught up with me at last. But why hadn't they killed me? I did not want to think about the reasons, but my guts shriveled with fear.

After a time—I don't know how long, but it seemed interminable, and the light in the room indicated it was by now full day outside—the door was opened and swung back roughly. A Chinese stepped inside—a man of medium height in a khaki shirt and trousers and pink rubber sandals, the left half of whose face was a purple patch, with a wrinkled slit where the eye ought to have been—and gestured that I should follow. I wrapped the sheet around me and walked behind him into the next room.

This was lit by a smoking kerosene lamp and what little light crept through the cracks in the shutters. Two Chinese stood flanking a table. The man with one eye stood behind me. Seated at the table was an Occidental, who was, as far as I could tell in that light, very fair, with rosy cheeks and blue eyes and brush-cut light hair. He was wearing a white shirt open at the collar and tan trousers. I thought that he was probably a good deal older than he looked. There were shadows around his eyes. He nodded at One-Eye, who tore the sheet off me.

"We're sick of playing games, Henriksen," he said with an American accent in a youthful voice that belied the threat his words carried. I was proud of my detachment. I could not admit the inevitable.

"We're entrepreneurs, chief. Very anonymous, get me? We got a nice business in Asia. We don't believe in free enterprise and competition. Your boys come fucking around here, we blow them away, get me? Good. Your cop buddies told you what's happened to the *Rose*? Never mind. We could mash you like a goddamn bug and put you where they'd never find you." The blue of his eyes was vivid and totally opaque. I could not imagine where his monologue was leading.

"We blew away the wrong man, didn't we?" he said suddenly.

Ah. I was standing naked and sick and in pain in front of one of the people who had murdered Paul Johansen.

I answered by instinct. "Yes."

The response seemed to satisfy him. "What is the source of your intelligence?"

"Agents," I said. I could feel his tension at my response. "Ship agents. Not our official ones. Small outfits. Fringe outfits that could use the extra cash." Pray God I had protected Norbulk. But he seemed to relax.

"How have you gotten to the cops?"

I had to think fast. I slumped a bit to give myself time. One-

Eye gripped my arm and held me up. "Not difficult," I mumbled, as if coming out of a daze. "We already had some leads. Give them what they want. Money, women, drugs. Boys. The cover is that it looks legitimate for us to have protection. And we have a legitimate business."

"Yes," he said, almost to himself. "Boy, you're a piece of work, Henriksen. Tell you what. We're going to give you a break. You've got ships, and you've got connections; we can use both. We're going into an expansion phase. We've got more work than we know what to do with. There's a big market out there, and with no complications like export licenses or taxes or passports or any of that shit, we get paid top dollar. This is a quality organization, chief, run by quality people who come from one of the best outfits in the U.S. of A. and who know what end is up.

"Let's get down to business, sport. You guys are amateurs. We've proved that seventeen ways from Sunday. You got a little bit of the market for a time, and you came on like gangbusters. That's why Johansen bought it and that's why you almost did. But my principals aren't unreasonable. Man that covers himself like you have can't be all bad.

"And you run a legitimate shipping company.

"So we're going to make you a proposal. You all continue to do your business, but we're going to kind of fold into it, see—put some extra cargo on here and there; M-16s for Discovery Bay, freedom fighters for Lebanon, or coke for Tyneside—that's a joke, son. That crazy fucker Qadaffi will buy almost anything, and we got a lot more customers. Wait till you see the stuff that Amin and Mobutu order.

"What I'm telling you, chief, is that we're going to cut you guys in because we want to use your ships and we want some of those lines that you've got to the fuzz out here. Call it your technical knowhow. And we'll give you ten percent."

The American looked at me expectantly. I hesitated because I didn't know what I was supposed to do.

"Shit, man," he said, "you ain't got a choice."

I looked at his opaque eyes and nodded.

He grinned boyishly and stood and came around the table and offered me his hand, which I took. "Thought you'd agree. We can have one of the best goddamn operations going." The childlike smile disappeared. "Now you get your business done here and you get your ass back to Oslo. We'll be in touch there. But we'll be watching you all the time, hear? Any funny business, chief, and we'll put you away in Sumatra or some place, and it'll take you an awful long time to die."

The last he said very quietly, as if he were discussing the intricacies of a sales contract. My flesh crawled despite the heat in the room.

"Now, Henriksen, when you leave here you go through that door and turn right and sooner or later you'll get back to Hong Kong. And don't worry about people looking at you. They're going to avoid you like the plague."

Then he hit me very hard in the stomach. I went down like a stone and began to vomit. When I stopped retching, the American leaned close to my ear and said, "This is going to be a limited partnership, chief. That's just so's you'll remember which of us is the limited partner. See you in Oslo."

What got me out of there was rage. I heard the footsteps leaving and the door slamming shut. I lay on the floor awhile, gathering strength, then heaved myself up, the sheet wrapped around me, and stumbled half blinded by the light into the street. It was more an alley and in deep shadow, but it was much brighter than the room I had just left. All around were faces of poverty and fear that avoided looking at me. But despite the American's implication, I was able to hobble along the slimy cobbles to a busy street in a few minutes. Here people stared boldly at the foreign devil emerging in a sheet from a hideous stinking alley.

In moments, a police car pulled up to the curb. Both constables got out and approached me warily from either side.

"My name is Henriksen," I said. "I think Lieutenant Goldsmith might be looking for me."

One of the policemen held my arm lightly while the other used the car radio. Then I was put into the back seat, behind the wire cage, and the car tore off through the streets, lights flashing and hooter going. I had been somewhere in Kowloon or the New Territories. We went through the Harbour Tunnel and back to the hospital, which I recognized only when I was once again inside, never having seen it from the outside in daylight. I was examined, given a number of shots, and made to shower with strong soap.

I was in bed and nearly asleep when Goldsmith and Potter appeared. Goldsmith was apologetic.

"We would not disturb you, Mr. Henriksen, if it were not important."

I told them my story in rambling fashion. They interrupted from time to time with a question. The only thing of interest to me then was sleep. All my mental and emotional defenses had been raised, and I might have been talking about something that had happened to a mutual acquaintance.

When I finished, Goldsmith and Potter stayed some moments locked in thought. At last Goldsmith said, "That confirms it, doesn't it, Stanley?"

Potter's eyes flared briefly and he looked at me and back at Goldsmith in warning. It meant nothing to me; nor did I care.

"There aren't many strangers who walk out of Kowloon walled city as if they hadn't a care in the world," Goldsmith said with fragile cheerfulness. Then he looked somber. "I am deeply sorry for the collapse of our security. I assure you it won't happen again. Cold comfort, I realize, since it shouldn't have happened in the first place."

He had jogged my memory. "There was a constable . . ."

"Dead," Goldsmith answered. And seeing my reaction, he said, "Weep not. Brought it on himself. He took a bribe. They stuffed a fifty-dollar note into his mouth." Goldsmith stood and motioned to Potter. "We'll be going, Mr. Henriksen. Stanley and I will have a natter about what to do with the information you've given us. And some of my people will assist you moving into the Furama tomorrow.

"One other thing, Mr. H. Not a word to anyone about your sojourn out of hospital. We've kept it out of the papers, and it's probably best that way. Ta, ta."

The anger I had previously felt when lying doubled up with my face in the dirt had subsided. What took its place was as blank as the ceiling of my hospital room, which, moments after Goldsmith and Potter had left, spun away as I watched and was swallowed up by the darkness.

On the following morning, two constables took me out to Repulse Bay Road to collect my things. Sven was not at home. The children were arguing with their mother, and the amah was looking sour. I thanked Elisabeth awkwardly and bid her good-bye, but she was hardly listening. The policemen then drove me back to Central to the Furama Hotel, where I registered. The man at the reception desk looked closely at me after I had filled out the card. This was the Henriksen who was in the papers:

> The police believe that a bomb being carried by the assailants exploded prematurely, destroying the car and killing the occupants [one article had said]. Mr. Henriksen could give no reason for the attack made on him. He is in Hong Kong on business connected with his firm, P. Johansens Rederi A/S, a medium-sized Norwegian shipping company. Four weeks ago, the chairman of the same firm, Mr. P. Johansen, was gunned down in Oslo's main street. It appears that the Oslo authorities are as much in the dark as the Hong Kong Constabulary. "We have not yet established the connection," says Hong Kong's Lieutenant "Vicar" Goldsmith, hero of the Triad raids two years ago, "but it's only a matter of time. We are, of course, on to Oslo."

I could not recall having spoken to anyone from a newspaper, but I was not sure I could trust my memory about that morning.

Mike Price came to my room in the afternoon with two cold bottles of beer and some paperback novels. "Tried to see you yesterday, old chum, but they wouldn't let me." We talked about the cost of energy and about the holiday he was planning in Penang. He avoided asking me about the attack.

The Mandarin desk informed me that Miss Nielsen was out for the evening. I went to bed at eight-thirty.

It is remarkable how one's aches and pains cease to be the center of the universe once one has had a bit of rest and the healing process has begun. My first thought when I awoke was whether I was the best possible representative for the firm in negotiations with T. T. Lee.

The room was pitch black. I could hear some traffic in the road below and running water and the occasional clank and thump of the lift bank near the room.

Questions intruded themselves. Who was the American? What had Potter meant by "bloody meddling fools"? What was one of the best outfits in the U.S.A.? And what would happen if, having delivered their ultimatum, they decided to go underground for a while—for weeks, months, a year perhaps? Would the police continue their interest and protection? And what of the other thread? Where did it lead? The American thought "we" were rivals in a lucrative trade. Raymond Bechmann, Pappas, and someone in Oslo.

I had a strong premonition then and was afraid. Afraid for Oslo and for Fredrik. I looked at the clock. It was between four-thirty and five, which is to say between nine-thirty and ten the previous evening in Oslo. I placed a call to Norland.

"Lars, is everything okay in Oslo?"

"Yes, certainly, John. How are you? That's the important thing. There were more reporters in the office yesterday than when Johansen was killed."

"I'm fine, Lars. I simply had a feeling that all was not well at the office. You've taken security precautions?"

"Oh yes. The office is being watched all the time. So are we. It's a great bore, really."

"Have you heard from Fredrik?"

"We have. He ought to be flying in tomorrow."

"You'll let me know when he arrives, won't you?"

"Absolutely, John. And for God's sake, take care of yourself."

"I am sorry I'm being so officious, Lars."

"I understand completely my friend. By the by, what have you done with the *Rose*?"

I was instantly on my guard.

"Why do you ask?" I said curtly.

"No need to snap, old man. But I am nominally responsible for the finances of the company in the absence of the other officers, both of whom are dead, and for the sake of good order, and particularly for my relations with the income tax people, who have started sniffing around, I'd like to know whether I'll be seeing any revenue coming into the account."

"I think you may, Lars, but it may be irregular in arrival. I've put her back to work."

"Have you indeed?" Norland said. There was a peculiar tone to his voice. I couldn't imagine what he might be thinking.

The next morning I hobbled next door to Sutherland House. I rang T. T. Lee for an appointment that morning and reviewed the telex from Karl Wessel. Lee had offered a total of fourteen million dollars for *Star Aster*, *Iris*, and *Ivy*. He made no mention of the *Zinnia*, but indicated he might be interested in the vessel at some nominal sum—he could not have been serious, of course, because she was the largest and the newest of our four tankers, and the one with the biggest debt—if he got the other three at his price. Wessel thought that the fourteen million might be divided three, four, and seven for the three vessels. If this was the case, Lee was not far off the market for *Star Aster*, one to two million low for *Iris*, and two to three million low for *Ivy*. The comment about *Zinnia* was absurd. Karl went on to say that it was his guess that *Zinnia* was really the vessel Lee was interested in, which I found an intriguing thought, but I was not convinced.

The three tankers together had thirteen-odd million dollars in mortgages outstanding, so accepting Lee's offer would cover the debt and accrued interest, with enough left over to buy an inexpensive bottle of Beaujolais at the Vinmonopolet for the office celebration. It was not enough, by a considerable margin, nor did the offer address the issue of the additional thirteen million outstanding on *Zinnia*.

I told Mike Price I was seeing T. T. Lee at eleven and asked him to tell me something about the man.

"He was a banker in Shanghai," Mike began. "Left in 1949, losing most of what he owned and couldn't carry. He settled in

Hong Kong, last bastion of *laissez-faire* capitalism in the world, and became very attached to floating assets. So much so that he has one of the biggest fleets in the world—independent anyway—and ranks right up there with Pao and Tung and Wah Kwong."

"How is he likely to negotiate?"

"The story is that his banker's background has made him cautious. He still wants to see how his banks are going to be paid back before he invests their money. Particularly since he demands a lot of it: one hundred percent financing and no equity—how do you like that gearing ratio?—his argument being that his long-term fixtures warrant it. That can be a mistake sometimes; I've seen a lot of shipowners gobbled up by interest payments. On the other hand, he is a very rich shipowner with a house full of precious *objets d'art,* and I deem myself lucky when I can buy a pint for a friend at the Mandarin. Which reminds me, can I buy you lunch there today?"

"Absolutely."

"Good. About one. If something comes up and you can't do it, not to worry. We'll catch up later. In any event, what I am saying is that if Lee is interested in the tankers, then he has a reason. And that reason is that one of his Japanese friends or Brazilian friends, or, God love you, one of the majors, wants them. And they don't want to charter Norwegian vessels because they cost too much to run."

"Have you seen Wessel's telex?"

Price shook his head, and I passed the message to him. When he looked up from reading it, I said, "What he pays for the ships depends on what he can earn with them and how long his bankers will give him to amortize the debt."

"Precisely. And these guys operate on pretty thin margins while they're paying off the mortgage. I think he will end up offering you a fair price for today's market. Don't let the prices in the telex worry you—they're just the opening salvo. But I shouldn't push him hard, John. There's an awful lot of tonnage for sale, and he can pick and choose. You've got two things going for you. The first is the reputation that P. Johansens has for maintaining its vessels. Your off-hire and your insurance records are impeccable. The second is sheer luck, but combines nicely with the first. Wessel's original offering telex arrived in Hong Kong at the same moment a couple of Japanese delegations were calling on T. T. Lee. That's why I think the prospective charterers may be Japanese. What else can I say, except good luck? One thing more. I don't think he has any interest in the *Zinnia* at all."

Lee sent a car for me, into which I was accompanied by a policeman in plainclothes, to go the few hundred feet to Gammon House, the new high-rise office building at the edge of the business district to which Sven Lygren was going to remove the Norbulk offices.

The entrance foyer to Lee's office was filled, as is often true of shipowners, with large scale models of his ships in glass cases. I counted a dozen vessels with Lee's distinctive red and green colors. In the old days, the yard provided a model along with the real thing; it was part of the contract. Those days were never coming back.

After a couple of minutes, T. T. Lee appeared. He was a short, round man with twinkling black eyes, a flatish nose and a broad smile. His hair was coal black, and he looked a good deal younger than his sixty-odd years. He shook my hand warmly and inquired after my health.

"I can't comprehend such things, John," he said in barely accented English. "In fact, I find the older I get, the less I understand. Please come this way."

I followed him along a quiet, softly lit corridor to a small sitting room, brightly decorated in cheerful colors. As soon as we were seated, a young man appeared with tea. He pulled the door shut after him when he went out.

"I have learned," Lee began, "just recently, that one of my charterers—people I've been doing business with for years, absolutely first class—has a need for three vessels very similar in size to those which your Mr. Wessel telexed us about. These people are very specific about their requirements, and the vessels you are offering nearly fill the bill. I know the reputation poor Mr. Johansen had for keeping his ships in tiptop condition. I need not tell you that there is a lot of tonnage overhanging the market, some of which can be had for a song and some of which is not worth the song. But I like the idea of *your* vessels. The problem is, of course, that my charterers and my bankers both have very sharp pencils. Both of them know the market; neither is going to be especially generous. The bankers have told me what they're willing to lend and at what rate; the charterers have told me what rates they are willing to pay. The rates do not lend themselves to expensive ships. More tea? So I telexed Mr. Wessel offering fourteen million for the three tankers, subject to inspection, of course, and financing, and subject to the *Ivy*'s having had special survey. Mr. Wessel has since confirmed that she had it last year."

T. T. sat back and regarded me with a pleasant expression. He had offered us less than half of what the vessels had cost, and they had been delivered at a time when prices had been reasonable. But nothing he had said was outrageous. The price he offered would give us a book profit of something under three million dollars, although actual profit would be virtually nothing.

"Thank you for your candor, T. T. I understand what you are saying, and I appreciate your concerns, which are similar to mine. Paul Johansen used to accuse me of being too conservative. In any event, I don't think we could afford to let the three tankers go for anything under eighteen million dollars."

"Oh, John, for eighteen million, I should expect to get the big ship as well."

"I thought you had no interest in the *Zinnia.*"

"I don't really."

"Well, it's a moot question, because the *Zinnia* has a lot of debt on her. It's no secret in the shipping community, my friend, that P. Johansens Rederi is not in the best financial condition." Lee nodded and looked solemn. "Giving her away for four million dollars would cause irreparable damage. We would then have to start selling ships that are turning a profit. I don't think I would have my job very long after I sold you the *Zinnia* on those terms."

"Well, John, let us both think about these matters and meet again. Say tomorrow at the same time?" I nodded. "Good. Now can you join me and my sons for lunch?"

"I should be delighted, T. T. If I could just ring my office."

"Certainly. You can use that phone. It goes straight out, no need to dial 'nine' or anything. I'll be outside."

I told Mike that I thought it would be important for me to lunch with T. T. Lee. He said he understood completely, but he sounded a bit distracted. "Say, old man, when you're through with old T. T., please don't go wandering off before nipping in here. I'd like to have a brief chin wag."

The Lees used a dining room in their own office. I was introduced to Lee's two sons as we had a sherry together. T. C. was the older and bore a strong resemblance to his father. T. F., on the other hand, was tall and slim and while he was polite and deferential to both his father and his brother, one had the impression that he paced inwardly, like something caged. He said little during the course of the meal, and I don't think he paid much attention to the conversation either.

We did not talk a great deal during lunch, but T. C. did speak about the progress of their container operation. Up to that point they had encountered no difficulty with the Soviet liners in FESCO, and the Transsiberian Railway, because they were trading to the U.S. West Coast, but they were on the edge of expanding the service to Europe, in concert with a couple of Continental operators, and it had them a bit worried.

"At some point," T. T. said, "they are going to find that the money they are losing is not worth the game. Then they will be charging closer to our rates."

"I don't know," T. C. said. "Political rates can go on for a very long time. Particularly if you want to end up controlling international commercial shipping. And all they are losing is rubles. They are earning hard currency."

His father shrugged. "I hope you're wrong, T.C., but I fear you have a point."

We went to a room adjacent to the dining room for coffee.

When we were seated, Lee said, "Tell me, how is Mr. Lindstedt?"

"Do you know Per then?"

"I met him once a long time ago, but I can't say I know him. I should like to. I am, shall we say, an observer of the Norbulk operation."

"He is very well indeed, bubbling along, full of ideas as always."

"Yes, that is how I've imagined him. You know, I've talked with Mr. Lygren from time to time, but he has always seemed, how shall I say, very busy and preoccupied." I took that to mean that Lee had tried to initiate a dialogue with Norbulk, and Sven Lygren had either missed the point or simply didn't care.

"I hope you will give Mr. Lindstedt my personal regards when you next talk with him," T. T. continued. "Now I think we ought to let you get back to work. The car will take you to Sutherland House, John. Until tomorrow then. We shall both consider the matters we have discussed."

Price looked very grim indeed and asked me to close the door to his office.

"They found a bomb in the Oslo office, John. The police defused it, so no one was hurt."

"I was told the office was being guarded."

"That's what we understood as well. They don't know how it was placed."

"Thank heaven they found it in time."

Price ran a hand over his eyes. "That isn't all, I'm afraid. Fredrik has been hurt."

"The poor boy. Badly, Mike?"

"We don't know. He was shot at Charles de Gaulle Airport in Paris."

"Do they know . . ."

"I don't know anything more. I'm getting all this from your copper friend Goldsmith. They got the man who attacked Fredrik. Goldsmith asked that you ring him up as soon as you can."

"I had some things to tell you about my conversation with Lee, but they seem meaningless now."

"That can come later. Why don't you ring Goldsmith? John,"

he said, as I started to leave his office, "what in Christ's name is going on?"

I could only shrug and shake my head. When I left him, Price was sitting very still, his hands folded on his desk and his eyes fixed vacantly on his hands.

There was a roaring in my ears as I walked the short distance down the corridor to Baker's office. Hadn't they done enough? The roaring continued until Goldsmith came on the line.

"Sorry about the bad news, old fellow. Are you on your way back to the Furama now?"

"I could be."

"We'll see you in your room in, say, half an hour?"

I waited in the room for Goldsmith to appear. I felt utterly drained and unable to move, frightened for Fredrik, for myself, for all of us. What were they doing, reinforcing the ultimatum they had given me? Would they hurt or kill whomever I was with, so that I wouldn't hesitate? I must not see Alice again before she left. I wondered also whether I could take it on myself to endanger the people at Norbulk or at Lee's office.

There was a pounding in my head that began to drive these thoughts from my mind. Then I realized that someone was banging on the door of the room.

"Gave us a bit of a start there, Mr. Henriksen," Goldsmith said as he came in. Potter followed. "But your shadow outside couldn't believe that anyone could have got by him, so we took it that you just hadn't heard us. Good that you answered though. I'm getting a trifle old to be breaking down doors, not to mention its being beneath my dignity. Mr. Potter here has never had to break down doors in his line of work. Have you, Stanley?"

"For heaven's sake, Goldsmith, get on with it," Potter replied.

Potter's answer brought me quickly out of my heavy headedness, and I noticed then Goldsmith's weary, solemn expression, one that belied his jaunty words.

"Get on with what, Lieutenant?"

"I'm very sorry about your young colleague, Mr. Henriksen. He died before they could get him to the hospital."

The light in the room seemed to go dim; I felt as if I were

choking. "He was just a boy," I said stupidly.

Potter was sitting on the bed staring at his fingernails; Goldsmith was standing next to my chair. "Why?" I said. "What good did it do them? What threat was he to them?" Goldsmith put a firm hand on my shoulder. Tears started, but they did not come.

"The attack is incomprehensible, Mr. Henriksen. We know that he was not followed from Tokyo, because one of Inspector Watanabe's people was with him all the way. He was fingered, as they say, in Paris. Would anyone have known he was going through Paris? Aside from yourself?"

I shook my head. "He should not have told anyone. That was the plan."

"But he may have, of course."

I was having great difficulty speaking, so I simply nodded. "A colleague knew when he was coming," I managed, "but I don't think he knew how."

Goldsmith nodded. "The assailant was wounded in his attempt to get away. He's a hired froggie killer who knows nothing. He simply fired at whomever he was told to. The French authorities are not convinced they yet have the whole story, but I think they're wrong. Nonetheless, they are applying the thumbscrews—I'm speaking figuratively, of course. May I continue, Mr. Henriksen, or do you want us to go away and leave you alone? Good." Goldsmith began to pace. "The bomb that was planted in your offices in Oslo was crudely made and might not have gone off even if it hadn't been defused."

I had to ask the policeman to repeat what he had said. I simply had not heard him. When he finished, I said, "But isn't that surprising?"

"In what way?"

"Everything else about these people seems so well organized and meticulous. It seems out of character for them to be using crude devices."

"My thought exactly. Very good, Mr. Henriksen. You may be on the brink of a second career. Your Inspector Frogh thinks it a mistake, but has not explained."

I could see Frogh then, mumbling to no one that it was a

mistake and staring into the middle distance, pipe smoke spiraling around, his eyes looking watery through his thick lenses.

"Have you ever heard the word *ronin*, Mr. Henriksen?"

"Not that I recall. Is it English?"

"Japanese. It means masterless, and in some cases renegade, samurai."

It meant nothing to me. With a glance at Potter, he said, "It's a word that occurs frequently in certain notes that Tomlinson made."

Tomlinson again. The suicide from Singapore. "Sergeant Ng thinks Tomlinson was a British agent," I said.

There was an involuntary intake of breath from Potter. Goldsmith said, "Why, my dear fellow, of course he was. I shouldn't think that would surprise anyone."

"Be careful, Goldsmith," Potter said.

"Tomlinson was on to something; that is clear. And either they murdered him, or, through blackmail, forced him to do away with himself. Whoever it was he called *ronin.* Putting together what you learned with Tomlinson's notes, I think it's a safe bet that the *ronin* and the people who kidnapped you are one and the same. Beside whom our local triads seem like callow schoolboys."

"Really, Goldsmith, I do think you've gone too far."

"Please do fuck off, Stanley."

At which Potter left, slamming the door behind him.

"Absolute fucking twit," Goldsmith said. "Foreign Office mumbo-jumbo. Where do they get them? I'm sorry, Mr. H. Where were we? Yes. The only masterless warriors in Asia just now were once connected with Vietnam. A lot of flotsam still around from that. But Tomlinson, poor old boy . . . Will you be in Hong Kong much longer, Mr. Henriksen?"

"I'm not certain; I have a good way to go with Mr. Lee, I think. Although at the moment it seems monumentally pointless."

"Yes, I can understand that," Goldsmith said, but it was simply a professional nicety. What could he understand? "I want to warn you, Mr. Henriksen, that the longer you stay here, the unhealthier it may become. Perhaps in killing Fredrik Johansen they were underlining their ultimatum. Or they may have changed their minds. I confess I am puzzled by their actions, because the pattern was broken almost as soon as it had begun to form.

"There will be a constable at your beck and call. I should, if I were you, go out only when absolutely necessary, and take the constable with you. Do not see your friend Miss Nielsen again, for her sake. Have your meals from room service. As soon as you've completed your business here, get out of Hong Kong.

"When you're ready to leave, let us know—not before then, mind, because I don't want your plans leaking out—and we will send someone with you for the first leg of your journey. I'm not certain that we can count on the 'meddling fool' to be there all the time."

"Who is this person that bothers Mr. Potter so much?"

Goldsmith looked blank, as if he hadn't heard.

"I would like to know a great deal more than I've been told, Lieutenant Goldsmith."

He seemed to be inspecting his shoes.

"Paul and Fredrik Johansen are dead. I have been kidnapped and nearly killed. The lives of those around me and those with whom I deal are in danger. I've done my job. I've held up my end of the bargain. But I'm not being told everything I ought to know."

"I doubt very much that what more we know would be of any help, Mr. Henriksen."

"I'll be the judge of that," I snapped.

Goldsmith walked to the window and looked out for a while, his arms folded in front of him. He began to speak before he had turned completely round. "I'll tell you the rest, Mr. Henriksen, not because I think you need to know—it would, in fact, be healthier if you didn't—but because I think you deserve to know. The man who troubles Stanley Potter so much—and there is probably more than one—is from the CIA. They have an interest in these *ronin* as well, but we don't know what it is. Potter, who is famous in Whitehall for having not one diplomatic bone in his body, has so infuriated their station chief here that he won't let

Stanley have the time of day, much less information of a sensitive sort. I think Potter ought to be replaced so that we can work cooperatively instead of at cross-purposes. But I am an officer in a police force that has special problems, and what I think about such things doesn't matter. Now, does that help you?"

"No. But it astounds me."

"The other stuff is horrifying. The Vietnamese, via the Swiss embassy in Hanoi, have informed the Liberian maritime wallah in New York that the *Rose* was found adrift in Vietnamese territorial waters and taken into custody. That is why your friend saw the ship in Haiphong. In fact, we learned the location of the *Rose* a little before you first called me. You don't have to say anything, old chap. I can appreciate your frustration entirely. Let me continue. On board the *Rose* were twelve dead crewmen, all of whom had been killed with automatic weapons. Officers, the rest of the crew, all gone, no trace. The Vietnamese would not have known about any supernumeraries. The radio and the engine had been destroyed with thermite grenades. Well-organized, well-equipped, ruthless. Shoot a man in Paris, murder twelve people in the South China Sea, attempt to kill a man in Hong Kong, then kidnap him. What's involved is big money, Mr. Henriksen, very big. So they are trying to eliminate the competition, either by forcing it to join them or by destroying it."

"And that is why they shot Fredrik?"

"That is the assumption we are working with." Goldsmith did not meet my eyes.

"You have doubts, Lieutenant?"

"My life is filled with doubts, Mr. Henriksen. But that's as may be. I am sorry if you have felt that you weren't being kept up to speed. It was certainly not deliberate on my part. Unfortunately, there are the Stanley Potters of this world who believe that less is always enough. That is only sometimes true."

How much of Goldsmith's little peroration was true, how much merely self-serving? The image of Jensen, the man from the Norwegian government, went through my mind, the pale expressionless face watching us over Frogh's shoulder at Oslo Airport.

Goldsmith left, after entreating me again to call him at any time. I was completely alone and with time to reflect. I could no longer hold off the grief, and I cried quietly for the young man whose life had ended when it was just beginning. But the grief began to turn very quickly to anger: the bomb in Oslo, Fredrik, British and American agents, *ronin.* Goldsmith's doubt nagged at me. Had the *ronin* murdered Fredrik or not? And if not, then who? Could it have been Raymond Bechmann's man in Oslo? But why?

I drifted in thought, but nothing came. I ordered a sandwich from room service, but when it came I could not touch it. I called Alice, who again was not in. I forced myself to ponder my meeting with Lee. It had to be done, but all the interest had gone out of the effort. However, since there was no getting anywhere with one problem, I persuaded myself to try the other.

As Price had said, I could not push Lee very far. The only possible leverage I might have, and it was modest, was Lee's professed interest in Norbulk, which might be mostly smoke. There was no doubt that T. T. had not found Sven Lygren helpful, but how much of a dialogue did he in fact want?

It was a little after one in the afternoon in Oslo. I placed a call to Lindstedt and ate some of the sandwich while I waited for the call to go through. The operator rang back shortly, and in a moment Lindstedt was on the wire. "How are you feeling, John? You had quite a wide press here in Oslo. And now so has Fredrik, poor boy."

"I'm well, Per, thanks, but I'm very sad about the boy."

"Of course, my friend. I am saddened and disgusted by the senseless things that go on."

"Has there been any more information in the paper?"

"Only the journalists' endless repetition of the same facts and semifacts to hide the truth that they have learned nothing new. But you didn't call to talk about Fredrik, did you?"

I was taken aback by his abruptness, but it was something one had to expect with Lindstedt. "I'm calling about T. T. Lee. Is he the sort of owner you had in mind to bring into Norbulk?"

"Why are you asking?"

"It came out in conversation today that he admires the Norbulk operation. And he would like to talk with you at some point, that's quite clear."

"As long as he understands that a voice in the operation does not derive from the amount of tonnage chartered to the company, I would be delighted to consider the possibility."

"Per, it's not anywhere near that stage. All he said is that he would like to know you better."

"Please tell your Mr. Lee that when he has something of substance to discuss, I would be pleased to meet him."

I could not believe the harshness of his tone. He must be in a bad mood.

"Per, I must explain. Lee has not asked me to contact you. I'm asking you for a favor. I have almost no leverage with Lee, and I want to use our connection with Norbulk. I want to suggest that I can, for example, prepare the way for a substantive meeting."

"You can do that, John. It is, of course, entirely without commitment."

"Of course."

"I might even change my mind and decide against it."

"I understand," I said, although I didn't. Before he hung up, perhaps to mitigate his waspishness, Lindstedt mentioned it was snowing in Oslo and very cold.

Alice rang up at a quarter to eleven. I told her about Fredrik. I also told her that I ought to keep away from her and why.

It was some time before she spoke.

"But I must come to you, John. I know how you must be feeling."

"I would love it if you came here, darling, but they probably know you by now and might try to hurt me by hurting you."

"They might try something anyway."

"I don't think so, Alice. Not if we don't tempt them."

Again she did not answer for what seemed a long time.

"All right, John," she said at last.

"You're going to Paris?"

"Yes. And London."

"Have a good flight, Alice. I love you."

"Do be careful, John. I'll be back in Oslo in ten days, and I want to see you there. There's something I want to discuss with you when we're both back and there's nothing else on our minds."

"You are unbelievably wicked, Alice. By the way, it's snowing like mad in Oslo."

"You've been talking with someone?"

"Lindstedt."

"Ah yes. Dear Per. Not precisely my favorite among your associates."

"I thought you hardly knew him."

"I know him well enough, John. Have you ever seen my photograph of him?"

"The one he has hanging in his sitting room?"

"Yes. It's one of my nastiest. Goodnight, John. Sleep well. A hundred kisses."

It was no doubt the nasty quality that Lindstedt treasured.

I had a hideous dream. I was walking on a crowded city street. Everyone ignored me, and people I knew—Alice, Lindstedt, Norland, Ritter, even Goldsmith—turned away as if they wanted nothing to do with me when I tried to greet them. It grew dark, and I was back in the corridor with no beginning and no end. The thing was behind me again, and I began to tire from trying to escape. When I looked to see if there were anywhere I could hide and rest, I saw Fredrik far ahead, pale and beckoning, and the corridor had turned a glistening wet blood red.

I woke to the dark room with my heart pounding. The hotel was quiet, and gradually my heartbeat slowed to normal. But I passed the rest of the night hovering uneasily between sleep and wakefulness.

18

I was exhausted when I went to the Norbulk office the next morning at nine, but managed a chat about the fine weather with my constable. Mike Price was in the office, looking as if he were taking an infusion for a head cold over his steaming coffee. I had a vision of Oslo winters forty years before, my mother mixing a hot bowl of strong-smelling stuff, myself leaning over it at the kitchen table with a towel over my head. It was a strong memory, and I had consciously to bring myself back to that dimly lit air-conditioned room.

I closed the door. "Fredrik is dead, Mike."

"Yes, the poor lad. We got word from Oslo over the telex last evening. Doesn't seem to have made the papers." He looked into his coffee. "I wish I could do something to get the bloody bastards that did it." Then, as if shaking off a chill, he said, "To whom does P. Johansens pass now?"

"If Fredrik followed my advice, to a trust for the benefit of his cousin, with Per Lindstedt and Oslo Credit Bank as the trustees."

"So Lindstedt now controls the company?"

"Yes."

"I could think of far worse things. Tell me about your conversation with Lee."

When I had finished, Price said, "I told you he's tough as nails. What makes it even more difficult is that he's so pleasant a man." He was surprised at Lindstedt's cool reception to Lee's interest in Norbulk. "And why the bloody hell has Lygren never mentioned it, in the first place?" And as if in answer to his own question, he shrugged. "Can I give you lunch one of these days, John?"

"I'm not sure it's advisable."

"They won't try anything in a place they can't get out of easily, John. And we can bring your copper along to stand outside the door. Look—I had some unpleasant moments in Burma with the bloody Nips on my tail. Let me take my chances."

I gave him a thumbs up sign and started to leave. Price sighed audibly. "The poor lad. What a bloody shame."

A few minutes before eleven, I was taken again by Lee's car to Gammon House. T. T. greeted me warmly, as if we were old friends meeting for the first time after a long separation, and led me to the same sitting room we had used the day before.

"I have thought hard about what we discussed yesterday, John, and I've also had a word with one or two of my bankers. I think a cost of fourteen million seven hundred fifty thousand may not put too great a crimp in our cash flow."

T. T. sat back and folded his hands comfortably. The increment, in excess of five percent, was not ungenerous. But if I wanted to match him, I would have to bring my price down by nine hundred thousand, and I was not prepared to give in quite that easily. I had trade creditors to satisfy as well.

"Thank you, T. T. I think the eighteen million I mentioned yesterday is a reasonable price; even so, I might be prepared to come down a bit. But in order for your revised offer to be acceptable, it really would have to be part of a package including the *Zinnia.*"

Lee did not change his posture at all. "John, I would like very much to be able to assist you with the *Zinnia,* but I really don't think . . . How much debt has she?"

"Thirteen-odd million remaining. Final maturity is mid-1981."

"And the rate?"

"Seven-eighths over London interbank offered."

"I promise to give it more thought, John, but I would be less than candid if I let you think there was a lot of hope. VLCCs are close to a drug on the market. Well, let us put some numbers together, and I shall talk again to my bankers. How are you feeling?"

"Still very sore, thanks, but on the mend, I think. By the way, T.T., before I leave, I must tell you I called Per Lindstedt and mentioned that I was talking with you."

"That's very kind, John." Lee smiled. "Shall we meet then tomorrow at three? I'm sorry it's so far into the afternoon, but I have a conflict in the morning. The car will come for you as usual. And I do hope you will consider the fourteen and three-quarter million seriously, even without the *Zinnia.*"

When I returned to the office, I found a message had come from

Goldsmith asking that I ring him. As there seemed to be no particular urgency, Price persuaded me to wait until after lunch. Mike took me to a grill in the Mandarin for British beer and roast beef; we listened to the plummy voices of expatriates around us, some of whom gestured at waiters as if the war had never taken place and a good part of the East still belonged to Europeans.

"Damnedest thing happened," Mike said. "We received a telex that Lindstedt is coming to Hong Kong in a month's time. I think your phone conversation had more of an effect than you thought."

"Does he have the dates? I'd like to let Lee know."

"All in the message. The old man does not hem and haw."

"Is Lygren upset?"

"I think he will be when he finds out. I haven't seen him this morning. Don't even know if he's in the office. Not, to be candid, that I care a great deal. Let's talk about something more pleasant. What are you going to say to Lee tomorrow?"

"I'm toying with the idea of letting him take the three tankers he seems to want for fifteen million five, if he'll take over the *Zinnia* for the debt and three million."

Price leaned back in the leather banquette shaking his head. "Never work," he said. He pulled a cigar from an aluminum tube, cut off the end, and got it lit. "Forgive me, John, but you're being unrealistic. Did you bang your head in your little mishap? No? Look at it this way. The Japanese needed you more than you needed them. Lee doesn't need you. Yes, he likes the ships; yes, they're the right size; blah, blah, blah, blah. But they're not the only ships around. If he has to, he'll look elsewhere. He might be a bit inconvenienced, but he can afford it. You can't. My advice to you is to forget the *Zinnia*. He doesn't want it. Get rid of that racialist idea that T. T. is a wily Oriental. He's a straightforward businessman who drives a hard bargain. If he offers anywhere between fifteen and a half and sixteen and a half, grab it. Forget the *Zinnia*. Further than that I cannot go, my friend."

"Let's see what happens tomorrow." But I felt in my bones that Mike was right.

Goldsmith was calling again just as we returned and said he wanted to pop over. When he arrived, he was alone. I inquired after Potter, which elicited no response at all.

"The Vietnamese are getting quite hot under the collar, what with this bit of scrap metal littering their harbor. We are given to understand the Liberian maritime commissioner has been on to the registered office for the owners in Piraeus and also to the bank in Geneva and has gotten no response—surprise, surprise. I am therefore turning to the only authorized representative of the *Rose* whom I know to ask how you wish to proceed."

"Believe me, Lieutenant Goldsmith, I do have other things on my mind. The *Rose* is the last thing that's worrying me at the moment."

"Fully understood, Mr. Henriksen. Nonetheless, they want the vessel removed."

"And what do you want me to do?"

"It's a heaven-sent opportunity, old man."

I said nothing; I simply stared at Goldsmith.

"Nip up to Haiphong in an ocean-going tug out of Singapore? Who knows what flies you might attract? It could be just the funny business you were warned against."

"You're suggesting *I* do it? Haven't I been through enough? By your own admission?"

"Look, old thing, you're already deep into a mug's game. The degrees of danger are academic at this point."

Goldsmith was singing a different tune from our last meeting, and I wondered why. But there was something more important still.

"And what significance has any of this, Lieutenant? Will it capture Fredrik's murderers?"

There was a perceptible pause before Goldsmith answered. "I don't know. It may. It will certainly go some way to getting at Paul Johansen's killers. You wouldn't be on your own, you know. You'll be accompanied by any number of heavily armed chaps."

"And if anything goes wrong?"

"Dear boy, you could slip in the shower and fracture your skull."

"And who is going to pay for all of this?"

Goldsmith beamed. "The taxpayers, dear fellow, as always.

How much longer do you think you have with T. T. Lee?"

"I have no idea."

"We do hope you can get on with it."

"Would the taxpayers like to take a two-hundred-thousand-ton tanker off my hands as well?"

"Sorry?"

I went that afternoon to a doctor Price had recommended; he was somewhat put off by the policeman in his surgery. He took the corset off and poked me in the ribs until I winced, put the corset back on, and changed the dressing on the back of my neck. He told me I would be all right if I would do nothing energetic for a while. I was tempted to inquire whether he thought an ocean voyage in the South China Sea would be salubrious.

When we met the following day, T. T. Lee began by stating flatly that he had no interest in the *Zinnia*. "We tried to weigh possible interest among our contacts against the debt outstanding. The problem is simple, John, and you are as well acquainted with it as we. While there are certain short-term fixtures available that could cover operating expenses and debt service for the currency of the fixture, the future is uncertain, grossly so. I am, I'm afraid, a very conservative shipowner. There are enough uncertainties in this business already. I'm not prepared to add speculation to them."

"Thank you for considering the *Zinnia,* T.T. Shall we discuss the others?"

"Indeed." He sat back and folded his hands.

"We are prepared to discuss a price of sixteen million five hundred thousand."

"We had concluded that fifteen million was a reasonable level."

"I'm afraid we simply cannot let them go for that figure, T.T." I sipped a glass of tea. Had I pushed him too far? "On another matter, I learned this morning that Per Lindstedt is planning to come to Hong Kong on the twenty-fifth of next month."

"That's very good news, John. I would like to give him a dinner while he is here. We'll send an invitation to the Norbulk office straight away. To whom shall I direct it?"

"Michael Price."

"Ah yes, Mike Price. I've enjoyed discussing the market with him on occasion." He sipped his own tea. "On the matter of the tankers: my final offer is fifteen million five hundred thousand, subject to inspection and finance."

I waited long enough so that I wouldn't sound overeager in accepting his offer. "We'll have a memorandum of agreement delivered to you first thing in the morning."

"Excellent, John. I hope you will be available for a dinner party at my home this evening?"

"I would like that very much, T.T. But I must refuse. I fear my presence jeopardizes the safety of others. It is only because I have been assured by Lieutenant Goldsmith that your offices are being protected that I have come here at all."

"Lieutenant Goldsmith is an old friend, John. Let us not worry about security measures. They will be ample. Please do come. If you wish to bring someone with you, please do so."

I looked at my watch. Alice had been gone for nearly thirty hours. "No, T.T., there's no one."

As soon as I returned to the office, I rang up Norbulk's lawyers to have them prepare a memorandum of agreement to be delivered to Lee in the morning. I sent a telex to Lars Norland informing him that I had agreed on a price with Lee and asking whether he had been contacted by the Geneva bank concerning a matter of mutual interest. Then I told Mike about my talk with Lee.

"Well done, old chap. As I said, a fair price in this market."

"I wonder if the trustees will think it fair. Or Torvald Johansen. After all, it's his inheritance I'm playing with."

Price smiled rather sadly. "I can't speak for Torvald, but you can answer for one of the trustees." He handed me a telex. "Fredrik ignored your advice."

The telex was from Oslo, from Frederik's lawyer, Kjell Borgensen. Frederik had made me, not Lindstedt, a trustee of his estate, along with the Oslo Credit Bank. For a long time I could not speak.

"I cannot imagine this chap Torvald will have any complaint either. I doubt if there are many people who could have done as well."

"Thanks, Mike. You had a good deal to do with it also."

He made a circle with his thumb and index finger.

"Why should Lee call Lieutenant Goldsmith an old friend?" I asked.

"Hong Kong is a small community, old chum."

"Is that all there is to it?"

"Rumor has it that Goldsmith once got the kid—what's his name, T.F.?—out of a scrape once. I don't think it'll matter much in the long run. From what I've seen, the kid is headed for trouble."

"He's nothing like his father or brother."

"Too much money, and his wits are all addled by whatever it is he smokes or sniffs. I'm told it was a drug charge Goldsmith got him out of."

"Why should he do that?"

"The Hong Kong Constabulary are famous for doing things like that—fixing this a little, fixing that a little. It's free enterprise. Every copper is his own law enforcement entrepreneur. Cash transactions only. No credit cards, although I'm told they're coming. It's called 'squeeze.' Actually, if there was someone I would think of as not taking bribes, it would be Goldsmith. I think maybe he's just a nice chap."

T. T. Lee lived in a large flat in a circular apartment block in Midlevels. There were fourteen for dinner. I met all of them, Chinese, British, American, French, and I recalled none of their names. My dinner partner was an extremely attractive French woman whom I bored by being so distracted. I thought a good deal about Fredrik, and the room seemed to go silent when I was thinking about him. It troubled me that I had not succeeded in placing the *Zinnia.* I had also not been able to get a flight to Singapore until the day after next. I hardly thought of Lieutenant Goldsmith's scheme for the trip to Haiphong. I didn't believe it would come off. It was too mad.

Late in the morning of the day following, I returned to Lee's office. We each reviewed the memorandum of agreement, made corrections, transcribed the corrections onto all the copies, initialed them, and finally signed the agreement, after which T. T. gave me a check for one million five hundred fifty thousand dollars U.S., the ten percent payment required under the MOA upon signing.

At the Norbulk office, I signed the check over to the company and asked Mike Price to arrange cable transfer of the funds to our account in London. He wished me godspeed, asked me to give his best to everyone in Oslo, and said that he looked forward very much to Lindstedt's visit.

"I ought to say good-bye to Sven."

"He's not come in yet, old chum," Price said evenly. It was nearly lunch time.

That evening I had three strong whisky sodas before my room service dinner. The sense of impending disaster that had burdened me all the time I had been in Hong Kong had left me that morning, to be replaced by something close to euphoria, coupled with a bittersweet sadness: Fredrik was gone and could not be brought back. It may simply have been that mentally I could no longer tolerate the constant tension and so had replaced it with a wholly unrealistic emotion. It could also have been that the sixth sense I had developed with respect to danger had detected that I was no longer being watched for an opportunity to murder, but to discover what I was going to do next.

Goldsmith was in the unmarked car that came to collect me at eleven the following morning.

"Wanted to have a final chat and see you on your way, old boy," he said. The morning was hazy and sticky with humidity. "You'll be met at Singapore airport by a regular city cab, number 304. The driver will identify himself to you. You'll go straight to the boat." My feeling of euphoria was draining away.

"Tell me, Mr. Henriksen, did you know of any travel plans that your Mr. Lygren might have had?"

Lygren? "None," I said.

"As we thought. We've already talked with the office and also with Mrs. Lygren. Mr. Lygren tried to leave the Colony rather abruptly last evening on a flight to Taipei. My chap assigned to watch over him thought it odd, and I must say so did I. So we've asked him to have a chat with us."

"You've arrested Lygren?"

"Taken him into protective custody. His solicitor is on his way, so we've not been able to have our little talk yet. We don't know whether it will lead anywhere, but I think it might. I was interested to learn that he has been acting quite unusually for some months now."

We drove in silence the rest of the way to the airport. Goldsmith used the opportunity to nap lightly, but he woke in time to say, "Well, here we are. Good-bye then, Mr. Henriksen. Good luck and thank you very much indeed. The constable will see that you're checked in properly and send you on your way to immigration. Good-bye again."

The flight to Singapore was pleasant and unpleasant. It was the first time in well over a year that I had not had the immense financial problems of P. Johansens Rederi hanging over me; and while I was disappointed that the *Zinnia* remained, I felt that somehow this could be sorted out and would not remain a problem much longer.

But Sven Lygren kept coming to mind. Could he actually be involved in this horrid matter? If so, how? Was it with Raymond Bechmann and Pappas? Was he the person Bechmann had gotten to in Oslo, in my definition of Oslo as including Norbulk worldwide? Or was he connected with the *ronin*? Was his lending me his car that night—it seemed months before—a setup? I could not believe that Sven Lygren, as cold as he had been, had arranged my murder. On the other hand, had he been so frightened by the attempt on me that he panicked and tried to run away? Had he perhaps been playing a double game?

I was surprised to find we were starting the approach into Singapore. I had no answers to the questions I had posed, but there were two things I intuitively knew. One was that Lygren was mixed up in it somehow, and the second was that Lygren was not the man in Oslo to whom Pappas had referred.

19

As soon as I stepped from the terminal building into the heat, a young Chinese appeared at my side. "Mr. Henriksen. I drive the cab you ordered. Number 304. Nice to see you again, sir." Goldsmith's mad scheme was coming true. I had never seen the driver before, I was certain. But the number of the cab was correct. The wheels had started spinning.

When we were well on our way toward town, the driver said, "Sergeant Ng sends his regards and looks forward to seeing you."

These little touches were comforting: the right number for the cab; Goldsmith's information confirmed; the mention of Ng's name—all presumably designed to reassure me and put me at my ease. But nothing would accomplish that until the end of this business.

I did not pay any attention to Singapore during the ride, but stared straight ahead at the hot sunshine glinting off the automobiles in front of us. I could imagine wanting to live year-round in such sunlight if one came from a place like Norway. Or Germany. Sunlight is why the Germans are so fond of Italy and Spain.

But when the Germans came to Oslo, there was no sunlight. I reflected back to the war years. That was the only time I could remember my father punishing me physically, other than with a slap on the backside, more startling than painful. My friends and I had been having a snowball fight. We thought of the wonderful idea of putting rocks inside some of the snowballs and, under pretense of throwing them at each other, trying to hit whatever Germans—vehicles or individuals—happened down our road. When I mentioned the scheme to my father in a great flush of excitement, he slapped me twice hard across the face, saying, "Never, never even think of doing that or saying that again. They'll shoot you, John, because they're animals." The tears came to my eyes, and he pulled me roughly to him and wept himself. It was the closest I ever came to my father. It was one of my happiest memories. I could not imagine what brought it to mind in that sweltering taxi.

I woke from my reverie when we entered the area of the Port of Singapore Authority. We drove by several quays until we stopped, facing an enormous ocean-going tug, bottle green in color, with a pale blue seven-pointed star on the funnel. She was called the *Monterrey* and flew a Panamanian flag at her stern.

"I'll help you with your bag, Mr. Henriksen."

There were a half dozen Asian crew members on deck, who paid us no attention, and a European officer in a dirty khaki uniform, who approached us as we came up the gangway. The cab driver put my bag on deck, held his hand out, and said, "Twenty-five dollars."

"You are . . ." said the European.

"Henriksen."

"So? No Sing dollars? I'll take care of it." He stuffed some bills into the driver's hand and waved him away.

"My name is Schmidt. I am master. Come, I will show you your cabin." His English was heavily accented.

I followed him down a passageway, but to what was a smoke room, not a cabin. There were five men sitting at a table in the narrow compartment, two of whom I recognized. One was Y.C. Ng, who nodded and smiled. The other was Stanley Potter, who looked through me.

"Here is your man Henriksen, gentlemen," Schmidt said. "Let me have your case, Mr. Henriksen, and I'll put it by your bunk." He banged out of the compartment and slid the door shut behind him.

Sergeant Ng leaned across the table and shook my hand. "I hope you had a pleasant flight, John? Good. It's nice to see you again. I believe you know Mr. Potter?"

I acknowledged that we had met.

"These gentlemen, I am told, are called Mr. Green, Mr. Brown, and Mr. White."

I shook hands with each, and each said a word of greeting in an American accent.

Green said, "We are all getting a bit testy and stale, Mr. Henriksen, because we've had to remain below decks, so occasionally you might hear some things you'd best forget. First off, though, let me say we're very grateful to you for consenting to participate in this exercise. We're certain this is going to smoke them out. We'll be casting off about ten tonight. Would you like some coffee?"

"No, thank you. What I would like is that someone tell me, at last, who 'they' are. The people who killed Paul Johansen and his son and tried to kill me, and who did kidnap me? Who murdered all those men aboard the *Rose*? Who tried to bomb our Oslo office?"

"That's not quite right, Mr. Henriksen," Green said. "We're pretty sure they had nothing to do with the bomb. Or with killing Fredrik Johansen. Your police are looking into all of that." The implication was more hideous than I could have imagined.

"But who are the *ronin*?"

"Why don't you tell him?" Stanley Potter snapped. "He knows almost everything already."

Potter was certainly giving me far more credit than I deserved.

"Potter," the man called Brown said, "if you're going to remain in this emotional state, you could compromise the mission. We may have to ask you to leave."

"In the same way you got Herbert Tomlinson to leave?"

"You know very well we could not let him proceed on the path he was following. We warned him. He wouldn't listen to reason."

"Why should he have? You were from the same company. How would he have known you weren't implicated as well?"

Green looked at me with sorrow. "I'm sorry you and Sergeant Ng are witnessing this friendly squabble, Mr. Henriksen." He looked genuinely embarrassed.

Ng spoke now. "I am very interested in what further you know about the Tomlinson matter, Mr. Green. I speak as an official representative of the Republic of Singapore, by whose courtesy, may I remind you, you are all present on board this vessel in the PSA without a Singapore visa in your passports. In another context, you would all be subject to an arrest."

"Very simple, Sergeant Ng," Potter said. "These men didn't like some things Tomlinson was finding out about some of their former colleagues. They claim they asked him to stop. Be that as it may, he continued to pursue his investigations—as he ought to have. So these gentlemen showed Herbert photographs of himself taken when he was most vulnerable. Tomlinson was, you may remember, homosexual; I gather he was once a bit less discreet than usual. And on that occasion they were present with their cameras, their long lenses, and their infrared film. It was too much for a man who had spent the bulk of his life gathering intelligence, interrupted only from time to time with a bit of what he must have thought of as meaningless dalliance. Before, that is, these gentlemen showed him what it looked like to others. So he used his cyanide pill."

"We tried very hard to make him stop his investigation," said the hitherto silent White. "You are making it all sound a lot more cold-blooded than it was, Stanley. He had gotten hold of an *idée fixe*, and he would not let go."

"And what was it that Mr. Tomlinson had found out, Mr. Potter?" Ng said.

"Tomlinson had discovered that a handful of CIA agents and hangers-on who had done their best to preserve democracy in South Vietnam and Laos were very disillusioned by the actions of their own government and the resulting outcome. They were so disillusioned, in fact, that they turned renegade—turned their backs on God and country and went into business. With their unique contacts and knowledge of Southeast Asia, they were ideally suited to conduct the kind of business they had in mind: drugs; arms of all kinds, stolen or purchased; discreet transportation for terrorists and mercenaries. It is very big business. Very American, I should think. Free enterprise carried to its logical extreme.

"Tomlinson had most of the pieces of the puzzle. Knew the names of ships' berths and so forth. He was bothered by the *Rose,* however. He couldn't understand how it fit in because it did not follow the *modus operandi* of the rest of the organization, which he chose to call *ronin.* We know now, of course, that the *Rose* didn't fit in at all, because it represented a new group of entrepreneurs who had nothing whatever to do with the *ronin* but did recognize a good idea when they saw one."

I found myself thinking of Raymond Bechmann, Captain Pappas, Stratis Evgenides . . . probably Sven Lygren. Who else?

"But if Tomlinson had found all this out why was he," Ng groped for a word, "pressured into killing himself?"

"Would any of you like to answer that?" Potter said with heavy irony. "No? Then I shall. Tomlinson was about to blow the whistle on many former CIA people. It would have got out. It would have looked very bad in the world press. No one would have been able to tell anymore whether an agent was working for the American government or for someone else, including himself. And this on top of the already bad news about the Agency's spying on the American people and acting as handmaiden for International Telephone in Chile."

"Enough is enough, Potter."

"I quite agree. Look. You have what you want. You're running the show. I'm only an observer. But paint pretty pictures of others. I'm too close to the truth to believe your lies or to be silenced or to be forced into taking my own little cyanide pill. Go to hell."

This last was said quietly, almost entirely without heat. Potter looked around the table, then at his hands. The compartment was silent except for the hum of the air-conditioning machinery.

Green said, "I did say we were all a little short-tempered, Mr. Henriksen. I want to set the record straight, though, and then I want us all to forget it. We were on to these same people. Tomlinson would not cooperate, and he would not get out of the way. He saw the chance of an intelligence coup and he forgot everything else. He stopped acting like a professional."

Potter shook his head sadly and continued to look at his hands. I was beginning to doubt his sincerity. I confess that my initial poor impression of him remained. And it seemed to me he was playing an elaborate game, scoring points off Brown and Green and White—for whose benefit?—and that he didn't care a fig for Tomlinson.

"I suggest that we all get some rest," Green said. "Mr. Henriksen, I ask that you take one slow walk around the deck before you turn in." He and his colleagues left. Potter waited a moment or two, then left also. Ng rose and went through a doorway into a tiny galley and, a moment later, handed two open bottles of beer back through the serving hatch.

When he had sat down again, I said, "Do I understand correctly that Paul Johansen was killed by former CIA agents?"

"Yes."

"And that this is the same group that has been following us in Asia? And delivered its ultimatum?"

"Yes."

"Do you know any more about this voyage to Haiphong?"

"A little. We have no intention of going there."

I could not conceal my astonishment.

"Can you imagine our sailing into Haiphong, John? Three American agents, a British agent, a Singapore policeman, on a vessel heavily armed, equipped, and manned by the Central Intelligence Agency? You are," he continued, "a bit of raw meat on the point of a large hook. They hope to attract the sharks. The big ones this time."

"Why now?"

"Our friends are guessing, John. The *ronin* have been watching you since they let you go. But they warned you to return to Oslo as soon as you finished your business in Hong Kong. You have not done that. Why not? Why have you ignored the warnings? How powerful are you? As I understand it, Green and Brown and White think that the *ronin* are going to want to talk to you before they kill you. So rather than blowing us out of the water, they will probably try to board us and take you alive—which might give us a chance to take one or more of them alive."

"So we're simply going to cruise into the South China Sea and let them come after us."

"That's correct."

"And the Vietnamese never contacted the Swiss embassy about the *Rose*."

"Not quite. The story is true up to the part about the dead crew. But the Vietnamese never asked for the vessel to be taken away."

Technically, I supposed, we had to pursue the matter of the *Rose* in due course. The vessel did, after all, belong to the trust. But she had brought us nothing but catastrophe, and I felt it just as well she was away from us. I would have recommended to the board that we make a formal inquiry and then do no more.

"How soon will they attack us?"

"We don't really have any idea, but everyone thinks it will be quite soon. In any event, I think Green had a good idea about getting some rest. I'm going to turn in. May I show you where your bunk is, and suggest you do likewise after your walk on deck?"

I walked once round the deck and no one topside paid the slightest attention. When I returned to the tiny, dimly lit compartment, there were huddled shapes in three of the four bunks. I lay on my own with a wool blanket over me and tried to think of nothing, and soon total darkness came.

I awoke when the overhead light was turned on. Green was standing in the doorway of the compartment with a look of that kind of professional concern one often sees on ministers.

"Sorry to wake you so abruptly, Mr. Henriksen. It's near eight-thirty, and we thought we might have some supper."

I rose and had a wash and then went along to the smoke room, still somewhat groggy from sleep. Ng was there, and Potter, and Green with his two companions. Captain Schmidt was at the head of the table, and there was a very young man at the foot.

"Quite a first-class cruise we have, Mr. Henriksen. *All* the passengers dine at the captain's table. Will you have a drink?" When I nodded and asked for whisky soda, Schmidt said, "Lownds." The very young man got up and went into the galley. "Lownds is my first officer," Schmidt continued. "This is Mr. Henriksen, Lownds." The young man handed me a large drink full of ice, in the American manner, and said, "So I surmised. Pleased to meet you, Mr. Henriksen." Lownds said nothing further, but tapped lightly on the table with his fingers and fidgeted in his chair.

We had a very plain dinner that reminded me somewhat of school—there was very little conversation of substance. Schmidt talked a good deal about the weather, which would be no problem, although we were forecast to get a brief shower the next afternoon. Potter was most withdrawn.

While we were finishing coffee, Schmidt took himself off, saying it was time to begin. Lownds went with him.

Green offered us after-dinner drinks, which none of us wanted. He said, "In case you are wondering, Mr. Henriksen, we are certainly not expecting you to take part in any of the active operations."

"I understand," I said. "I should hope not. I wouldn't be of much use in any event."

"Nevertheless, do you know how to use a revolver?"

"I fired them when I was in the army twenty-five years ago. But not at anything other than a paper target."

"Quite. That will do nicely. Given the firepower on board this vessel, we cannot imagine your needing a weapon, but we'll give you one anyway, just in case."

Shortly after that, I went out on deck to watch us cast off and to get away from the macabre quartet below. The engine growled contentedly at a low rate of speed, and the quay slipped back from us. Very quickly the lights of Singapore began to recede, although they would remain in view for the next couple of hours. The sky was a profusion of stars, and the phosphorescent waters of the strait were like glass.

I was frightened, yes—the kind of fear that grips the bowels—but I was angry also. This mad exercise had no meaning for me; it was the business of the four ghouls below. I had honored my obligation to Paul Johansen. I did not need revenge for what the *ronin* had done to me. The rest, as far as I was concerned, was superfluous. The answer for me lay not in the South China Sea, but in Oslo. Because the *ronin* had not killed Fredrik. Someone else had. Someone I knew.

Hour after hour we chugged along. I slept very little that night and was back on deck with coffee in a thick mug when the sun came up. The sea was smooth as a lake and the air was already warm, although the movement of the vessel created some breeze. When the sun rose higher, it became most uncomfortable on deck. I spent most of the day reading (the suspected murderer of Antony Bayes-Lawless was himself discovered drowned in the fish pond) or playing cards in the smoke room with Y. C. Ng.

In midafternoon we turned away from the active shipping lanes in which we had been traveling, and the sea became empty. After four o'clock, the watch reported an object on the radar screen moving at high speed behind us. As one, we all moved out on deck, and by the time we had assembled there in silence, it seemed that we could hear something above the sound of the *Monterrey*'s engines. It was not long before a blue-green vessel was spotted perhaps two miles to our stern. It was obvious that it was moving fast, and I guessed it to be a very large cabin cruiser.

"Time for you to go below, Mr. Henriksen," Green said. I needed no convincing. As I descended the short set of steps, a bell rang throughout the ship. Silent Asian crewmen moved past me in the passageway, carrying weapons, including rocket launchers. The lights were turned off below, and there were blackout curtains pulled across the portholes. I returned to the smoke room with the revolver that Green had given me, and pulled one of the curtains partly aside. The sky was deep blue, with mountainous white clouds very high up; the sea was an even deeper blue. I could now hear the roar of different engines not far off, and then a cabin cruiser, seemingly randomly painted in sea greens and blues, hove into view perhaps two hundred meters away. She slowed to the speed of the *Monterrey* and gradually moved closer. There were several dull thumps and a cloud of smoke from the bow of the cabin cruiser, and the tug slowed perceptibly. They had fired across our bow. The cruiser moved much closer. She flew no flag and had no markings of any kind except the sea camouflage.

A voice distorted by an amplifying device said in English, "Give us Henriksen, or we'll destroy you." Green's gamble had paid off.

For a few moments the only sounds were the low rumble of the engines and the water lapping at the sides of the boats.

"Sorry," I heard Captain Schmidt say, shattering the silence. "Impossible. Please get out of our way." Over the amplifier, his voice seemed to quaver.

There was a short burst of gunfire from the cabin cruiser, designed to show us they meant what they said, and a motor launch pulled out from behind it and headed directly for us. It was full of armed men. When it had covered half the distance to the tug, there were several loud cracks, followed by a continuous roar of weapon fire from the *Monterrey*. Flashes appeared along the length of the cabin cruiser and I flattened against the deck of the smoke room. An enormous explosion shook the tug, and we rolled as if in a heavy sea. But I felt no shudder in the vessel to suggest she had been hit. An engine sputtered to life and died. The firing stopped.

I looked through the porthole. The cabin cruiser was on fire and looked lifeless. There were gaping holes in her sides and flames licked out of them. As I watched, a form lifted itself slowly over the rail and dropped into the sea, preferring death by water to death by fire. The motor launch drifted between the cruiser and the tug, apparently helpless, although it looked untouched.

"The party's over, George," our amplifier said. It was Green's voice now. "Throw your weapons into the water and come aboard."

In answer, the engine on the motor launch roared into life and the boat started moving away, while its occupants began to fire at the tug. There were three loud cracks, and the boat disappeared in a cloud of smoke and flame.

Flames shot high from the cabin cruiser, and I could see her shake. Then she went down like a stone.

The whole thing had taken less than five minutes. Perhaps, I thought, your death has been revenged, Shipowner Johansen. But there remained much to do.

I waited in the growing darkness until Ng entered the smoke room and turned on the lights. He was followed by Potter and Green, the latter of whom looked depressed.

"We are grateful to you, Mr. Henriksen," Green said. "Had you not voluntarily put yourself in danger, we would not have accomplished what we did today. I can't say we're a hundred percent finished, but we've made a start, yes sir."

"Made a start," I repeated woodenly. I thought of how I had been living the past weeks.

"I appreciate your concern," Green said, "but we can never be absolutely certain, Mr. Henriksen." He shrugged.

Brown and Schmidt entered the compartment; we had a quiet drink. I learned later that Lownds and White were searching the water from a small boat looking for other Occidentals. A number of crewmen from the cabin cruiser were hauled aboard the tug, given medical treatment, and confined uncomfortably below.

When White and Lownds returned, the former said, "We couldn't find George."

"No?" Green said.

"The whole goddamn area is full of sharks happy as pigs in shit," Lownds said.

Ng asked, "Who was George?"

"George Bettencourt," Green answered. "A man I worked with for twelve years."

White looked through the porthole. Lownds drummed on the table and fidgeted in his chair.

We returned to Singapore in the same stately manner as we had traveled on the way out. Green, after he had recovered from the action, became expansive. It was almost overbearing, but understandable. He was greatly relieved that things had gone as well as they had. There had been no deaths—only a few wounds, none serious—among the crew. The *ronin* had not anticipated encountering a military vessel, which is virtually what the *Monterrey* was.

Green was especially forthcoming with Potter, who, at lunch the next day, finally could tolerate it no longer. "Good heavens, Green," he said. "It was masterful, masterful. There. Is that what you wanted me to say? But in fact it was a triumph of economics as usual. Give *me* an unlimited budget and lavish weaponry, and I'll show you what *I* can do."

When we had docked, about ten o'clock, Green said, "The four of us have some things to discuss, so we'll say good-bye here, Mr. Henriksen. I can't seem to recall where you left the pistol we lent you."

I had thought, foolishly, of trying to leave with it, but had already come to my senses. "On my bunk, Mr. Green. Unloaded, safety on, cylinder open."

"Excellent. Good-bye then, Mr. Henriksen. Sergeant Ng will see you safely away."

Schmidt nodded as Ng and I went down the gangway. There was someone standing next to him in the shadows—the taciturn Mr. Lownds, I guessed.

I followed Ng to a waiting patrol car. "I think we may be able to reach the airport in time for one of the European flights, John. Would you like that?"

I nodded. He asked what route I wanted to fly, then radioed his headquarters to find me a flight with a stop in Frankfurt. Ten minutes later, while we roared through the streets, I was confirmed on Qantas.

"Are you worried, John?" Ng asked after we had spent some minutes in silence.

"I was thinking about the boy," I told him.

Ng did not respond immediately. When he did, he seemed more to be thinking aloud rather than talking to anyone in particular.

"I thought you might be upset by Green's comments. By the ambiguity." I demurred. Ng said, "I wouldn't do anything precipitous if I were you."

It was as if Ng were reading my thoughts. He knew I had been only partly present on board the *Monterrey*; he knew I had entertained thoughts about the pistol. It was a very gentle warning, but warning it was.

When we reached the airport, Ng came with me while I

checked in. Then he said, "Good-bye, John. I hope some day we shall meet in different circumstances." An awkward little wave and he disappeared into the crowd.

I cabled Lars Norland from the airport, giving him my flight numbers and arrival time in Oslo the following day; I also cabled Alice, asking her to dinner the same night.

The tables were laid for supper after we had taken off. While I ate, the questions I had pushed to the back of my mind now came forward. There was no question that Green's ambiguity troubled me, but what troubled me more was what lay ahead. My instinct told me the *ronin* were finished with me. Having suffered the blow they just had, the ancillary criminals they hired to carry out specific tasks would move on to other things—they would have no vested interest in remaining with a shattered organization to which their only ties were financial and occasional. Further attempts against me or against Johansens Rederi seemed improbable.

There remained the man in Oslo, the person whom Pappas had spoken of, the man who had arranged the murder of an innocuous young man in Paris. I knew suddenly that the man in Oslo was my old friend and colleague Lars Norland—quiet, painfully diffident, always in his worn cardigan, who must have hated Paul Johansen beyond comprehension. The realization made my head spin, and I had difficulty breathing. Oslo was drawing me and repelling me at the same time. The flight that lay ahead seemed endless.

I had several more glasses of wine and fell into a troubled sleep, half waking, half dreaming. I dreamed or thought again of my father in Oslo during that first German winter, and I wondered why. I was aware of the landings in Delhi and Tehran, but I remained half asleep.

When I woke to breakfast, the first officer announced that we were two hours from Frankfurt and estimated to arrive at 0900 hours, or thirty-five minutes behind schedule. The weather was overcast and the temperature minus one degree Celsius or thirty degrees Fahrenheit. The late arrival would not interfere with my making the connection to Oslo.

We circled beneath a heavy gray sky over cold-looking fields of dark earth on which there were still traces of snow. After four weeks of sunshine and heat, with only a bit of cool weather in Tokyo, it was a shock to be reminded that weather could get to be the way it appeared outside the window. Why on earth did one live in Scandinavia instead of in that perpetual sunlight? Simply because it was in the blood, I decided; anything else was compromise. And as far as I personally was concerned, because Alice Nielsen lived there.

We landed and taxied smoothly. By the time we reached the Frankfurt terminal, it had begun to sleet, and I was reminded of the day Fredrik and I had left Oslo. It was exactly the same sort of weather. Despite my overall weariness, I was feeling a growing anxiety as I got closer to home. I would have to confront Norland, but I did not know how, and I was, in my tiredness, having some difficulty in thinking it through.

As soon as I got off the plane, I went in search of a television screen or a Solari board that would tell me the gate for my connection and whether there was any delay.

I was walking along, feeling quite lightheaded, my raincoat open, carrying my briefcase with the precious Dai Ichi Zosen contract and the Lee memorandum of agreement in it, when a voice very close behind said levelly, "Mr. Henriksen, you and I are going to go very quickly through immigration and outside to a dark blue Mercedes that is waiting for us. You will not make your SAS flight to Oslo. If you don't cooperate, I will shoot you dead here and now."

PART 3

Home from the Sea

20

All the old horrors came back at once, and I wanted to laugh in terror. I cursed myself for having cabled my plans to Norland.

"Say nothing," the man behind me warned, "and keep walking, quickly please."

The health officer looked at our immunization records; the immigration officer gave our passports only a cursory glance—How long will you stay in Germany? Business? Two businessmen arriving from the Far East: what of it? We went through customs, through the terminal, and outside. It was cold and damp, but the sleet had stopped. Across the road, beyond the taxi line, was a large dark blue Mercedes. A man in a dark coat and uniform cap got out of the driver's seat and came round to hold the door for us, two businessmen being met by the company car. The chauffeur was Pappas.

"So nice to see you again, Mr. Henriksen," he said, without a trace of irony.

As we started off, Pappas said, "Well done, Raymond. Any difficulties?"

I had completely forgotten about Bechmann.

"Thank you, none. I'm very pleased. You will know, of course, what we want to discuss with you, Mr. Henriksen."

"I find everything that has happened since I got off the plane to be incomprehensible."

Bechmann removed the automatic pistol from his coat pocket. How the devil had he gotten that through the security check?

"Pappas and I want the answer to one question, and when we have found it, you will be free to go. Where is the money?"

"I have no idea what you are talking about."

"I was afraid you'd take that attitude," Bechmann said. "Our friend in Oslo told us you would. Never mind. We'll find out soon enough." Keeping the gun aimed at me, Bechmann settled comfortably into the corner.

Pappas turned the car north onto the autobahn toward Kassel and Hannover and held our speed steady between one hundred twenty and one hundred thirty kilometers an hour. The sky was dark and very low. We passed truck after truck, all with their lights on. One of them was trailing a forty-foot container with the name TTL Container Lines Ltd. on the side. That was Lee's container service.

"They were expecting me in Oslo this morning. They'll be wondering where I am."

Bechmann shrugged slightly. "No doubt," he said.

Kilometer after kilometer passed. The air inside the car was warm and the hum of the tires on the road lulling, and I began to doze. I hovered between consciousness and sleep for what seemed a very long time, but Bechmann was always wide awake, the gun level and steady. He had been waiting for me in Frankfurt—had bought a ticket, no doubt, had checked in, gone through immigration, and waited until my flight landed. And Norland had told him where I'd be. Bechmann, Evgenides, Pappas, Lygren, Norland.

"Norland," I said aloud, becoming alert. "Lars Norland's your friend in Oslo."

Bechmann said nothing. His eyes were gray and expressionless; his nose was sharp and his lips thin. His hair was black. One had the impression of the monochromatic about Bechmann, as if he rarely were seen in daylight and so had no need of coloring, like those blind creatures in the darkest parts of the ocean. But even they, as I understand it, give off a phosphorescent glow.

We took an exit for Kassel and went carefully through the town, past where the tram line stopped, to where buildings became small and farther apart, and finally we were out in the country again on a two-lane road that ran between wide, low rolling hills covered with a light dusting of recent snow. We pulled off the road into a driveway that ran between two high stands of hedge, through which could be seen a small house with an orange tile roof and muddy white stucco facing. There was a green Volkswagen Passat standing next to it. Pappas parked the Mercedes in front of the door. Bechmann motioned me out, and I preceded him into the house.

What I could see of the house was sparsely furnished, and it was very cold inside. Bechmann waved me along with the barrel of the pistol. I went through the sitting room—a couple of straight-backed chairs, an upholstered sofa, a table, a stove with a pipe vented through the wall—into a dark room that had no furniture at all, simply a window that had been boarded over.

"We shall have our first discussion after Pappas and I have eaten," Bechmann said, then closed and locked the door.

The room was perhaps two meters wide by two and a bit long. It was cold and damp, and in the dim light that showed through the cracks in the boarding over the window, I could discern mold growing in the corners of the room on the roughly plastered walls and on the linoleum tiles. Fortunately they'd left me my coat and gloves. I walked back and forth to generate a little body heat, then slowed down so that I would not begin to sweat. I did a circuit of the room first clockwise, then counterclockwise. Then I walked the diagonals, devising different ways to get to the starting point each time. At one point I removed my glove, and touched the wall. It was clammy. I put the glove back on and resumed my walk.

Through the door I could hear the sound of a lid on a pot and the rattling of plates and cutlery. A few moments later I thought I detected the smell of cabbage, and realized that I was extremely hungry, which I had been denying up to that point.

I was not frightened. I *was* most uncomfortable, from the cold and the hunger. And I was enraged that after all that had happened I should be locked in a room in the middle of Germany, that I had been prevented from getting to Oslo, from reaching Fredrik's murderer. As soon as the police stopped following me around, as soon as I had been exposed, something had happened. Must I spend the rest of my life being protected? The anger worked to hold off the jet lag that eventually would overtake me, but it was not making me particularly clear-headed. I did not, for example, recognize that the rest of my life might be a very short period indeed.

At a quarter before two, Bechmann unlocked the door and told me to come out. The sitting room was very warm and stuffy and smelled of paraffin. I kept my coat and gloves on, however. I would probably not get them back if I removed them.

"Sit." Bechmann pointed to one of the straight-backed chairs. It was in the middle of the room facing the sofa. Pappas was sitting on the sofa in a pair of khaki trousers and a heavy, rough woolen pullover. There was a large window behind his head that looked out over a wide field. It had begun to snow lightly.

I sat down.

"Where is the money?" Bechmann asked.

"I don't know what money you're talking about."

Bechmann whipped the barrel of the pistol against my right ear. It stung, but not unduly. I didn't realize that the ear had been somewhat anesthetized by the cold; I did not know it had been ripped until I felt blood running down the side of my neck.

"I'm not joking, Henriksen. We want that money. All right. Let us assume you've had a lapse of memory—due to the long flight perhaps. I'm talking about the three hundred thousand dollars you had Evgenides steal from the account of the *Rose*."

My ear had begun to hurt.

"I tell you, I don't know what you're talking about."

Bechmann hit me in the ear again with the pistol. This time I felt it all the way down to my hip.

"I instructed Evgenides to transfer the balance in the account. It was nearly four hundred thousand dollars. We received ninety-seven. Where is the rest?" This last was shouted into my injured ear.

"Let him think about that, Andrew," Bechmann said. "Get him out of my sight."

Pappas hauled me to my feet by the back of my coat collar and pushed me back into the small room. The tumblers of the lock turned over.

My ear was by now a searing mass of pain and must, I thought, be a bloody mess. As soon as I touched it with a handkerchief, a wave of nausea swept through me, but I fought it back. I resumed my peregrinations in the room. I had been so warm in the sitting room that it took some while before I began to feel the chill again; it came eventually, however. My walk was slower as well, because I was feeling quite dizzy. The nausea came and receded.

Some time later—I had no idea how much later, but there was no longer any light in the room except for a thin crack of yellow beneath the door to the sitting room—I heard the front door slam and, not long after, the sound of an automobile engine starting and fading away. In a few minutes the door of the room opened, and Pappas said, "Come out."

I stumbled into the light and heat and sat back down onto the chair. Pappas said, "No time for that now." He held out a large chunk of bread. "Come."

I took the bread and began to eat as I followed him out the door. It tasted wonderful. Pappas pointed me to the passenger side of the Passat and got into the driver's side himself. We moved quickly out of the driveway into the road, turning back, it seemed to me, the way we had come.

I finished the bread and thought I had never eaten anything so wonderful. Pappas was bent over the wheel, concentrating on the city streets to which we were now coming, the night leaping back from the orange glow of the street lights.

"Bechmann," I said.

"Let me get out of Kassel, my friend," Pappas responded tensely, "and then we can talk."

As far as I could tell in my stupor—I felt drunk—Pappas kept off the main streets of the town. When at last we came to the autobahn, he took the entrance leading south back to Frankfurt. The road was comfortably full of vehicles moving at high speed, among which we lost ourselves in short order.

"Bechmann had some errands to do," Pappas said at last. "I thought it was a good time to leave. I've done many things in my life, my friend, but murder is not one of them."

It took some time for me to understand Pappas' words and more time to connect them with myself. Despite the warmth in the car, I shivered.

"You think Bechmann had no intention of letting me go?" I asked slowly and with difficulty.

"When I saw him start on you, I knew. He's mad."

He turned off the autobahn into a brightly lit petrol station, gave his order to the attendant, and motioned to me to follow. In the toilet, he helped me clean up my ear and the side of my head and applied some plasters. Just before we left, while I sat in the car, I watched Pappas inside the station making a telephone call. I was feeling a litle more alert after walking a bit in the cold, fresh air.

"How did you get away from the *Rose*?" I asked him after we'd started off again.

"Ah," he said. "I didn't. I never sailed on her." He paused for effect. "At the close of our interview in Singapore, if you'll pardon me, John, I smelled a rat. You gave up one-third share much too easily. So with my considerable powers of persuasion, I convinced the first officer, a most untrustworthy man, that the show was his . . . that I had, how you say, other fish to fry."

"Wasn't he suspicious?"

"Ioannis was always suspicious, hence indiscriminate. He would not have recognized truth from the mouth of a bishop. Dreams of money got in the way of his suspicion. He was also very stupid. Like Evgenides. Greed is fine as long as it is tempered with intelligence. What happened to the *Rose*?"

"It was attacked."

"And the crew?"

"Many were killed. I don't know anything about the rest of the crew or the officers."

Pappas clucked. The wind rushed by the car. "Poor Ioannis might have gotten away. But I doubt it. Who did it?"

"A very big operation."

"Yes. We knew our competitors were a big operation. We had hints, but we paid no heed. There was certainly enough business for all of us, we thought. Then they got on to us, and things got very confused. But Oslo ordered us to continue. It is easy enough to be brave when you are sitting in Europe and don't have to stare into the barrel of a machine gun that's pointed in your face."

"You're talking about when the auto parts were taken?"

"Yes." Pappas fell silent. It was a palpable silence, as if he were reliving a terrible memory.

"Why did Evgenides go to Bechmann after Paul Johansen was killed?"

Pappas started out of his reverie. "I asked Raymond the same question. I was wondering about that myself. Even before our talk in Singapore. It doesn't hang together really. Why should Evgenides have put his head in the mouth of the lion when, if he *had* stolen the money, he could have ended his days fornicating nonstop in Rio?"

"Amadeo da Silva?" I asked.

We slipped smoothly around a gigantic tractor trailer.

"An account we were all supposed to be able to use. No, my friend. Poor old Evgenides didn't take that money. He lacked the imagination. He was frightened and went running to Bechmann for protection. And got a bullet for his trouble. He was only a stupid Greek, after all." He continued in a musing tone. "But someone was playing a double game. Lars Norland—you are right there—or the other one."

I did not think I heard him—I was very close to losing consciousness. "Someone other than Norland?"

"Yes," Pappas said in response to my question, "there is someone else in Oslo connected with this whom only Bechmann knows. Someone who has a very good information source, someone who found out about the interesting trade that was going on in Southeast Asia and managed to get into it. It's someone who's used to pushing people about like chessmen. From what Bechmann has let slip, and from what I know, I think whoever he is is a shipowner."

Pappas' voice came to me as if I were far back in a cave and he were standing in the mouth calling to me. The words seemed to echo in my ears, and I slipped back into that first German winter in Oslo and my father embracing me with tears in his eyes. And then I was sitting upright, watching taillights rush at us and fall aside, and I realized who it must be. I had known for some time, but I had not allowed myself to recognize it. I suddenly felt shriveled and very old.

"Lindstedt," I said.

"Per Lindstedt? The Norbulk man?"

"Yes."

"Why on earth should a man like that involve himself in this sort of business?" Pappas sounded genuinely surprised.

"It doesn't matter why. He must be destroyed."

"That kind of thinking leads to trouble, my friend. Why don't we simply ring the Oslo police from Frankfurt? Like the surprise I arranged a while ago for Raymond?"

"It's something I must do myself." The conviction lay painfully in the pit of my stomach.

Pappas said, "That sounds dangerously like a principle, John. Principles are best abandoned when they interfere with comfort or convenience."

I do not recall much of the next twelve hours. I remember thanking Pappas, absurdly, when he left me off at the Frankfurt airport. Somehow I managed a plane to Oslo and slept deeply until we arrived. At immigration at Fornebu I was asked to step aside. My obvious exhaustion checked their questions. I acknowledged I had been delayed and told them I intended to get in touch with Inspector Frogh the following day. They helped with my suitcases, which had preceded me by thirty-six hours and had been kept in the unclaimed baggage area, and took me home in a police car.

I remember nothing of the ride home. The house smelled musty, and it was cold. I recall walking into the bedroom and turning on the light. When next I was conscious, a feeble gray light from the windows was warring with the lamp, which was still on. I was fully dressed, including my coat and shoes. It was a little after six. I was nauseated and had a massive headache, but I remembered what I had to do.

It was not going to be easy. There was a man in a car parked in front of the house—obviously someone Frogh had sent to watch me. But I deceived him. I slipped quietly out the back door into the chilly air, went across my wretched back garden through patches of dirty snow, and lifted myself over the low fence into the next garden. It was perhaps half a kilometer to Drammensveien, and it seemed to take me a fearfully long time to reach it, although the cold air invigorated me.

The counterman at the early morning cafe in Drammensveien looked at me suspiciously, I thought, as I ordered a coffee, so I deliberately paid with a fifty-kroner note to shut him up—dreadfully clever I was. I asked him to ring me a cab while I sipped the hot coffee, which did my stomach no good at all, and tipped him five kroner when it arrived.

Unlike the man in the cafe, the young man driving the taxi was too absorbed in himself to notice me. He did turn down the rock music on his transistor radio long enough to hear my direction, then turned it back up. He passed a comb several times through his shoulder-length blond hair, regarding himself the while in the rearview mirror; he then lit a fresh cigarette from the one dangling from his lips, and we set off.

I had to tell him to slow down. There were still patches of ice and snow on the roads, and he was driving stupidly, like so many of the young who know they are immortal. I did not care what happened to him, but I did not want a gratuitous accident preventing me from getting to Lindstedt, especially having come so far already.

There were two beings in the back of that cab going to Lindstedt's: an exhausted middle-aged man, feverish, unshaven, dirty, near collapse; and with him, an alert, cunning animal, something like a fox, with a single object in mind. The fox had been created in the past weeks, while I was the object of the hunt; his instincts had become well developed, so that he could sense danger.

Lindstedt answered the door himself and was astonished to see me.

"John, you look dreadful. Come in, my boy, come in. I'll call a doctor straightaway."

"No. Please don't, Per. It's unnecessary. I'm on my way now. I simply wanted to have a little chat with you first."

The fox knew at once that Lindstedt was suddenly *en garde,* but it took a while before I realized it consciously. He led me into the sitting room, where I slumped into the sofa.

"Can I get you some coffee?" he said, somewhat distantly.

"Thank you, Per, no. Please sit down. I want to tell you what's happened."

Lindstedt sat on the edge of the upholstered chair across from me, a coffee table between us, resting his arms on his knees and folding his hands together.

I looked into his eyes. "I have just escaped from Raymond Bechmann." The eyes did not change, except to express mild curiosity. "He was holding me in a house in Germany. He was beating me to find out where I had hidden money he thinks I stole from the *Rose.*"

Lindstedt began to tap lightly on the coffee table. "Very interesting, my friend. But why are you telling me this? It means nothing to me."

I looked again in his eyes. There was nothing there but kindness and concern, and I began to be unsure of myself. But the fox noticed how the other was sitting, how he was rolled into a protective ball. I had to go on.

"I'm sorry, Per. I should like to believe your denials. I have loved you as a friend and as a mentor. But I cannot any longer. I know almost everything now."

"I think you are very ill, John."

"It was Sven Lygren, wasn't it, who told you about the trade in arms and drugs and terrorists in Asia?"

"I'm seriously concerned about you, John."

"It was you who set Bechmann onto Norland, wasn't it, because you knew how much Norland hated Paul, and that he could be suborned?"

"I'm not sure how much of this I can take, my friend."

"You couldn't lose, could you, Per? If the scheme succeeded, there was a lot of money to be made in a very short period of time, none of which Johansen would see, of course, because he thought he was running a legitimate cargo vessel. And if the scheme failed, you lost nothing. Either way, you were likely to wind up with Johansens Rederi at a bargain price because of our tanker problems."

"This is preposterous. It's time to go to the office."

"But there's one thing I don't understand, Per. I don't understand why you murdered Fredrik."

He stood up, and I stood with him. "Ridiculous," he said icily. "I have other things to do. If you wish, I'll drop you off at the hospital. Or you can call a cab from here."

"You're not going anywhere, Per, ever again." He had started around the coffee table and came within reach. I took him by the throat and began to squeeze. The surprise in his eyes was genuine. I was weak, but after all, the man was over sixty; I regretted only that it would take time because I was so tired. He was flailing at my arms but I took no notice.

Behind him, on the wall, was the large photograph of Lindstedt triumphant at a shareholders' meeting. The photograph had been taken by Alice Nielsen, whom I had entirely forgotten. And whose love I was destroying now as surely as I was destroying Per Lindstedt.

I pushed him away and sat back down on the sofa. All the hatred was draining out of me. I could hear Lindstedt gagging, but I did not look at him. The fox was leaving me . . . fading . . . fading . . . and was gone. I was finally alone and thought that at last I could sleep. Per was standing next to me. I looked and thought distractedly that I had never seen him look like that before—he looked quite mad. He had in his hand one of the small ship models mounted on mahogany that he kept in the sitting room. It was taking me a terribly long time to sort things out. He was raising the model high over his head. I put my arms up, but my head exploded into stars, and then everything went dark.

21

They kept me in the hospital for several days for concussion, and they patched my ear and filled me with antibiotics. Inspector Frogh came to visit on the third day. He kept worrying his pipe without lighting it.

"Two things happened within less than forty-eight hours," Frogh said. "The first was that Norland reported you missing."

"Norland reported it?"

"He had to. He didn't know whom else you might have told when you were landing in Oslo—which was good thinking on his part, because we also received a telex from Sergeant Ng telling us when to expect you. Well, we traced you up to the time you arrived in Frankfurt. Then nothing else. There were no witnesses to your abrupt departure from the airport. Then we received word from the German authorities. They had received a call giving them very clear instructions where to find Raymond Bechmann and telling them that you were on your way to Oslo."

"That was Pappas. I watched him making the call from a petrol station on the autobahn."

"A Volkswagen Passat with Kassel plates was found parked near the railway station in Innsbruck."

"And Pappas?"

"Disappeared."

"I can't say I'm sorry."

"*Chacun à son gout,* Mr. Henriksen. The man is a criminal."

"How did you get on to Norland?"

"The man Sven Lygren confessed. Told us the whole story. We had, I may say, been watching a number of people in Johansen's office, including Lars Norland. We did not take that bomb as a serious attempt to destroy the office—much too crude. Sand in the eyes. I had also been troubled ever since you'd received that letter threat. There was no way it could have gotten to your desk without someone noticing unless someone from the office put it there. So I had a more than passing interest in the people at P. Johansens Rederi."

"And Norland hated Johansen profoundly."

"Yes. There was greed as well, but I think the hatred was the driving force. Johansen had taken to bemoaning his fate to Norland rather than to you, because you had become too critical of him. At the same time, Bechmann, coached by Lindstedt, surfaced with full knowledge of Johansen's financial problems, and bit by bit he corrupted Norland, the one man in the organization who was prone to being corrupted. With Bechmann as financial adviser, Norland advising him on the operations side, and Johansen thinking you were too conservative—in addition to which he could not bring himself to admit that you had been right about the tankers—it could not have been too difficult to persuade him to take a chance with cargo liners. Evgenides was just Bechmann's representative. Bechmann even financed the purchase of the *Rose.* Another seven hundred fifty thousand pounds in his pocket."

"I seem to recall the *Rose* was bought for cash."

"Not so. She was not encumbered, that is so, but there is on the books of Multinational Capital Limited a demand loan to Paul Johansen in the amount of seven hundred fifty thousand pounds for which we have not been able to find any other use Johansen might have put it to. It certainly does not appear in the books of Johansens Rederi, which you would know far better than I. Multinational Capital, by the way, made a handsome profit as well on the conversion from sterling to dollars."

"But why should a man like Lindstedt engage in such activity?"

"I don't have a complete explanation. I don't think we ever will. But Lindstedt grew more and more acquisitive and power hungry as he grew older. His rooting in the wreckage of small Norwegian shipping companies was an example of that. And you yourself mentioned his messianic tendencies. He saw an opportunity for profit in which he would have almost nothing to risk and he went for it. He did not anticipate two significant problems. One was the ferocious response from the *ronin.* The theft of the crates in Malaysia was an early warning that no one paid any attention to. The other problem was your insistence on sorting out the problems of your firm before you talked terms with him. He admires you for that, by the way."

"How did the *ronin* find out who owned the *Rose*?"

"They knew Evgenides was the manager. That was a matter of public record. They frightened him into telling them who the owner was. Evgenides then told Norland that the *ronin* were onto the scheme, although he did not tell him how they knew. Lars Norland, ever keen for the main chance, then started stealing from the account of the *Rose,* and he also made contact with the *ronin,* we think."

"You think?"

"Someone must have let them know when Johansen left the office on his way to the Grand."

"And the letter to me?"

Frogh simply nodded.

"And the bomb in the office?"

"An attempt to take the heat off. He knew he, and a number of others, were being watched."

"How did it happen that Evgenides' office in Piraeus was bombed?"

"We have to guess at that. We think that the *ronin* told him they would do it so that his employer would not be suspicious of him. In fact, Evgenides realized that there was no need for them to keep him alive after he'd been of use to them. So he went running to Bechmann. But Bechmann had already been informed by Norland that Evgenides had betrayed them. And so Bechmann eliminated him."

My head was swimming. "And what has become of Bechmann?"

"He was arrested as soon as he returned to the house outside Kassel."

"Inspector Frogh . . ."

"Please, after all this time, you must call me Arne."

"All right then, Arne. Why did Lindstedt have Fredrik killed?"

Frogh looked for what seemed a long time into the bowl of his pipe before he answered.

"Lindstedt has told us he thought the boy might prove troublesome when the time came to take over Johansens Rederi."

"God in Heaven, Fredrik was no longer interested in the

company. He would have sold it to anyone who made him a half decent offer."

"He was taking no chances, John."

"How did he find out how Fredrik was returning to Oslo?"

"We surmise that the boy knew telling his own office was dangerous. So he telexed Lindstedt instead."

"Did you have someone watching Lindstedt's house?"

"Yes. And when we found out you had gone there, we had an idea that you would try to confront him with what you'd learned. We waited a bit to see what would happen."

"What in fact did happen? I don't remember."

"We arrested him in the act of trying to kill you."

22

Alice came to see me the following day, bringing me three paperback mysteries in English. She looked simply wonderful. I was as much in love with her as ever and told her so. She smiled, rather wistfully, I thought, not quite her old self. She said she would like to have a talk with me as soon as I was out of the hospital.

"That all sounds rather ominous, Miss Nielsen," I said with a jauntiness I did not feel.

"Not at all, John." She kissed my eyes and mouth. "Let me know when you are home, and I'll come to you."

She arrived in a taxi and entered the house with a broad smile, her wonderful hair windblown, her cheeks bright. She had with her two string bags full of packages and boxes and bottles, which she put down in the middle of the foyer floor while we embraced—or rather, while she embraced me and I held onto her. I began to speak, to tell her what had happened, but she put a finger to my lips and told me she did not want to hear it yet.

She pulled a bottle of very good champagne from one of the bags and gave it to me to open while she hung her coat in the foyer closet. I poured it and we drank to each other silently. We took the bottle and the glasses and went into the bedroom. She told me she wanted to hear nothing about any of it until we'd made love.

So Alice Nielsen and I made love and drank champagne in my house off Drammensveien. Then she asked me to tell her the rest of it.

She did not interrupt, but let me chatter on. In fact, the only sound she made was a sharp intake of breath when I got to the part Lindstedt had played. When I finished, she did not say anything for a long time. She touched my bandaged ear gently and nestled beneath my left arm.

"Do you think it's over now?"

"I don't know, Alice. Mostly, I think. Maybe I have to think so to stay sane. But I think our involvement is at an end. For heaven's sake, why are you crying?"

Her body was pressed closely to mine, and I could feel her shaking. "It's nothing," she said.

I kissed her eyes. She snuffled a little and smiled and kissed me on the cheek. "Let me open another bottle and I'll start dinner."

"Let's make love again," I said.

"Satyr. After we've eaten."

We had a lovely dinner of veal scallops and new potatoes and salad, and drank rather more champagne than was absolutely good for two middle-aged lovers. But if I was a little less than sober, it was not because of the wine. I felt we must be very near to that time she and I had had together in Athens, when we had come so close to a commitment. I did not intend to let the opportunity slip through my fingers again. But a discussion along those lines did not go with the washing up. We finished cleaning up the kitchen, closed up the house, and returned to bed.

We did not make love then. I could tell she was tense. I lay next to her and stroked her shoulder while she stared at the ceiling and was far, far away.

"I love you, Alice," I said. I wanted to go on, but she interrupted me gently.

"Please don't continue, John. I think I know what you want to say, and I'm grateful. I want to tell you that I'm leaving Oslo."

I felt an icy ring close round my heart. "But why, darling?"

She held my hand tightly. "I could say all manner of practical things. The communications are too difficult. It's got much too expensive. I'm not nearly as fond of the cold weather as I used to be when I was younger. All of these are true, but they're not the reasons. The reason is that I love you also, John, but I don't want to marry anyone. If we married, I know we should cease loving each other, and I don't want that. I want to love you always."

"But you needn't leave Oslo," I said, sounding probably as desperate as I felt.

"Yes I must. I've thought about it a long time, especially since we were together in Hong Kong. I know it's right."

I was terribly hurt, and I wanted to hurt her. What I wanted to say was, "You're afraid of commitment," but I could not bring myself to do it. What I said instead was, "Alice, you sound as if you're afraid of making a commitment."

"I think not, John. I think rather I'm afraid of going through motions. I'm afraid of routine. I always have been. I am especially afraid with you. I don't want my love for you, or yours for me, to become routine, rote, a conditioned reflex. Which is what would happen if we lived together or were too close."

I had no answer. "Where will you go?"

"London. I think I've found a situation that will keep me in one place more. Travel has become tiresome . . . routine," she added, almost inaudibly.

"Another high tax environment," I said irrelevantly.

"John, you *are* romantic," she laughed.

"I shall go into bankruptcy paying for plane tickets."

"I'll love seeing you in London."

"Will you love me as much in London?"

"At least as much."

It was Henriksen's turn to cry, and I did—inside. Alice saw only the brave, plucky chap beside her. She did not see the darkness into which I gazed.

Things moved quickly over the next year or so. Norland's number two did an admirable job filling his shoes, which did not surprise me. Norland had trained him well. He worked particularly hard with Karl Wessel to insure that delivery of *Iris, Ivy,* and *Star Aster,* set for the end of April, would come off smoothly.

The board of Johansens Rederi, including Fredrik's heir, Torvald, agreed with my suggestion, and instructed me to proceed with negotiating the sale of P. Johansens Rederi to Norbulk A/S.

The board of Norbulk, after recovering from the shock of losing its chairman and managing director, particularly in that way, quite sensibly promoted one of their own number chairman, and chose Haakon Ritter to become the new managing director. (Mike Price was transferred to take over in Singapore.) So it was with Haakon that we negotiated the sale of the firm and the transfer of the new Dai Ichi Zosen contracts.

In the course of preparing for our talks with Ritter, we inquired into the fate of the *Rose*. We discovered that the insurance had lapsed, because Transoceanic Maritime had not bothered to pay the premiums; in fact, the putative owner was still subject to a call from the Protection and Indemnity Club. We found also that the *Rose* herself no longer existed. The Vietnamese had regarded her as a pirate ship and so eligible to be exploited; they scrapped her because they needed the steel more than they needed a cargo liner in a state of disrepair. My finance director's heart winced at the loss of well over a million dollars; but it was, after all, Multinational Capital Ltd. that had lost the money. That situation would have to be dealt with in the future and, from the sound of things, probably by the bank's liquidators.

T. T. Lee had been horrified to learn about Lindstedt, and he and I discussed it at length over the telephone, just after we had completed delivery of the tankers. It was during this same conversation that he said he might be in a position to reopen discussions about the *Zinnia* in the near future, which was good information to have just as we were about to start talking with Haakon Ritter. The discussion went, in fact, very smoothly and quickly, the *Zinnia* not causing Haakon nearly as much concern as I thought she might. My mentioning T. T. Lee's interest helped a great deal. In the event, Ritter paid the trust nearly seventeen million dollars, entirely in cash, as Torvald Johansen totally rejected any equity in Norbulk, and the name P. Johansens Rederi A/S disappeared forever from the commercial register.

Alice left for London in May. We had a small party for her the week she went, and I had dinner with her the night before. She asked me quite specifically not to take her to the airport or see her off. She looked wonderful that evening, and we did not speak Norwegian the entire time.

I had to return to Kassel, with Frogh, to give a deposition in the matter of my kidnapping by Bechmann and Pappas, but it has not come to trial yet and may never do so. Frogh told me there were a number of countries who were interested in Pappas, if ever he were found, and Multinational Capital Ltd. had sworn out a writ on Bechmann in the United Kingdom.

When Ritter bought Johansens, I went to work for him directly as chief financial officer of Norbulk. He did not increase my salary by much, because in Norway it would only have increased my taxes more, but he recommended, and the board approved, my being given a share in the operation. It was an exciting job, with a great deal more responsibility than my old one. Now I was drawing plans for growth and expansion, not conducting a rescue operation. The damage Lindstedt had done in his acquisitive last years was minor and quickly remedied. An exciting job, as I said; and I couldn't stand it. Oslo without Alice Nielsen became a place totally devoid of interest for me.

I thought at first it was living alone out of the center of town that had finally gotten to me, so I did what I'd vowed never to do and moved into a flat near the office. It was, actually, quite a nice flat, but I was almost never there. I spent more and more time at the office, including Saturdays and occasionally Sundays. I had one or two liaisons with attractive women that ultimately bored me and, I'm certain, must have bored them.

I did see Alice occasionally because my work took me to London from time to time. She had two cheerful rooms and a kitchen near Regent's Park. She was warm and welcoming and loving as always. But it was not enough for me, and I told her as much. I told her that I would be moving to London as quickly as I could arrange it. She said nothing when I told her, simply looked pensive.

Haakon was upset when I told him I was resigning, but I think he understood. He was not happy himself in Oslo, because Joan was unhappy. I knew he'd had misgivings about moving back from Singapore, although it had been impossible for him to turn down the opportunity he had been offered. They are more settled now, and I think—I hope—happier.

In any event, when Ritter realized there was nothing he could do to prevent my leaving Oslo, he offered me the job of running Norbulk's London office, which is not a bad job at all. There was an appreciable reduction in salary, due both to the position and to the difference in the cost of living, but we get along quite nicely.

Alice relinquished her independence at last, and off we went to the registry office one Tuesday afternoon in July. We are still living in her old flat, but are looking for something larger, perhaps with a bit of garden. We do not seem to love each other less, as she had feared. If anything, I think we are more in love than before—there seems to be a glow around everything we do together. Why she weakened finally and decided to marry me, I'm not certain. We are, after all, two years older than we were when all this happened. And perhaps, at the end of the day, she saw the darkness outside the two cheerful rooms in Camden Town.

The Lutine Bell at Lloyds is rung when a ship is lost at sea. Nearly two years after I returned to Oslo, and about a year after I came to London, the Lutine Bell was rung for the ocean-going tug *Monterrey*.

It appears that the *Monterrey* was on her way to assist *Ocean Explorer Number Three,* a drill ship that was working off Sarawak and had lost her power. In full view of the drill ship, the *Monterrey* was shaken by a series of tremendous explosions, caught fire, and sank in three minutes, with a loss of all hands.

From time to time over the next two months, a short note appeared on the "Marine Casualties" page of *Lloyds List* concerning the progress of the investigation into the destruction of the *Monterrey,* but the final determination was "Cause unknown."